BRUTAL PLAY

ALISON RHYMES

This is a work of fiction. Unless otherwise indicated, all the names, characters, businesses, places, events and incidents in this book are either the product of the author's imagination or used in a fictitious manner. Any resemblance to actual persons, living or dead, or actual events is purely coincidental.

Copyright © 2022 Alison Rhymes

All rights reserved. No part of this book may be reproduced in any form or by any electronic or mechanical means, including information storage and retrieval systems, without written permission from the author, except for the use of brief quotations in a book review.

To request permission, contact: alison@alisonrhymes.com

Editor: Zainab M. at Heart Full of Reads Editing Services

Cover Design: Temys Designs

Formatting: Triumph Book Covers

Content warnings for this book, and other titles by Alison Rhymes, can be found on her website alionrhymes.com.

This book is dedicated to anyone who ever needed a second chance and to those of us who struggle to give them.

PROLOGUE

This morning, Noah was late for practice. Again. It's weighed on me all through my classes and cheer practice. I haven't spoken to him since he left his room today. But I'm back now, and he should be, too, soon.

His room has been a lifesaver for me. Though, I go to school a dozen miles away at USC, my dorm is a quad. And every one of the other three girls that live there are a distraction to my studies. With my background, I can't handle that. I have to do well. I have to graduate. There is no other option.

There is no backup plan. If I can't support myself straight out of college, I'm screwed.

Noah's room gives me the quiet space I need to study. Or nap. At least until he returns. Then my focus will shift to him. He works hard. Harder than anyone I've ever known. Regardless of how fit he is, and he is, he comes back beaten-up and bruised more often than I'd like.

He's the quarterback here at UCLA and he has big dreams of the NFL. Dreams I know he'll fulfill since he's the type of guy that doesn't give up. Noah deserves such success. A good, caring guy, who looks after me better than anyone has before.

I'm a bit obsessed about his well-being, too. Well, obsessed about everything when it comes to Noah Anders. I've never been so close to anyone, male or female. He makes me feel different than I ever have. Safe. Cared for. Maybe even loved.

Though, we haven't made those proclamations. Even after nearly a year together. I'm terrified to tell him the words I've never said aloud to anyone.

It's also terrifying to think he could say them to me. There's so much he doesn't know about my past. Every day I want to tell him. Every single day. The problem is that he already has so much pressure on him; I don't want to add to that. He's the type to take on the problems of people he cares about. He can't take on my issues, though.

Noah and I aren't sustainable this way. However, it can't be wrong to enjoy him while I can, though. I do so enjoy him. I never believed in soulmates before I really took notice of him.

During the first two years of college, I stayed focused on my studies. Back in Utah, at high school, I'd lost my virginity to a boy just as nervous and curious as me. It was a fumbling mess in the backseat of his Toyota Corolla. I didn't care to repeat the experience with him. Sophomore year of college, I tried again with the football team's wide receiver. He came almost as soon as he penetrated me.

Then there was Drew McKenna, my own college's quarterback. He at least knew what he was doing and gave me my first, non-self-induced orgasm. Drew's a great guy, but he's not for me. Not only because he's in love with a girl he grew up with—even if he hasn't admitted that himself—but there isn't anything there more than friendship. Drew is sexy, sure, but we don't have that *thing*. I know he's not who I want to spend my life with. But I do trust him more than I do most people. And in my life, that's invaluable.

Last season, when we played UCLA, I noticed Noah. Of course, I'd seen him at games before. And there's no way to ignore the chatter from other women about how good-looking he is. That game changed something for me. After their loss to us, Noah stayed on the sidelines. He didn't immediately retreat to the locker rooms with the rest of the team. Removing his helmet, he sat on the sidelines and stared at the barren field.

His expression wasn't sad, or mad, or even disappointed. It was contemplative. As if he was reliving every play one by one. Trying to find the flaws so that he wouldn't make them again.

I watched from the entrance to the tunnel. Transfixed. Envious, even. I've never been good at recognizing or fixing my flaws. Something told me he could teach me. That he would, if I could just catch his attention.

Noah Anders was a notorious non-dater. Until me.

He *has* taught me a lot. He's taught me how to put someone above myself. He's taught me how to love.

I try to continue reading. This week, it's Jane Austen's *Northanger Abbey*. My eyes trail the words.

I have no notion of loving people by halves, it is not my nature.

Reading the line over and over doesn't change the impact it has on me. I didn't know love as a child. Not until Aunt Alice. Love was something I felt for her, but my respect for her overshadowed it. She got me out of a terrifying situation, after all.

That love was different than what I feel for the man whose bed I currently lounge in. I'd shatter my own soul for Noah. It's wholly encompassing, as if he's the rod in my back holding me upright. And if ever that rod was too heavy for him to hold, I'd let it fall away to lighten his load. Even if it means I fall to the ground. It's probably not healthy for me to be so enraptured by him. It can't be helped.

Noah Anders is my reason.

I don't love him by halves. He has my whole heart.

He strides into the room, shoulders slumped with fatigue. Until he sees me, and he schools his posture. He does this often, not wanting to show me how tired he is. Or battered. I wish he'd stop pretending and be vulnerable with me. Maybe then I could be with him, too, and the thought wouldn't fill me with fear.

I'm working on my degree in physical therapy. It's a dream of mine to eventually work up to sports medicine, or nutrition. But that all takes time and money. I received a scholarship for cheer, and I'm making the most of that. Extended schooling would take more scholarships and grants than I've been able to secure just yet. Someday, though.

"Come here," I call, laying my book on the nightstand next to his bed. It's usually where I do my studying, so if I doze off, I'm already in a comfortable spot.

"Let me go shower first. I probably stink."

"Noah, come here."

He steps to the side of the bed and leans over to give me a kiss, careful to keep his body away from mine. As if he'll soil me. He couldn't possibly. I wrap my arms around his neck and pull him down on top of me.

"Baby, I smell."

"You smell like you," I say.

"Fuck, I hope I don't always stink like this." He laughs against the skin of my neck.

"It's always good; whatever it is you smell like."

"You're twisted," he says, then blows a raspberry along my collarbone, making me giggle and squirm.

"How was practice?"

He stands back up, removing his t-shirt and throwing it in a pile in the corner. I notice when he turns his back to me that he's trying to hide the haunted look in his eyes.

"It was good. We're ready for the game this weekend." He is. I know he is. But I also know the coach rode his ass today for being late to morning practice. "I have an away game, remember? Do you have plans?"

We have a home game this week while Noah will be traveling. I hate it when that happens—him gone, and I'm left alone here. He always asks this same question, and the answer doesn't usually change.

"No. That theater downtown is doing a midnight showing of Rocky Horror Picture Show. I might see if one of the girls will go with me. But you know how that goes." They only like to do things when members of the team are present. College girls are horny as hell.

"I hope you find someone; you didn't make it last time they played it either."

"Yeah, but there's time," I say with a shrug.

He moves back to the bed now, dressed in nothing but athletic shorts. "Mind if we order pizza tonight? I'll call in a veggie."

"You hate vegetable pizza." I scoff.

"But it's the only pizza you'll eat, and since that's the easiest thing to have delivered here, pizza it is. I don't feel like sharing you with the world tonight."

"You say the sweetest things, Noah Anders."

"We can even put on a scary movie if you're done with your reading."

Noah knows how much I love horror movies. He's not a fan, but he indulges me.

"*The Babadook*?"

"I don't know what that is, but sure. Whatever you want, Lorelai."

Later, I fall asleep with Noah behind me, his arms securely wrapped around me. I dream of a life I never thought obtainable. Pictures of wedding dresses, a home on a quiet street, and blonde-headed children clinging to my hands. So different than the life I grew up expecting. My dream life is safe and filled with happiness, with Noah by my side, every step of the way.

The dream is always the same. It's only in waking that I know it's a beautiful delusion. An unobtainable fantasy. And that someday, likely soon, I'll have to leave Noah. I'll have to free him of the burden that is me.

1
LORELAI

My mother had told me I listen to my heart with impetuous violence. I was only seven, and I had no way of understanding what she meant. She wasn't right about much in life, but this was something she got right.

Mistakes are made every day.

Not like mine, though.

Surely, not with such regularity and severity.

Simply stated, I'm a fuckup. In the most epic sense.

It was a mistake having an affair with a married man. It wasn't my first mistake. Certainly, it won't be my last.

I once thought Drew McKenna was my future. Not as a husband. I always knew he'd never be that to me. But something else; a friend, a security I'd never had before, never dreamed of having before. Because of that belief, I betrayed people.

Delusions drove me to spitefulness.

Fear drove me to my delusions.

Abuse drove me to fear.

None of that excuses my behavior. It doesn't absolve me of my sins. Nor did it get me any closer to my goal. Only further away.

My emotions reign over me. I'm rash, impulsive, and nearly always regretful. Though that never seems to stop me.

This time… this time, I've really fucked up.

I feel it the second I see Drew across the room of Noah Anders' Super Bowl party. It's a big party, exclusive, so I had to sneak in. Noah would never dream of allowing me entrance—the woman who broke his heart all those years ago. The woman who had an affair with his co-host's husband this past year.

He fulfilled his dream of the NFL, as I always knew he would. Unfortunately, he was only able to play a few years before an injury took him out of the league. He moved back to his home state of Louisiana and works for the New Orleans' Saints as some sort of consultant, I believe. He's also recently taken on a position with ESPN co-hosting a show with Drew's wife, June.

June is up on stage singing some ridiculous karaoke pop song. If I let myself admit it, June's an amazing woman. She's stronger than I gave her credit for, much more forgiving, too.

So, I don't let myself think about it. At all. I can live with the choices I've made if I attempt to see her as an obstacle in my way. Even if it's not at all true. She's nothing more than an innocent woman who didn't deserve any of this.

Drew's all dreamy eyes and cheesy smiles while he watches her, unbeknownst that I move through the maze of bodies between him and me. A quick scan tells me half the damn room is having the same reaction to June. The other half is gaga for June's blonde friend.

Leighton. I've followed Drew and June's lives enough to know they've been close for years, even if I didn't have vague memories of her tagging along with June to several of Drew's college games. Their friendship is just one more thing for me to be jealous of. I've never had a girlfriend like that. In college, I had fellow cheerleaders that I occasionally hung out with. Except they came along with all the petty bullshit you'd expect. I had little in common with them, and absolutely no patience for them. I tried once; I really did. It was a complete carnage.

Much like the scene I know I'm about to cause, the one I seem helpless to stop. All it would take is for me to turn around and leave. Except I have nowhere to go.

Desperation is the devil, and it fuels my every step.

June's brother is the first to see my approach. His wide smile fades, and he mouths a name in warning.

Drew.

I'm on him, swinging my arms around him before he has the chance to turn and cut off the interaction. Altercation? Probably, altercation.

Impetuous violence.

"Hey, Drew," I purr in his ear with nothing left to lose. Tension sets in the muscles under my arms, and I fight the instinct my body has to it. It tells me to run and hide. It doesn't understand that there is nowhere to go and no money to do it with.

I have little left in the way of options, with few funds and fewer friends. Any reputation I had is obliterated now that I've been publicly branded as a homewrecker. That wasn't something I set out to be. Truth be told, I'm ashamed of it. Of course, I don't tell that to anyone but myself. Outwardly, I embrace my monikers.

Villain. Clinger. Trash. Whore.

"Get the fuck off me, Lorelai," Drew growls.

"Oh, come on. I thought we were friends."

All I want is a chance to explain. When you only have one friend in the world, even if that friendship is built on a fragile foundation of lies, you hold on to it with everything you have. I wasn't trying to betray him or make things worse for June when I went to the tabloids about Drew and my affair.

It wasn't about that. It was about survival. Drew's never been unreasonable, I think he'd understand, if he'd only hear me out.

"Fucking hell," Reed, June's brother, mutters as he glances up, probably looking for his sister who's no longer on stage.

"Were. We're nothing anymore."

"Can we talk, please? I just want the opportunity to explain."

"What the fuck are you thinking?" He seethes.

"You wouldn't answer my calls. What was I supposed to do, Drew?"

"You were supposed to fuck all the way off. I'm sure I've told you this already," June butts in now that she's found her way back through the crowd. I barely grant her a glance. Mostly because she looks gorgeous, glowing with a new confidence, the likes I once possessed myself.

"I'm not here to talk to you, June," I throw back at her.

"Oh honey, I don't care what your intentions are. You need to leave."

"Lorelai, just go," Drew pleads.

"Not until you let me explain why I did it, please…"

"Nobody wants to hear it. Leave." June is quite comfortable, no longer letting Drew do all the speaking for her. She used to remind me of a spineless creature, always cowering behind Drew or Reed. She's not that same woman anymore. I noticed the spark of it when I confronted her all those months ago. That spark is a bonfire in her now.

The straighter her spine grows, the brighter the fire in her eyes… the more I feel the volatile pit stir inside me. I don't see June in front of me. She morphs into another figure altogether. One I don't know how to react to in any way except one.

Anger. Fight back. Survive, survive, survive.

Red bleeds over my vision and I no longer know where I am or what I'm doing. There is no thought, just action. Or reaction, more like. I feel the words as they flutter out of my throat with a stinging speed. I don't know what I say, but they burn and burn.

But then it isn't them burning me any longer. It's something new as a small, yet strong, fist takes me by surprise. I stagger back, unable to keep upright in the stupidly high heels I have on. The ones that make my feet look elegant. The ones I kept on the last time Drew fucked me into a mindless stupor after he spanked my ass to a pretty beet red.

I'm not sane in this moment. At least I know that much.

The fight instantly drains out of me. Easily. Since I never truly wanted it anyway. I don't stand, even as I feel the trickling blood. The heat of embarrassment keeps me low, right where I belong, I suppose. Down here on the floor, sticky from spilled booze, and dirty from trampled feet. Maybe it suits someone like me just fine.

Drew's shoes come into view as he lifts June back. Removing her from my radius. Maybe he's afraid I'll infect her with whatever disease lives inside me that makes me this way.

It's not Drew's feet that concern me, though. It's the new set beside me. Perfectly polished and pristine, they can only belong to Noah Anders.

My breath hitches, and I try to control the trembling that wants to shake me wholly. I'm afraid to let it, scared of what might escape with it. My ego has already left; my self-confidence gone. What else can I afford to lose?

As hard as it is being reduced like this in front of this crowd, Drew, and June; it's infinitely worse with Noah here.

I start to stand, ready to flee fast and far, when his voice hits me like a whip.

"What is she doing here?" The disgust in his voice makes me wince more than the split in my lip when I try to lick away the blood.

Once upon a time, I thought I loved Noah.

That's a lie. I knew then that I loved him. That was a long time ago, back when I still had some goodness in me. Like everything else, I fucked that up. It makes what I did to him even more horrible. Much more unforgivable. Facing Noah... well, that's one thing I'd hoped to avoid tonight. Or forever.

"I needed the money," I say softly, no longer able to keep the tears at bay. "I need the money."

"Enough, Lorelai," Noah clips. His brutish words affect me more than I would have guessed they could. "Apologize."

This isn't the Noah I knew. Noah was soft-spoken and kind. He treated me gently, raised me on a pedestal that he held up with kid gloves. Now he's hard, commanding, his words too reminiscent of my father.

"No," I say, in denial of the image playing out in my head. I blink hard to clear the confusion. I'm not responding to Noah's order, but he doesn't see what I see and takes my words as a refusal to his demand.

"Noah," June says, her pity putting me further in my place.

The last thing I want from her is fucking sympathy.

When Noah snaps at me again, I can't get the words out fast enough.

"I'm so sorry." I need out of here; need air and a quiet space to numb the humiliation and my scattered thoughts.

With my first step toward the stairs, I stumble slightly. Noah's large hands reach for my waist. At first, I'm shocked he would even try to stabilize me instead of just watching me fall again, this time without the help of June's right hook. But then he bends at the knees, just enough to ram a shoulder into my abdomen and easily lift me off my feet.

There's no point in fighting him; he's twice my size. I don't protest or scream for him to stop; nobody here will help me anyway. Resigning myself to be escorted out and dumped on the street is all I have going for me right now.

My view is full of Noah's ass encased in perfectly tailored black suit pants. In any other circumstance, I'd be impressed, probably even turned on. That would get me exactly nowhere. If I've been successful at anything tonight, it was making myself the most unappealingly lowest creature in the building.

Nobody would want me, least of all Noah. Why would he? I was unfathomably cruel to him all those years ago. Deceiving him as I did. Even if it was to benefit him.

In another desperate move, I had asked Noah to spank me. I didn't explain why, instead I taunted him into doing it. I used the aftermath of that experience as a catalyst to end our relationship. That, too, wasn't something I explained to him. There's a bigger story there and I've never admitted it to anyone.

A few wayward tears stream out of my eyes and run down to my hairline while I bounce on Noah's shoulder as he takes the stairs down. They're surprising, the tears. I'm not a crier. But I can't blame myself for them. My life hasn't been easy. If anyone deserves some tears, it's me. Well, that's a lie.

The noise of the crowd and the music quiets, and the light that penetrates my watery sight dims and dims.

He carries me through a doorway and kicks the door shut behind us. The room is still, silent, and pitch-black for a second. Foreboding settles over me, causing me to shiver uncomfortably. Being in situations I can't predict freaks me out. Takes me back to a time I would rather never revisit.

Back to when my raging bull temper wasn't something I possessed. All I had was self-preservation, and a fit of any kind would only cause me more trouble. Which, I suppose, all things considered, is still true.

Fuck, I just don't learn.

Noah unceremoniously dumps me into a hard chair. I slump in it as the blood rushes back to all the places it's supposed to be. My hair acts as a curtain around me. I don't bother pushing it out of my face. It will only make me witness to whatever hard expression Noah is wearing. I don't need to see it to know it's there; I feel it. He's moving around the room like a storm waiting for the perfect place to strike down its thunder.

His tension fuels the worst parts of me. The ire starts in my stomach, then creeps through me, blotting out anything calm, anything remorseful. I want to rage as my fists clench and my neck tightens so much; I stretch it—pop my shoulder back until I hear a crack.

"Stop," he barks, and I shiver for another reason now. "Relax. Eyes to me."

Relaxing isn't exactly an option. But I lift my head just enough to see the shape of him through the waterfall of my white hair; still making no effort to brush it away.

I've never seen clearly. Why start now?

Dragging another chair in front of me, Noah sits close enough to touch me, but far enough that he isn't in any danger of being tainted by my presence. At least, that's how I take it. I don't presume to know Noah these days, but his disapproval of me is clear enough.

His fingers brush away at the strands still covering my face, and the touch makes me flinch. I don't fear that he'll hurt me. But I don't want his physical contact all the same. Though I allow him his firm grip of my chin, tilting my head up further, I close my eyes before his face comes into view.

"You really fucked up this time, Lorelai." My name on his lips is as cold as the piece of damp cloth he presses to my mouth. It stings as he cleans up the damage June inflicted, but I take it. I deserve it. We both know it.

"I'll get you cleaned up and get you back to wherever you're staying," he continues, and that does make me wince.

"I don't have—" I begin but quickly retreat. "You don't need to worry about me."

"I'm not worried about you. I'm worried about how much more damage you'll cause," he says. "Seeing you safely put away is the best thing for the well-being of all my guests."

Put away. Like I'm a feral dog.

"I'll leave. I won't come back," I say, sounding more dejected than I'd like.

"You'll have to forgive me if I don't believe a single word out of your vicious mouth."

Forcing myself to look at him, I open my eyes. As I expected, the gaze staring back at me is hard, chilled, focused on the cut he's still tending. When he meets my eyes, there's something else there, too. It's quick, just a flash of an emotion, as if I startled him just by looking back.

It's been so long since I've seen him in the flesh. Since I've been this close to him. My heart screams that we're home. Even my damaged brain knows better.

Noah has always been very good-looking. In college, every girl I knew crushed on him in some capacity. He's turned from an attractive all-American boy to a downright handsome man. He's broader than the guy I knew and infinitely sleeker in a suit that was obviously made for him. His once dirty blond hair has darkened a few shades, parted just off center in perfectly styled waves. Neatly trimmed facial hair blankets his powerful jaw. And those damned eyes of his.

Wolfish—that's what I'd always thought of the gold flecks that brighten them as they pierce into me. His current prey.

"I don't want your help."

"I don't care. Where are you staying?"

"Noah, stop," I plead. I don't want him to know what a bind I'm in. My money is so limited, even if it wasn't Super Bowl weekend in New Orleans, I'd have a hard time finding a safe spot to afford.

"It's not up for fucking discussion, Lorelai. Where are you staying?" Noah leans forward slightly, impressing his will and determination, his dominance, on me. The tendons in his neck tighten, and I focus on them instead of his stern expression.

"I... I don't." I fumble over the words as the last bit of my pride clogs up my throat.

He leans back again, removing his hand from the ministrations of my injury. He's quiet for a moment, and I use that time to bolster myself for what comes next.

"Hell, you don't have anywhere to go." It's not a question; it's a surprised admonishment.

I shake my head in silent agreement, glad that I didn't have to say the words myself.

"Did I miss you being this stupid all those years ago, or is this something you've learned since college?"

"Fuck you, Noah," I hiss. Yes, I mess up. A lot, recently. But I'm not dumb and I hate the accusation. Maybe it's my fault that he sees me as too stupid to live, but I've been living with the 'dumb blonde' stigma my entire life, and I'm anything but that. He knows it just as well as he knows how much the insult stings me.

"There she is," he mumbles with a sly half smile I know can't be trusted. He may not be the man I used to know, but some things never change. That smugness he carries so easily being one of them.

We study each other for a few hundred heartbeats. Me glaring and tight-lipped. Him relaxed and almost amused, which only fires me up more.

Finally, he rises, tosses the used cleansing pads into the trash before gesturing toward the door.

"When is your flight home?"

I balk a little because I don't have that either. There is no home, so there isn't a need to return to Seattle.

"You're joking, right?" Noah asks with a grimace, cluing into my reaction.

"No, Noah. None of this is a joke. None of it is funny! This entire situation is hard enough without your bullshit. Just let me leave." I stand, but he reaches an arm out to block my escape.

"Stop."

"You stop," I protest in petulance.

"Let's go," he says, laughing at my expense. "I have a place you can stay, you toddler."

"Where?" I ask wearily.

"Follow me. I'll fill you in on your new ground rules on our way home."

What the actual fuck have I gotten myself into now?

2
NOAH

Someone should probably diagnose me with a mental disorder for thinking it was a good idea moving Lorelai Simmons into my home. Fuck that, skip diagnosis and move me to an institution.

Good idea isn't the right sentiment, either. I know it was a horrible idea taking her home last night—one I'll pay for in regret and despair, if history has any bearing. She is the only woman who ever broke my heart, after all.

Throughout high school and my first couple of years of college, I kept women at arm's length. My career goals took priority, as I was to be drafted into the NFL. I couldn't afford the distraction of girls, drama, or my libido.

I prided myself on my control. I still do.

But then I met her. She was a cheerleader for USC, our rival school. That didn't matter. Once those argent eyes of hers pierced mine, I was done for. I wanted her. Needed her. More than animalistic desire, or physical attraction, took over me. Deeper inclinations were at play.

I *had* to know her.

We were heading into the off season. That didn't mean my schedule would be much lighter, but I made time when she walked into the bar that night. It was a UCLA hotspot, a dive really. Complete with shitty fried food and drinks that contained more water than booze. She wasn't a regular, but a few teammates recognized her. She was hard to miss. Still is with that mass of blonde hair and legs for days.

I was a good-looking quarterback for a top-ranking Pac-12 school. Beautiful women came out of the woodwork for guys like me. It wasn't her looks that attracted my attention; it was her attitude. The way she walked into the place like she belonged there, like she owned it. Passing by every other woman in the place ignoring the curious glances they gave her. Ignoring all the men gawking at her as she entered the bar all by herself and scanned it before she settled on me.

Except for the one idiot who dared to block her path with a "hey baby". The look she gave him was enough to wither the balls of half the men in the place.

She was there for a singular purpose and didn't hide it. Instead of being annoyed, I found myself flattered. A novel sensation for me. When she elegantly sat on the bench seat next to me, I knew she was about to turn my world upside down, and I couldn't find a reason to care.

"I grow tired of you not introducing yourself to me, Noah," she said with a small pout.

"Is that so?" She amused me. While I recognized her as one of my rival's pom-pom girls, I had not paid her, or any of the others, much attention. Because… football, NFL, career. I didn't fuck our own school cheerleaders, let alone anyone else's.

I wasn't a saint, or even virginal.

Discriminatory is what I'd call it. My hookups had been women above college age that did not know who I was and wanted nothing but a quick fuck.

"Yes." She sighed as a smile formed on her sweetheart lips.

"How can I make it up to you?" I asked, wanting to see if her attitude matched what my mind conjured. She was confident, but I sensed it was armor. A tough shell hiding something else. The fixer in me wanted to splay her open, find the weak points, and solder them back together.

"Buy me a drink?" she suggested.

"Sure. What will it be?"

"Just water."

I pushed my glass to her with a raised brow. I hardly ever drank in those days.

"Thank you," she said. "You still haven't introduced yourself."

"You already know who I am."

"True," she said. "But you don't know me."

She was right. I hadn't known her then. Months later, after she'd spent more nights in my bed than hers, I can't say I knew her any better then, either.

I certainly don't know the Lorelai that is currently waiting for me as I drive back home after the Super Bowl game at our local stadium. It was a big day for my city, for the team I work with as a recruitment consultant. I should be out enjoying the afterparties with friends and co-workers. Instead, I'm rushing home to the bane of my past and the woman who broke the heart of one of my dearest friends.

For all I know, Lorelai's wiped my home clean of any valuables, trashed the place, and fled.

Something tells me that isn't the case.

We said little on the walk from the party last night to my condo several blocks away. By the time we got there, her lip was fatter with more of a purple bloom. She looked like a ragged barbie doll with her bruises and messy hair, as she dragged her small suitcase behind her. The only possession she had stashed at the coat check before infiltrating my party.

I'd shown her to the guestroom and let her settle herself while I grabbed her an ice pack. She was half asleep by the time I made it back to that side of the condominium. My ground rules could wait until morning. But before I left for the game this morning, she was still sound asleep.

I'd left a note and then spent my entire day wondering if I'd placed too much trust in her. She doesn't deserve any, but she is also human and someone I once cared a great deal for. Leaving her to fend for herself on the street isn't something even I am capable of.

That doesn't mean I'm happy about the whole situation.

Walking through my front door, I'm met with some awful rap music. To top it off, she's singing along. Following the screeching sound, I find the source in the kitchen.

She doesn't hear me enter, so I use the opportunity to watch her for a minute. Lorelai is wearing leggings and an oversized tee, her hair all wrapped up on top of her head while she dances around the small space, cooking something that, admittedly, smells delicious.

Thinking she's by herself, she's relaxed. Comfortable and at ease. That all changes when I reach over to the speaker on the counter and reduce the volume. Her entire demeanor shrinks, as if being in the presence of another person makes her several inches shorter.

"Your taste in music has gotten no better than your tone deafness," I say once the music is low enough for me to be heard. She doesn't stop cooking or spare me a glance.

"Sorry."

"For what?"

"The music. And the singing," she answers on a nervous exhale.

"House rule number one, don't apologize unless you have offended me with the intention to do so."

Lorelai turns off the burner, then finally turns to me, eyes wide. A tingeof fear in them, only highlighted by her defined, darker brows. They're naturally that way. She doesn't need to enhance them with makeup. It's always given her a slightly severe look, still beautiful, just with a veil of something edgier to it.

"How many rules are there?"

"As many as there needs to be."

She stares back at me, still too tense. She's ready to run, like a scared rabbit staring unblinkingly at the predator scenting its prey. There isn't a reason for her to be afraid, but I like that she is. I take a step forward; she retreats by the same distance. I'd smile, except her skittishness makes my dick twitch with excitement.

And, well, that just pisses me off.

Lorelai enticing me is not part of the plan. She's a viper, one whose venom I don't want. I'll keep her housed, fed, and safe until I know what the hell is going on with her life. Long enough that I can help to get her out of June and Drew's lives, therefore, out of my life. I won't be fucking her.

"Are you hungry? I made enough for two," she says hesitantly. "Your note said I could help myself. I… I hope it's okay."

"It is. I ate at the game. Besides, you look like you could eat it all."

"Do I look that bad?" she asks, looking down at herself.

Even as battered as she still is from her altercation with the wife of the man she'd been having an affair with, she is gorgeous. Another thing I don't need to tell her.

"You've gotten scrawny. Too much extracurricular activity, perhaps."

She flinches, but her mouth pulls tight. That temper I've always admired kindling on the surface.

Game on, Lorelai.

"Maybe I should just go."

"Maybe you should eat your dinner. It smells good. Sit. I'll talk, you eat," I say, nodding to the dining nook.

She plates her meal, a stir-fry of brightly colored vegetables. No lie, it does smell fantastic, and it gives me an idea. Sitting in the chair opposite her, I wait until she's a few bites in before I talk.

"Next rule. For as long as you are staying here and are without gainful employment, you cook the meals."

Her fork stalls on the way to her mouth.

"Am I supposed to be your housekeeper? Do I get a sexy little French maid costume?"

"You won't be the housekeeper; I have one of those. You will earn your keep, though."

"I'm not fucking you for room and board."

She brightens as her indignation rises. Cheeks become rosier, eyes flash with heat. She glows against the dark eggplant walls. A contradiction. The room is old, stately, classic—and her, everything but. Lorelai is jaded as hell, though she's always had an undertone of youthful naivete. Nearing thirty, you'd expect she'd have her life figured out by now. She clearly does not.

Nor does she have me figured out.

"We won't be fucking at all, Lorelai. I learn my lessons."

Her nostrils flare and though I'm baiting her, I don't let her see that I'm pleased by her reaction. This is only the first of many battles we'll wage against each other, and since we'll both be keeping a tally of wins and losses, I'm determined to be the first to score.

"Why am I here, Noah?"

"Do you want all the reasons?"

"Yes," she says immediately. It's not surprising; she was always brave.

"You had nowhere to go. Even though you're a treacherous little devil, I gave a shit once, and that means something to me. I'll help you out and then I'll get you the fuck out of June's life." I clock her reaction as I say it. She doesn't give me what I'd expected, and again, I get excited by that. I like the unexpected. "If I can even the score between us, all the better."

"What does that mean?"

"I don't know yet. I'll tell you know when I figure it out."

She ignores me and finishes eating her meal. I watch as she does, then as she cleans up her dishes and wipes down the stove. Putting everything back to the way it was pre-Lorelai. Like she never existed in my space at all.

If only she could have erased herself so easily all those years ago.

"I think I should go."

"I'm not forcing you to stay, but you should at least hear me out before you decide."

Determination is a double-edged sword. It can help you get everything you want out of life, or it can drive you to dangerous obsessions. I can't say with certainty which side of the blade I'm teetering on right now. All I know is that I'm not ready for Lorelai Simmons to walk out my door just yet.

"Have a glass of wine with me. We'll talk. If you still want to leave, I'll help you find a place."

She looks uncertain, but pads on her bare feet to the sofa and folds herself onto one side of it. I take my time pouring each of us a glass. Because I'm an asshole and I want her on edge. I know it worked when she takes the offered glass with an unsteady hand.

To further chip away at her sense of security, I opt to sit next to her. Her body curls into itself ever so slightly more.

"Should we start with why you don't have a job or a home to go back to?"

"Are you psychoanalyzing me or offering me a place to stay?"

"Both, it seems," I answer with a smirk.

"I quit my job in Seattle. The manager was… handsy. I had savings, but something came up."

She doesn't meet my eyes, which means she's lying or hiding something. Her perfectly painted pink-tipped toes disappear underneath her as she shifts in her seat. It's a subject we'll be discussing, but it can wait for now.

"Why were you in Seattle? You had a great job in San Francisco." Her mouth pops open in surprise. She doesn't hide it. "I may have kept tabs for a time."

"Then you know why I went to Seattle." She tips her chin up, trying to be proud of herself despite knowing what a colossal mistake it was to make that move.

"I know who you went there for. What I don't know is why. What made you think he'd ever leave June for anyone, let alone you?" It's harsh, I know. It's what she needs. Besides, placating her doesn't appeal to me.

"I knew he'd never leave her. He helped me, so I made myself available in return."

"You made yourself his whore, Lorelai."

"Fuck you, Noah." This time, her eyes meet mine. Steely and so damned stubborn.

"No need to be angry with me. I'm not the one who reduced you to pussy for hire." Her feet shoot to the floor, ready to bolt. I'm not having any of that. "Sit the fuck down, Lorelai."

With a tremble, she does.

"Good girl," I praise. Her gaze shoots to me, confusion playing on her brow. "I'm not the same man I was all those years ago, Lorelai."

"I'm beginning to see that," she says in a shaky voice.

"You'll stay here, and you'll follow my rules. I will reward your good behavior."

The effect my words have are clearly visible by the pebbled nipples beneath her t-shirt. I keep my smile to myself.

The night Lorelai walked into my dorm room, offering me a crop and begging me to spank her, it was this version of me she was hoping to find. He didn't exist then.

Now, I want no part in whatever her game was back then. Lorelai is my war, and I play to conquer.

3
LORELAI

I read a quote by some doctor once.
The difference between shame and guilt is the difference between 'I am bad' and 'I did something bad.'

I've felt guilty for longer than I care to remember. Noah makes me feel shameful in such a way that I haven't felt since I was a child. He makes me needy for his approval. Something that surges up lost feelings from when I was a cowering youth trying to avoid my father's spittle as he spewed his sermons over me.

I'll be damned if I seek license from someone who so easily degraded me just seconds ago.

I spent my childhood in that way. Every move, every action made to please my father. How I sat, what I wore, the way I held my fork, and chewed my food. If I made a simple mistake, punishment followed.

I crave punishment now, but that's a story for another time. Or never at all.

"What do you want from me, Noah?"

He takes his time answering. I'm on to him; he's keeping me guessing. Knowing he's doing it, and why, doesn't make my response to it any different. I'm down to my last few chess pieces here, and my only move is to sacrifice a pawn while I wait for him to give away more of his strategy.

Though I know we're playing, I don't understand his end game. He wants something from me. But if not sex, then what? If it was revenge, he could have easily left me on the street to fend for my broke-ass self.

"I told you already. For you to be stable enough to get out of June's life."

"How do you see me going about that, exactly?"

"I'm hiring you. You'll stay here rent-free while you save enough money to find a job in another state, preferably one without an NFL team. Then you'll go."

"Never to be seen again," I muse.

"One can only hope," he says, and it stings.

"What are you hiring me for?"

"Cooking, as we've established. I don't enjoy it, and you seem qualified. Also, I still need physical therapy. You'll handle that."

That is my profession. My dreams to one day continue schooling for Sports Medicine never happened. Life has a way of derailing all my plans.

"Anything else?"

"You'll also run basic errands for me and take care of grocery shopping. I'll let you know when I have other needs you can fulfill." His tone makes the words sound dirty despite already making it clear this isn't a sexual arrangement.

"How much?"

"More than enough to set you up somewhere else. Tomorrow, I'll set up two accounts for you. One will get a weekly allowance that you can access. Another where I will deposit the bulk of your pay. You'll get that when it's time for you to leave. I'll set a salary for the items we've established. If I add tasks, I'll add funds as well."

"Sure. But how much?"

A wide, toothy smile lights up his stern face. I wouldn't call it a cheerful smile. More of an evil sneer.

"Good girl," he praises, and I feel it like a tingle in my tits. *Motherfucker.* "Five hundred dollars a week allowance. More than adequate, since I'll be paying for your housing and food. Another thirty-five hundred a week in the separate account. We can negotiate anything else as it comes up."

Holy shit.

That's more than I made in San Francisco, and certainly more than in Seattle, where I worked ten-hour days with multiple clients. Mostly pretentious asshole clients. I guess I'd still be dealing with that, though. Even adding in personal chef duties, the money is more than adequate. Generous, even.

Noah's draft deal into the NFL was newsworthy. Larger than almost all other offers that came before, or since. He's a wealthy man.

However, he threw that number out easily. Too easily. While the sum is appealing on many levels, I'd be stupid to eagerly agree.

Surely, he expects negotiation.

"Five hundred as an allowance is fine. I won't need much. I want five thousand a week in the separate account, with your assurance in writing that you won't fuck me over when it's time for me to leave," I say, making direct eye contact so he sees I'm serious.

"I'm not the one with experience in fucking people over, Lorelai," he says flatly. "What will I be getting out of paying such an exorbitant salary?"

"The best care you can get since you'll be my only client. You still favor your right side. I felt it when you rag-dolled me out of your party. You're still feeling pain because you haven't taken proper care of it. There's likely inflammation, making the discomfort worse," I tell him with confidence. "I'll want to see your last set of imaging and a current blood panel. If you haven't had an hs-CRP test, I'll want one. As well as vitamin D, vitamin B, and a comprehensive food sensitivity test. After that, I'll tailor your nutrition. You'll be back in fighting form before I disappear into the ether."

"You have yourself a deal, Lorelai," he says after a moment of careful evaluation. "I'll have a contract drawn up tomorrow while we set up your accounts and get the medical documents you require."

Expecting him to counter my offer, I'm surprised by his simple acceptance. And again, I don't trust it. Probably wise not to trust anything Noah does or says based on the way he looks at me like I'm a calculation he hasn't yet figured out.

Remembering that about him, how he studies things from all angles, brings back a sense of nostalgia. We spent many lazy mornings, me wrapped around him in his bed as he studied game tapes, and I napped in between rounds of sex. Even then, young as we both were, he was an exceptional lover. He excited me and I enjoyed our time together. It was just missing something... more. Something dangerous and depraved. Things I didn't want to ask of him. I didn't want to taint or corrupt him. Instead, I ruined it all.

No matter how I've tried to ignore deviant desires, it had a forever hold on me. Therapy should be at the top of my list of things to do with the money I earn here. But like a good little ostrich, I'd rather bury my head in the sand than face my issues.

Noah knows nothing of the curses I've carried with me since childhood. There were many times I wanted to tell him, to open up to him or seek his help in coping with my demons. Life could have been different had I done so. Instead, like I often do, I let fear of the unknown rule my decision to keep it all to myself.

I've only ever told one person, and even he doesn't know much about it. I let him hold a small bundle of my secrets because I held all his biggest ones in return. Drew McKenna gave me a sense of security that way. He didn't love me; he didn't make promises of a future together. We both knew that was never in the cards. But I knew he'd help me, at least somewhat, because of what I held over him. Being someone's mistress allows you to hold a terrible power over a man.

Power isn't something a woman like me should hold too much of.

"Thank you," I say, keeping an even tone. "Do you have access to a gym we can use?"

Noah's right eyebrow raises at a controlled, steady pace. He probably practices that move in the mirror.

"What?" I ask.

"You didn't find the gym when you snooped through the condo today?"

"I didn't snoop. I only left my room to use the bathroom and kitchen." I wanted to wander the place, to peek in every nook and cranny. To find all the things Noah covets and hides away from the world. Then I remembered, I know nothing of Noah Anders and didn't want to risk his anger when I'm on such tenuous footing.

By tenuous, I mean I have a bank balance of $628.24. I need Noah, as hard as that is for me to admit.

"Come." I follow him toward the opposite end of the condo from where the small, but plush, guestroom I slept in is. The hallway is dark from the carved wood panels, lit up only by a few small vintage wall sconces. They cast ominous shadows as we pass. I can't help taking it as a foreshadowing.

"My office." Noah points to the first door we pass on the left. "Another bathroom is here. This is the gym." He gestures to the third door before pushing it open. There is one more door at the end of the hall.

"What's that one?" I ask, pointing to it.

"My bedroom."

I nod and walk into the home gym. It's not large. Well organized and looks to be equipped with everything we'll need. A massage table sits in one corner. The opposite corner holds an elliptical machine and a weight bench. TRX straps hang above where some various Pilates and yoga equipment are stored.

Strolling around the room, I examine everything.

"If you don't find something you want, let me know. We'll order whatever is needed."

"Sure thing. Is it okay for me to work out here in my free time?"

"Of course. While you're a guest here, nothing is off limits. There's a computer in my office, if you need to use that," he says with a shrug. As if it's a simple thing to put all this trust in me.

"Is that what I am, Noah? A guest?"

"Sounds better than a live-in employee."

"Right. Because that makes me sound like pussy for hire."

"There isn't anything wrong with sex work," he says, as if I am exactly that.

"No. But that's not something I've ever done. No matter how many times you imply it."

Yes, Drew helped me out financially, but not in that way. The money he gave was to help solve a problem I couldn't do on my own and it sure as hell was not in trade for fucking him. He gave the money out of goodness, not as payment.

The hurt I feel isn't for how Noah thinks of me as much as it is for his opinion of Drew. That man shouldn't have fucked around on his wife, but he isn't a bad guy. He has an enormous heart.

I'm not sure Noah Anders has anything beating inside his chest anymore.

"Is the suitcase you arrived with all you have?" he asks, effectively changing the subject.

"Yes," I say after taking a big gulp of air. Besides the outfit I wore last night to the party and the outfit I have on today, I have a few other pairs of underwear, a pair of jeans, a couple of tees, and a pair of tennis shoes.

There is nothing else. Except what little pride and attitude I still possess. That, and my pure determination to find my way out of this bullshit existence.

"We'll remedy that tomorrow."

"Why?" I can get by with what I have until he pays me my first stipend. It's not like I need anything fancy for cooking and working him out. "I'd rather not start off the week by already owing you money."

"I'll be supplying an adequate wardrobe for you to perform the duties I ask of you. I won't be docking your pay for it," he says, as if it's already been decided.

"If I fight you on this, is there any chance I'll win the argument?"

"No." The word is flat, but his eyes betray him. That gold spark says he's amused. Or turned on. Either way, I roll my eyes.

"Fine, Noah. You want to keep me; I won't stop you. You can be my Sugar Daddy. For now." It's not as if I'm able to say no. And why should I? He wants to pay me and buy me shit… fine. There is zero shame in taking what he's offered.

A low, yet genuine, laugh erupts from him. His head falls back a little with the effort of it. Once again, nostalgia kicks in. We had some good times, this man and me. While the memories bring a smile to my face, they make me heavy-hearted. Yearning for what might have been.

If only I'd not been such a horrendous cunt.

Noah leaves the home gym, and I follow, watching as he checks the front door before he makes his way room by room, switching off all the lights. He stops in front of me, where I lean, holding up the doorjamb to my new bedroom.

"I like breakfast by seven. Is that going to be a problem?"

"No. I expected you were still an early riser." He used to wake before daybreak without fault. No matter what we got up to all night long. Noah didn't believe in wasting time. I assume that hasn't changed. Some things never do.

"Good. We're calling it a night. Do you need anything before bed?"

"Do I have a bedtime, Daddy?" I ask in amusement, because seriously, what the fuck?

"Yes. You need structure, Lorelai. Rules and guidance. Possibly therapy. We'll work through all that. But for now, you go to bed at a decent hour because I need you to be up early. Understood?"

That flash of whatever makes Noah's eyes bright is there again. Mine flitter back and forth on him. Try as I might, I can't gauge what he's thinking. Let alone what he's planning.

"Sure thing, Noah. I'll play along," I say with a wry smile. "Sleep well. I'll see you dark and early in the morning."

"One more rule," he quietly says as I'm about to shut the door on his stupidly handsome face.

"What's that?"

"Your orgasms belong to me now."

I'm about to agree with whatever he said just to get him to leave so I can wallow alone in my bed when the words hit me.

"I'm sorry," I say with a laugh. "But what the fuck does that mean?"

"You always had quite the potty mouth," he muses. "It means, dear Lorelai, that you don't come unless I allow it. Rules. Structure. You need them in your sex life as much as anywhere else, judging by the trail of pain you leave in your wake. While you're here, I'm in charge of everything, including when you come."

"You're joking."

"I'm not. And I'll know if you try to skirt this rule. You need to get off? You earn it."

With that little bomb, he turns on his heel and strides off to his side of the condo.

Lines are clearly drawn now. If Noah wants a war, I'm happy to oblige.

4
LORELAI

Rising before Noah, I'm showered, dressed, and have breakfast nearly ready when he strolls into the kitchen. As always, he's impeccably dressed. Only slightly less dressy than the past two days. There's no crisp suit today, though I bet I could go check his closet and there would be a jacket to match the dark gray pants he's wearing below his black button-down.

In comparison, I'm woefully underdressed in my jeans and faded tee.

"Coffee?"

"Please," he answers. "Black."

Like that hole where your heart should be.

Probably, I should direct that thought to myself. Maybe neither of us has any heart left. I hand him a steaming mug, then plate the food of rice and beans, eggs, and side of fruit.

"Bacon?" Noah asks as he sits at the table where I set his plate.

"No. At least not until I see your blood panels."

"Jesus," he mutters while rolling his eyes.

"You're paying for a great job. Let me do it."

He side-eyes me, but digs in. I watch him eat every bite while I eat my smaller serving. And drink my coffee doused with oat milk I found in his refrigerator. Because only psychos and serial killers drink their coffee black.

"What's the schedule for today?"

"The lab opens at eight, we'll stop there first. Then the bank. We'll shop for necessities and eat lunch out before coming back here for a workout."

That all sounds fine. *Except.*

"Contract?" I ask before biting into a ripe strawberry. For the past few weeks, I've been on such a budget my diet has been complete crap. Reminiscent of my college days, full of instant ramen noodles and cheap macaroni and cheese. Fresh fruit feels indulgent.

Noah reaches out and wipes a drop of berry juice off my lip with his thumb. Then sucks that very thumb into his mouth, tasting it, and *me*. My eyes narrow on him, from both wondering what he's up to and because the tip of his tongue swirling around his thumb makes my pussy clench.

This bastard doesn't get to work me up, only to withhold orgasms. Which is another item we'll be discussing. At fucking length.

"I emailed my attorney last night. He'll have the contract ready this afternoon. We'll go over it together this evening."

"Sounds good. I'm ready to leave when you are," I say, taking both our empty plates to the kitchen to wash up. Gaining a little distance. Noah brings out far too many emotions in me. None of which I know what to do with. Keeping my armor strong around him is a necessity.

Once, I let it disappear altogether. Noah attracted me like no other guy had before. He had a confidence about him that differed from even Drew. Drew was the quarterback at the University of Southern California where I attended on a cheerleading scholarship. Noah was the all-star quarterback at the University of California, Los Angeles. Rivals, but equally talented and equally good-looking. While Drew was always charming enough to make sure he had a chick in his bed anytime he wanted one, Noah was aloof and uncaring about the gaggle of women constantly vying for his attention.

In my infinite stupidity, I found that attractive, and I became obsessive. I practically stalked him to the point of creepiness. Shit, close to criminal even. Before I ever uttered a word to him, I knew his entire schedule. Putting myself in his way got old quickly when it didn't work. He never took notice.

Until the night I didn't give him much of a choice. We were a whirlwind after that night. In short order, Noah and I became each other's everything.

And then we weren't. We were nothing. Or nothing good, anyway.

What we are now is anyone's guess.

"Lorelai." Noah's deep voice brings me back to the present.

"Hmm?"

"Ready?" he asks, holding up his car keys.

I nod and follow him, grabbing my handbag as we move to the door.

Noah gets blood drawn at the lab, and we go to the bank where he sets up both accounts, as promised. In one, he deposits my first week's allowance that I am issued a bank card for. The other, I don't. It's in both our names, but he's the gatekeeper of it.

Not questioning any of it, I go with the flow until we pull up at Canal Place. If he'd have asked me where I wanted to shop for my 'necessities', this wouldn't have been the place I chose. All the storefronts are high-end brands. But, hey, if he wants to spend all his hard-earned dollars on a piece of pussy he doesn't even plan on tasting… fine.

Heading straight for Sak's Fifth Avenue, I let Noah trail me this time. The confidence I had walking into the store dies a fast death as I swiftly become overwhelmed with the store. I knew it would be posh, but this is an enormous step up from where I typically shop. Which is Target and discount racks at lesser department stores. Occasionally, I'll splurge for higher-end fitness apparel online. But that's rare; I've always been frugal.

Scanning the space, I see athletic wear and make a beeline for it. Noah doesn't say a word for the first few minutes I peruse the racks. I've pulled a few sports bras and leggings, an array of colors and prints blanketing one of my arms. When I hold up a black lycra bodysuit, Noah finally speaks.

"No."

"What? Why? This would be great for yoga and Pilates," I say, imagining how nice it would be to not worry about a top riding up or leggings slipping down in certain poses.

"No," he says, this time with a raised eyebrow and a sterner tone.

This type of domineering bullshit should piss me off. But I'm Lorelai Simmons, the dumbass that gets hot and bothered by such things.

So, I put the stupid bodysuit back and tally one more point in Noah's column.

Pulling a handful more items, I turn to him and eye his large, strong, empty arms. "Care to help here?" I ask, raising an eyebrow of my own.

"Come," he says easily. After following him to a checkout counter, he unloads the items from my arms and drops them on the counter.

"Send these up to Eileen, please. Tell her there will be more items and Noah Anders will text her when he's ready for them to be brought out."

"Of course, Mr. Anders," the sales associate says, her pupils glassy as she grins from ear to ear.

Rolling my eyes, I turn and look for the next department to plunder. We repeat a similar process for the next half hour. Mostly, Noah stays quiet. Only occasionally replying with a short no. However, I have a much more expansive wardrobe waiting for me with the mysterious Eileen.

I'm covered for workout and casual wear. I don't expect to need anything else. Other than shoes and undergarments. I hit the shoes next, picking another pair of tennis shoes. Ones much expensive than I'm currently wearing.

A male sales associate asks which size and disappears to go in search of them. I sit on an upholstered bench to wait, but Noah stays standing, a small frown on his face.

"Take a load off, Noah. It might ease the pressure of whatever is stuck up your ass," I tease.

"Classy," he deadpans.

"Classy is overrated, Daddy."

"Stop," he clips, but there's a twitch at the corner of his mouth. Point for me.

The associate comes back, kneeling in front of me. I've already kicked off my worn shoes, making it easy for him to reach for my foot.

"She can do that herself. You're dismissed."

"It's no problem," the associate begins.

"You are dismissed. Thank you," Noah repeats with a hard edge.

"Uh, yeah. Okay, let me know if you need anything else," he stammers out as he retreats.

"God, Noah. That was rude."

"Polite is overrated," he says before taking a few steps away.

Huffing out an exasperated breath, I turn my focus to the shoes. Once laced up, I stand to bounce around in them. There's something to say about expensive shoes. They feel like they're made for my feet and I'm prancing on clouds. Smiling, I look up to let Noah know that these are a definite yes, but he isn't there.

He's standing across the department talking to a woman with long, dark, wavy hair. She's tall, taller than my five-foot-seven. Her elegantly put together outfit would make me look like a crack addict if I stood next to her.

Not that it matters. I'm not in competition with this random woman who has captivated Noah's attention. It's not like I want his hand dragging up my arm to clasp my elbow, like he's doing to her as he speaks with her. He doesn't need to make intimate eye contact with me or share air from standing so close.

Damnit.

I blink away the welling feelings. Finding the dude that Noah ran off, I wave him down.

"I'll take these," I tell him, shoving my old shoes into the now empty box. "Follow me."

I point out two more pairs of the dreamy tennis shoes and a few casual pairs of flats, not bothering to try them on.

"Send them all up to Eileen for Noah Anders, please."

"Of course, Miss."

Walking up behind Noah, I lay my hands on his shoulders and stretch on to my tippy toes.

"I'm heading to lingerie, sir," I purr, just loud enough for the woman to hear. Her eyes narrow and her mouth forms a soft O, and I score another point in my column.

By the time Noah catches up, I have my arms laden with panties, bras, and sleep things. For the first time, he seems to take an interest. He sorts through my stash, tossing a few items back on the racks. My eyes bounce from him to the items.

What the fuck?

He's returned all the most conservative pieces, leaving me with nothing but thin straps and bits of lace.

"What are you doing?" I muse aloud.

"Exerting my veto power."

I shrug and begin looking for even skimpier items. None of which he puts back.

"I hope I didn't embarrass you in front of your friend."

"Eileen doesn't blush easily," he knowingly retorts. Of course, Eileen is beautiful. And of course, it seems Noah has fucked her.

"I'm all done. Feed me," I demand, failing to ignore the weird twang of pain I feel in my gut. Noah has always affected me more than I like.

"Are you sure you have everything you need?"

"More than enough. Food. Now. Before I turn into a gremlin."

"A what?"

"Never mind." I sigh. I'm a horror movie fanatic. The more gore, the better. Noah always hated them but would indulge me. Since I'd often end up terrified and shivering in his arms.

We wait in some fancy valet area while my packages are brought out to the car, and I can't help but stare in awe at how much life has changed for him. Noah's family has money. He didn't grow up in the dirt the way I did. His current lifestyle is multiple steps up from where he was, though. He's adjusted to it well, too. People bending to please him has become second nature.

His bossiness is a new character trait as well. Yes, he always had a stern and determined vibe, it's a big part of what attracted me to him. But the man sitting in the driver's seat of a sleek luxury sedan has leveled up about a hundred times.

The Noah Anders I knew all those years ago was more of a confident frat boy. Now he's a card-carrying Boss Daddy.

I don't know what to make of it all.

"Are you craving anything?"

"Can we go somewhere with crawfish? I've never tried it."

"Seriously?"

"Yep. This is my first time farther East than Utah. Crawfish are hard to find on the West Coast."

He stares at me with a bit of confusion. Replaying the words over in my head, I can't figure out what I said that would have him stumped.

"What, Noah?" I ask, with no small amount of exasperation.

"I just figured… never mind. It's nothing. I know just the place."

We drive to a very divey looking place. I think we're just outside of the French Quarter, but this is my first time in New Orleans, so what do I know? I can say this place does not look like an establishment Mr. Buttoned-Up Anders would frequent.

I'm proven wrong when we step in and an elderly Creole woman sends him a wave with a big smile.

"Noah, mon beau," she calls.

"Hey, Babs. The usual, please."

"You got it," she says, and Noah leads me to a picnic table lined with a newspaper on the back patio.

"What's the usual?" I ask just as a young boy places two plastic cups down on the table, along with a roll of paper towels.

"The best crawfish you'll ever have," he answers.

The sweetness from my drink as I take a sip puckers my lips, causing Noah to laugh.

He's beautiful when he laughs. Even when it's at my expense.

"What is this?" I take another tentative sip. "Sweet tea?"

"Yes. Don't be rude, drink it." His eyes narrow and his mouth thins.

I'd already planned to, though it's not my taste. I took a ton of nutrition classes in college. I'm careful about what I put into my body when I can afford to be. But I'm not an asshole. It doesn't take a genius to guess that Babs is the owner of this joint. Or that she's proud of her hard work. If she puts in front of me, I'll down it with a grateful smile.

It's another reminder of where I rank on Noah's list of favorite people. I needed that reminder, as I'd gotten too comfortable after a relatively amicable, albeit strange, morning.

I ask no more questions. Instead, I busy myself by pretending to read the obituaries printed on the newspaper in front of me.

Thankfully, Babs doesn't take long bringing out a large platter of steaming food. She unceremoniously dumps it all onto the table between Noah and I, and I want to die from how delicious it smells. There are red potatoes, small pieces of corn on the cob, and sausages all mixed with the heaping pile of crawfish.

"Who's your chouchou, Noah?" Babs asks in her strong accent.

"No chouchou," Noah says with a slight grimace and a shake of his head. "This is Lorelai, and this is her first time having crawfish."

"No, ma Cherie, say it's not true?"

"Guilty as charged," I say apologetically.

"Let Babs show you how," she offers, picking up one of the little lobster looking things. "You pinch here and here, see?"

I grab one for myself and mimic her movements.

"Then you twist and pull the tail right off." She does it and I do the same. "Then you suck the head. It's the best part!"

She does exactly what she described, putting the open end of the crawfish head to her mouth and sucking loudly.

Again, I do as she does. Damn, that taste. Health be damned, I've found myself a new favorite food.

"Now, pull that tail meat out."

"Damn, that's delicious," I tell her after I've eaten the buttery meat and I pick up another.

"This one's a keeper, mon beau." Babs laughs, patting me on the shoulder before walking back into the small restaurant.

Noah rolls up his shirtsleeves. Slowly as if he knows it will have more effect that way. I'd love nothing more than to be able to admit that it isn't causing me distraction. But who am I kidding? It's an absurdly sexy thing, especially when he's always so covered and buttoned up. His skin glows golden around the slightly bulging veins that I want to...

Fuck.

Picking up another crawfish, I push out those carnal thoughts. I may be lonely, but Noah is not an option. For so many reasons.

Including his disdain for me.

"I can't believe you're sucking the heads."

"Why?"

"Most people not born to it dismiss it as disgusting," he says. "You wouldn't let me eat bacon this morning and now here you are sucking the brains of mudbugs."

"I'd be a pretty shit villain if I didn't suck brains, blood, and souls." I may as well play the part of the portrait he's painted of me. The one the world sees me as.

Drew McKenna's mistress. The would-be home wrecker.

"Excellent point," Noah agrees easily, making me want to wipe my messy fingers all over his pressed shirt, soil him up so he matches me.

I've been alone for a long time, but I've never felt it more than now. It's a desolate place, down here, beneath the soles of everyone I know.

5
LORELAI

There is zero conversation made after we leave Bab's and head back to Noah's.

I couldn't say what bounces around in Noah's brain during all the quiet time. I made the incredibly unwise decision to check some social media notifications I'd been ignoring.

Big mistake. *Huge.*

There is a resurgence of cyber shaming me since my antics at the party the other night.

If there is a dignified way to walk away from the wife of the guy you occasionally fuck finding you naked and washing her husband's spunk out of your hair… well, I haven't found that. I was doomed from the moment June walked into that hotel room and saw me naked with her barely dressed husband. It's not my proudest moment.

Bystanders caught photos of Drew saying goodbye to me outside the hotel and the press ran with it. Speculating a torrid affair. They weren't wrong, even if Drew and June never made public statements about it. There's always more to the story though. There's a lot more to mine, not that anyone would care to hear it.

I'm the other woman, forever doomed. Forever hated. I can't say how many horrific messages I've gotten from people wishing me a tragic death or telling me I should just kill myself. I've quit looking. They don't know me and they don't get to have that kind of power over me. It has been successful in making me feel more alone in the world.

The only people online that have my back in any way are the gross-ass guys that just want a taste of what I gave Drew.

Despite what it all looks like, my affair with Drew wasn't some elaborate plan. Just over a year ago, I had been in Seattle taking a two-week long intensive course at the University of Washington. The private club I belonged to in San Francisco has sister clubs in several other cities, including Seattle.

One night, I went looking to relieve some stress and ran into Drew. I hadn't seen or spoken to him in ages. Him being there looking for something similar felt like fate. Dealing with him instead of a random stranger was much more appealing. June hadn't even crossed my mind that first night.

Because I'm a horrible person. Because what I needed superseded the needs of anyone else.

Politely, Noah helps me haul my spoils of war into my room.

"Put your things away. I'm going to shower, then I'll meet you in the gym," Noah clips.

Setting to my task, I sort through the bags. Some items I recognize as the ones I chose. Many others, I've never laid eyes upon before. I think maybe they sent us with the wrong bags, except most everything appears to be the correct sizes.

By the time I have it all hung up or put away in the antique chest of drawers, I'm no less confused. There's only one explanation. Noah vetoed more than he made me aware of and somehow chose other items without me knowing. Perhaps that's what his intimate conversation with Eileen was all about.

Trailing my hand along the row of clothing perfectly hung in the closet, it's obvious what his intention was.

He's dressing me like the whore he believes me to be.

Every item is insignificant, showy, barely there. The only exception is the workout leggings.

My gut clenches at the hurt of the insult. The entire world is beating me down, and Noah won't even allow me the safe harbor of covering up my own skin. He replaced the casual pants and tops I'd selected with shorts, miniskirts, tanks, and crop tops. I hadn't picked dresses, seeing no need for them, but there are a handful of tiny cocktail dresses. All just scraps of fabrics.

I think Eileen found every piece of clothing in the store that could be described as trashy and bagged it up for me.

Refusing to let it break me down any further, I grab a few things and get ready for another battle with Noah.

Beating him to the gym, I take advantage of the free space, focusing on some Pilates to loosen up my chest and hips. I haven't had a good solid workout in over a week, and today's lunch, while delicious, is going to drag me down if I don't counteract it with some exercise.

Fitness, dance, and gymnastics are the only things I've ever been good at. Well, and screwing up, but I don't count that. Growing up on the ranch, I wasn't allowed much free time. My days were strictly scheduled with chores and the very basics of education.

I used to joke that Utah teaches girls to read and write, but I was lucky because I learned to count, too.

It's not so funny when you know the only reason they taught rudimentary mathematics to me was because I would be expected to keep a precise inventory of food stocks and calculate recipes, depending on how many were living on the ranch. It certainly wasn't to better my education or prepare me to enter the world when I became a young woman. That was never expected of me.

Gymnastics and dance were a luxury few of us girls were allowed. At first, it was something special to me. I thought it was a prize given to me by my father because I was a good girl.

However, that wasn't the case at all.

Noah strides in with confidence, and I falter in my side bend.

"Why are you dressed like a UFC character?" I ask, eyeing his tiny, tight black shorts.

"They're fighters, not characters."

"Are you sure about that?"

He laughs genuinely but eyes me with a sort of look I can't decipher. I, too, am in teeny, little black workout shorts, which I paired with a strappy electric blue sports bra. The most revealing one I found in all my many bags. It's a cup size too small. Eileen either misjudged or didn't give a shit. Either way, I'm all skin and exposed cleavage. He can take his fill; he'll be seeing it every day, it seems.

"First thing I want to do is assess. Just stand naturally for a minute," I say, rising to my feet and circling him. As I suspected, his right hip sits slightly higher than his left. It's not an alignment issue, it's muscular. His body is protecting the injured area in the only way it knows how.

Noah's injury replays in my mind. I'd been watching the game. I had watched all his games. Every single one he played as a professional. A secret I've never told anyone.

The hit he took while running the ball into the end zone was brutal, and I watched with bated breath for him to stand up and shake it off. Like he had with every hit he'd taken before. But I knew that would not happen. I felt it like I'd taken the hit, too.

I cried for the man I had once loved who had just lost the dream of his life that day.

That's another fact I've never told. I mourned with Noah in spirit that day. And I mourn a little more today as I reach out and run my fingers over his firm hip, the muscles tight underneath. A small silvered surgical scar lies just above his waistband. I touch that, and notice the way his ass tenses as I do.

Affected by the memory or by me, I wonder. Not that it matters.

I haven't had many goals in my life. After I was taken from the ranch, I spent a short time wanting to get back to the only life I'd known. Then that morphed into never wanting to return. Working as hard as I could to catch up to the other children in the public school my aunt enrolled me in, I quickly surpassed most. College was a must for me; getting out of Utah was another.

It's hard to imagine how heartbroken I'd have been if I lost the dream I'd worked at tirelessly for only six years. There's no way for me to know how hard it was for Noah to lose the one he'd had for so much longer.

"Take a couple steps forward," I say. He does, and I watch him with a trained eye, not a hungry one. There's no place for my libido in this room. Even if he stands in front of me looking like the gods delivered me my very own version of Thor.

I'm here to heal Noah's body, and if I can heal some portion of my guilt in the process... all the better.

Running Noah through various stretches and simple strength exercises, I quickly get an understanding of the condition of his body. He's still in excellent shape; his only hindrance is from the hip injury.

"It's been years since your injury. Did you quit physical therapy earlier than you should have?" I ask as I guide him through a few poses. To his credit, he hasn't complained about me keeping his routine to mostly yoga today. A few athletes I worked with in San Francisco threw fits if I even suggested it. Noah's taken it with grace. Honestly, his flexibility is light years ahead of where I expected it to be. There's still room for improvement, but it won't take long to get him where he should be.

"No, I think I just had a horrible therapist. She was a bitch. I didn't like her much," he answers.

"You don't like me much, either."

"I'll do my best not to run you off until after I'm healed."

"For what you're paying me, it will take a lot to get me packing."

"We'll see," he says ominously.

I finish his workout with a massage and some assisted stretching, aiming to further loosen his muscles. Once done, I retreat to my room as fast as I can. Being professional with Noah is going to be hard. Having my hands on him, running them along his taut body, reminds me of better times. Reminds me of what I gave up.

What I threw away.

I decide on a cool shower before I figure out a meal plan for dinner. By the time I make my way to the kitchen, I'm feeling less hot and bothered. Even if I'm dressed in light linen shorts with a matching wraparound crop top.

I feel almost naked in the thin, gauzy fabric. It's not like Noah hasn't seen all my goods before, anyway. Still, I'd rather be in something more substantial. Especially since it's still technically winter and not all that hot outside.

Pulling food from the refrigerator, I get to work on dinner.

Noah comes in as I'm plating. I wonder if he has cameras in here. I imagine him lurking like a creep in his dark office, touching himself while watching me julienne the carrots, and the thought washes away some of my sour mood.

He sits at the table, placing a stack of papers next to him. The contract, I assume. Bringing the plates in, I drop one in front of him and take my place in the chair across from him.

"No meat again?"

"We ate two pounds of protein for lunch. Or did you forget?"

"No, you ate a pound and three quarters. I got the dregs and I'm twice your size."

"You should learn to eat faster." I shrug. "Is that the contract?"

He nods, pushing it toward me.

I scan the numbers to make sure they're what we discussed last night, and the bite on my fork stills on the way to my mouth.

"This isn't what we agreed on," I say, looking at him in question.

"No."

"Why did you change it?"

"Keep reading."

There's a section detailing how to end the contract, stating mutual agreement or arbitration are the only ways. I can't choose to end it on my own without forfeiting all the money in the separate account, which should be concerning. But then again, he can't end it either. Not without paying me double what I've earned.

Then I get to the details of my duties. First are the ones we'd already discussed—physical therapy, cooking, grocery shopping. Then there are the ones that he will require occasionally such as picking up dry cleaning, prescriptions, random other things of similar kind.

None of which I have an issue with.

It's the next section that makes my stomach drop.

Under no circumstance am I allowed an orgasm without Noah's expressed permission. I'm allowed to date only if I get his approval prior in order to not cause conflict with his schedule. However, I may not have sexual contact with any said mystery men I may want to go out with.

I have a curfew. And a bedtime. Unless I am out with Noah on one of the occasions he requires me to accompany him to an event. This one I find particularly laughable. I can't see Noah wanting to be seen with me anywhere.

In return, he's upped my weekly pay to ten grand. One thousand allowance, nine to the other account. Every event I attend will prize me with more funds. There's a scale. Five thousand is the minimum for things like a dinner or a simple social gathering. An evening at a gala is worth twice that. Overnight travel is twenty thousand a night.

At the top end is something called Lupus et Agnus. I don't know what that is, but it would pay me fifty thousand dollars.

"There's nothing in here that says what happens if I break a rule," I state, looking in his direction but not making eye contact. Again, I wonder about his end game. Not knowing it makes me feel very unstable, and I don't want him to see that in my eyes.

"That's your first concern?" he asks coolly.

"It's one of them at least." I do my best to keep my voice casually even.

"I'll correct the behavior."

"By docking my pay?"

"No, Lorelai. You earn the money, you keep it. You earn the punishment, you take it." His tone is silky. I feel it like a cool finger down my spine as fearful excitement curls my toes and I hate him for that.

"What's my curfew?"

"Nine on the evenings I am at home. Eleven, otherwise."

"Bedtime?"

"Midnight."

"Unless I'm somewhere with you?"

"Correct."

"Is that something that would be a regular occurrence?"

"No."

"Have you become a sadist over the years, Noah?"

"Only when it comes to you, it seems," he says before taking the last bite of his dinner. Mine lays nearly untouched.

"Fucking wonderful," I snark.

"Would you like to negotiate any changes?"

"Is there a way to get you to back off the orgasm stipulation?" I ask.

"Not likely, but you're free to try," he says as he stands and takes his plate to the sink. "Do you have questions about the dating clause?"

"No. Contrary to what you seem to think, I rarely date."

By rare, I mean never. I don't go home with men. I don't let them come home with me. The only boyfriend I ever had was Noah. The only other relationship was Drew, but even I don't know how to classify that.

If I had a need I couldn't take care of myself before my affair with Drew, I only did it at the club. Structured and safe. Drew was a mistake. One I thought I had learned to not fall into again after our college days.

But fuckups never learn easily.

"Is that so?"

"Yes," I say adamantly. Defiantly.

"Fine. No negotiations, then."

"What do you hope to accomplish by withholding my orgasms?"

"Who says I'm withholding? I've only said you need permission," he says, pouring a finger of whiskey into a thick, block crystal glass.

"Noah," I say with exasperation. We're beyond this type of verbal play.

"What I hope to accomplish is for you to learn sexual discipline and some sense of fucking right and wrong, Lorelai. That should be obvious."

Right and wrong. Good and evil. Hero and villain. Virgin and whore. I can't say I've been on the winning side of those too often in my life.

Feeling properly admonished, I pick up the pen that lies next to the contract and sign my life away into the care of Noah Anders. Unbeknownst to him, he's just handed me a gift far more valuable than he knows.

6
NOAH

Lorelai's been here almost a week now and has agreed to everything I've set in front of her without much fight at all. Admittedly, I'm disappointed by that. Egging her on doesn't even work.

The whole reason I put that stupid dating clause in the contract was to piss her off. I wanted a fight. I still do. She's yet to give it to me.

The contract, in its entirety, was just a tactic for instigating a fight.

She follows the rules, even my arbitrary bedtime. I couldn't care less what time she goes to bed, so long as she has my breakfast ready when I want it the following morning. Not that I even care about that, either. I can cook my own damned breakfast.

There have only been a few instances when I notice her carefully built wall crack. When I blatantly treat her like a cheap whore or when she has her hands on me and is too lost in thought to remember the role she's trying to play.

The workouts have been professional, and she knows what she's doing. Already, after only a few sessions, I feel the difference in my hip. It's loose in a way it hasn't been since before the injury, and the constant, dull ache has faintly eased.

Her hands are magic. After each session, she massages the muscles she's just put through the wringer. I know the effect it has on her, because I feel the same.

Lorelai is hard to avoid and impossible to ignore as she flutters around my space in outfits that bare every luscious inch of her skin.

A miscalculation on my part. In my rush to keep her on the edge of discomfort and humiliation, I naively forgot how much my dick loved her body so long ago. She's even harder to resist now. Long gone is the body of a young woman still finding her stride. It's been replaced with a woman who walks with the knowledge that she's a fucking goddess and men should bow down in gratitude.

I've been close too many times these past days. And that just pisses me right the fuck off.

Tonight, things change.

This battle has become something close to amicable. Continually finding myself content with her cohabitation is unacceptable.

As is the fact that she hasn't asked for permission to get off. She could be ignoring my threats and coming every night. Of course, I have no way of knowing. That was all a bullshit bluff. Somehow, I don't think she's broken that rule either.

Which is why I went out tonight. Every night since we made this deal has been spent in. With her. Mostly, she's kept to herself. She's been reading a lot. She makes the occasional phone call but always heads outside to the balcony for those, piquing my curiosity, though I've yet to confront her on it.

I'm hoping this evening she made herself more comfortable while I was out. I want her at ease and unsuspecting.

Then I'm going to take her comfort away.

It's nearly ten o'clock when I walk back in the front door. Lorelai is curled up on the couch under a thick throw blanket. Screaming comes from the television as blood splatters all over the screen. I almost smile as the memories of her horror movie binges well up in me.

She thinks I hate them. I made her think I dislike them. That was never the case. I just loved when she would beg me to watch one with her. It was the most innocent thing about her, the only time she let me see her vulnerable or needy. I relished those moments.

Instead of smiling at her now, I remember how she ruined those memories. Tainted them with her betrayal and lies.

Intentionally, I slam the door shut loudly. Not only to startle her in her already amped-up state from the movie, but because I need her to look over her shoulder. First, I get a wide-eyed glance, then I watch as those stormy eyes narrow in confusion, or suspicion. Or maybe she's just pissed.

"Monitor the clock, Lorelai," I say sternly.

"Yes, Daddy," she says sweetly as I grab Kelly's hand and lead her to my room.

This is an exception to a very strict rule I keep. I do not bring people back to my home to fuck. Home is a safe space. A place random hookups don't get to know about because I don't want clingers showing up uninvited.

Kelly isn't a clinger, however. She's a paid professional of the highest order.

Leaving the door to my room open, I take a seat at the end of my bed, loosening my tie as Kelly strips. Over her shoulder, I can see down the hall. The television is still on, lights from the movie flashing in the darkness. My focus is everywhere at once. My eyes tracking Kelly's long, lithe movements. Ears tuned into the sounds emanating from outside the room.

"Remember your instructions?" I whisper.

"Of course, Mr. Anders."

"Good," I say, standing to kick off my shoes and remove my shirt. Everything goes except my pants. "You know how to start."

Naked, she settles onto her knees in front of me, hands coming to undo my pants. She doesn't hesitate to reach in and pull me out, running her hand up and down my length as I harden slowly. Kelly tends to me with a confident experience. Unsurprising for the price I paid for her.

"Open," I demand, letting my voice carry louder than necessary, wanting it to travel over the sound of bloodshed from the living room. "Taste me, sweetheart."

Kelly runs her tongue under my sack before trailing up and up. Slowly she traces my length, then around my head a time or two before I wrap her long brown ponytail in my fist and push forward.

Gagging at first, she adjusts her tongue and relaxes her throat. It eases her discomfort, but not fully. She came highly recommended and very experienced, though maybe she's used to… smaller clientele.

Nevertheless, she's noisy as hell, and that, above all else, pleases me immensely. It's what I told her I expected of her. If her performance meets or exceeds my expectations, she'll receive a large tip in return. No pun intended. Well, perhaps she'll get that too.

Fucking her isn't my plan. We discussed my plan might shift as the night went on, however. She's amenable to me shifting gears and sinking into her pricey pussy. She'll be compensated for it, after all.

Kelly's good at what she does, her mouth warm, her tongue talented. But what is really getting me off is the knowledge that the volume of the television is lowering incrementally.

Lorelai wants to hear the show.

"Nice, sweetheart," I say, projecting as best I can. "You like choking on my cock, don't you?"

Kelly moans loudly in between her gags.

"Can you take more? Yeah, there you go. Good girl."

I'm not into daddy kink; praising a woman with words like this has never been something that gets me off. But I've noticed how Lorelai reacts to it.

Football paid for my college career, but my back-up plan had been to be a psychologist if I didn't make the cut or had gotten injured before drafting into the NFL. I was fortunate that I could play a few seasons of pro ball. The money that provided meant it wasn't necessary to finish out the last few years I'd need for an alternate career path. I don't need a career. My interest in it remains though, and because of that, Lorelai's brain intrigues me.

Wanting to know what makes her tick, what molded her into the selfish creature she became, could keep me up at night if I let it.

I don't want to fix her. I want to know what sets her off so I can use it against her. Bitterness fuels my intentions where she is concerned. So, if being a 'good girl' is what she wishes to be, I'll happily give that to Kelly instead.

We carry on this way for a few more minutes until I hear the television shut off. Pulling Kelly's mouth off me, I again sit on the edge of the bed and sheath myself with the condom I tucked in my pocket earlier.

"Ride my cock, Kelly." She stands, then steps in between my legs. "Turn around."

Following instructions, she turns, and I get my first look at her ass. For how slender she is, she's got curves in all the best places. I swat it in appreciation, and the sound vibrates through the room.

"Sit," I say and let out a long groan as she does. Immediately, she bounces. Keeping up with the guidelines I gave her, she makes the necessary sounds, reminding me all too much of a cheap porno.

It's not hot. But it is working. I have my hands on Kelly's round tits, but my eyes are on the hallway. On the shadow that shifts at the far end. The one I know is Lorelai lurking and listening. Hopefully fighting the urge to touch herself.

That's what has me ready to blow. Images of the beautiful, blonde bane of my existence shaking with the need for me to fill her pussy instead of the one I'm currently encased in.

"Scream for me, baby," I whisper in her ear as I thrust two fingers inside with my dick and press the heel of my hand to her clit.

And scream she does as I bring her to her crisis, waiting for her to catch just enough breath before I push her off and back down to her knees as a door clicks shut on the other side of my condo.

"Tongue," I shout, and she sticks it out as far as she can get it. A pretty pink place for me to dirty up. "Keep those eyes on me while you taste every fucking drop."

She does that too, but the eyes I see staring up at me aren't a deep golden brown. They're cold steel, framed by dark brows and darker lashes, as I imagine it's a different woman entirely swallowing down my release.

It's been her face I've seen for years, only making me hate her more.

Kelly quietly leaves shortly after. I take a quick shower, then pad silently to the guestroom. Before opening, I listen at the door. Hearing nothing, I enter, leaving the door wide so a swath of light illuminates the inside. Shining just enough for me to see the body curled up tightly in the middle of the queen-size bed.

Passing that, I instead take a seat in the wide club chair set in the corner, and study her like a damned psychopath. Her uneven, gasping breaths give her away.

She's awake and knows I'm here.

"Lorelai."

A weak whimper emanates from under the blanket.

"Lorelai, do you need to come?"

"Fuck yes." She sighs quietly.

"Come here."

In a rush, she nearly trips from her legs tangling in the blanket. I reach out to steady her.

It's a mistake. Another miscalculation on my part. Her skin is flushed, her hand shivers like I know her greedy little pussy is too. And fuck, I want her.

Kelly did nothing to sate my desire for the bitch now standing in front of me in nothing but tiny panties and a threadbare tee from which her breasts are nearly completely visible through.

"Undress."

Her thumbs hook into the straps of her underwear. That, with the combination of an enticing shimmy, successfully drops them to her ankles where she kicks them off. Then she pulls the tee over her head and her blonde locks cascade in a mess back down. One thick strand comes to tickle her nipple as I watch it harden under my perusal.

"Have you earned this, Lorelai? Have you been a good girl?"

She shakes her head, that piece of hair tickling the spot my mouth desperately wants to be.

"No."

"No?"

"No. I'm a bad girl," she says in a pouty, shy way that shoots straight to my groin. Lorelai has never been anything close to shy.

"Do you need a punishment first?"

"Y-yes," she says with a heated gaze that travels the ridges of my naked body, pausing where she sees my semi-hard cock.

"Turn around and bend over. Grab your ankles." I waste no time. Once she's in position, I swat the underside of her ass. Hard. "How have you misbehaved?"

She doesn't answer. So, I repeat the action on alternate sides for a few minutes until the skin is a nice rosy shade.

"Have you touched yourself without permission?"

"No, Noah," she says without a hint of defiance, and I believe her words, though I don't know why. Villains can't be trusted to tell the truth.

"Why do you need punishment?"

"I let a married man fuck me."

Those fucking words... as if she's not culpable. As if she didn't want Drew to fuck her. She makes me want to spank her ass until she can't sit comfortably for days.

I continue to swat her ass, occasionally switching sides with no set rhythm so she doesn't know what to expect, all the while saying horrible things to her. I try very hard not to mean it. Because calling her a whore out loud comes easier than it should. I hate the moniker outside of this room. I don't believe women should treat sex any differently than men.

This is different. This is Lorelai. The only woman I ever considered mine. The only woman I never wanted to share. I plan on making her regret the day she betrayed me.

"Show me how wet you are for me."

Lorelai widens her stance and brings her hands up to her ass, spreading her tender cheeks apart for me.

"You shine even in the dark." I push a single finger into her folds, swirling it around in her readiness. Drifting it up, I lean forward so the air of my words will hit her most sensitive of spots. "You're as wet as I'd expect a greedy slut to be."

Another distressed whimper escapes her, but it turns into a groan of pleasure as I press my wet finger into the pucker of her ass. Not too far, but far enough.

"If you were anyone else, I'd bury myself so deep. Right here," I say, pushing further in. "You don't deserve that, do you, Lorelai?"

"No," she cries out.

Pulling my finger out, I press an upward swat to her cunt, and she yelps again.

Lorelai's distress is the best sound I've ever fucking heard.

I yank her down onto my lap, my now hard as a rock dick cradled in the warm crease of her perfect ass. With a hand to the front of her throat, I bring her back flush against my chest.

"You ready to get off now?"

"Please," she pleads hoarsely.

My other hand wraps around her body so I can harshly shove two fingers into her soaked pussy.

"Ride my hand, Lorelai. Fuck it like it's the dick you wish it was. Fuck it like it's Drew's," I growl with more anger than even I knew I held on to.

Her gasps are louder now, more reckless as her body moves. Grinding and arching to a fast melody only she hears.

My anger only grows. The wetter she becomes, the closer she gets to a climax. Images of her and Drew play like horror porn behind the eyes I keep closed tight. I don't see them as they are now. I see them as they were when she was mine.

If she fucked him while she was in a relationship with me, I don't know. I'd make bets she did, though. I imagine her running from my dorm to his. Or vice versa. Playing me for the lovesick fuck I surely was. Making a fool out of me.

"Noah," she rasps, bringing me out of my daze. It's not fear I hear from her; it's need and desire, making my fingers clench even more.

Fuck.

My grip on her throat is so tight I'm afraid she can hardly catch air; I immediately move my hand to her breast. Yanking on her nipple, I command her to come.

"Come now or lose your chance for tonight. Come like the wanton whore we both know you are."

Her body pulls tight as she grips my fingers inside her. Her arms raise above her head, her hands digging into my hair as her back bows up like some graceful dance move.

It takes everything in me not to blow like a fourteen-year-old virgin with his first glimpse into a dirty magazine.

"Fuck, Noah," she screams as she humps her way through it, my hand aiding her in every way it can.

Lorelai's head rests on my shoulder as she comes down, her puffs of sweet air mixing with mine. So close.

Close enough to strangle the life out of her.

I resist it—this urge to end her, to kiss her. To fuck her. Resisting the desire to be caught in her silky web is the only move I have left to play tonight.

"Go to bed." I wait for her to rise before I walk out, pretending I can hear soft sobs behind me. They're a lie though. Lorelai doesn't cry. She'd have to have a conscience for that.

7
LORELAI

If Jigsaw and Voldemort fucked and had a baby, it would be Noah Anders. He's equal parts mastermind of games and evil incarnate.

This morning, I hate him.

Mostly because I fell for his twisted plans last night. Hook, line, and stinging sinker. Leaving his bedroom door open was a dead giveaway. And like a dumbass, instead of cranking up the volume of *Midsommar*, I lowered it bit by bit, opting to listen to Noah's fuck buddy slobber her way through sucking his dick instead. She sounded like a professional. Probably was one, though, I know firsthand how incredible his dick is, so I'm sure she got some honest enjoyment out of it.

Eventually, it was too much to handle, and I tried to hide away in my bed and fall asleep. But memories and regret got in the way, and by the time he came and found me, I was too big of a mess to resist.

I wanted his hands on me.

And now I feel like a fish swimming upstream, exerting all my energy to get exactly nowhere.

This past week we've gotten along rather nicely, all things considered. We work well together in the gym. He takes instruction with ease, asks questions, and listens to the answers. Noah works harder to get into proper shape than anyone I've worked with before.

Outside of the gym, we've cohabitated with ease. Staying out of each other's way unless necessary. He hasn't gotten on my nerves, and I thought that was mutual.

That all changed last night when he walked in with that woman. I'm not mad that he dates or whatever that was between them last night. My problem is with his baiting me. Working me into a sexually frustrated frenzy, only to treat me like trash.

It hurts when he calls me things like whore and slut, that's not my kink. The kicker was him throwing Drew into the mix. Using my shame against me, all the while giving me what I so desperately desired.

I cried after he left the room. Not because Noah was cruel to me, but because of all the underlying reasons I am the way I am. I cried for the childhood trauma that has molded me into the smallest version of myself, the one that begs for scraps of attention. I wept for the memories Noah brought up.

The petty bitch in me wants to spit in his breakfast.

I concluded a few days ago that I should use my time here productively, so I'm trying to bury that part of me. To use this easy life as a time of growth and self-reflection. I can't be the person I was only months ago. Too much has changed. Too much is on the line.

Olivia deserves more from me.

Before Noah came home last night, I had a call from my mother. She doesn't sound well. Time isn't something I have on my side. If I don't earn some real money and find a way to support her and Olivia, she may do something stupid. Again.

I don't have the brain capacity to navigate through Noah's games when the weight of my mother and Olivia hangs so heavily on my shoulders.

From here on out, no men. No orgasms. No falling for Noah's bullshit. Certainly, no more temper tantrums.

Like every day, the psychopath walks into the kitchen the moment I've finished preparing his meal. Coffee is poured and waiting at the table. Black like his soul. I bring the plates full of vegetable frittata over without making eye contact.

"My test results," Noah says, pushing a stack of paper toward me.

"Oh great," I say in false cheerfulness. It's the best I can do.

"How was your movie?" he asks in a strange tone. Deciding not to analyze it, I keep reading through the results.

"Amazing."

"Glad you enjoyed yourself," he says with a healthy dose of smugness, so I know he isn't speaking about the movie at all.

Fuck you straight to hell, Noah.

"Like I suspected, your inflammation is high. It should be under a three, at least. Ideally under two. You're at 5.6. See?" I hand that test back to him as I move to his food sensitivity test.

"What should I be concerned with here?"

"Well, inflammation can cause pain, of course. But chronic inflammation can cause heart disease, diabetes, arthritis, bowel issues. It's a lengthy list. If your injury was recent, that could explain an increase. Since it's older, I'm inclined to think there's more at play. You've never been diagnosed with an autoimmune, have you?"

"No."

"Ahh, look here. You have several foods with an acute sensitivity. Gluten, cow milk, eggs. Fuck," I say, grabbing his plate from him before he can take another bite.

"Hey," he protests, as I rush to the garbage and dump it.

"You can't eat this, Noah. There's a full dozen eggs in it."

"I'm hungry, Lorelai," he says behind my back.

"Oatmeal or a smoothie. Your preference?"

"My eggs."

"Oatmeal or a smoothie?"

"Oatmeal, you wench."

"Charming," I snark.

Noah laughs softly, and my lips curl into a smile.

None of that.

Paying him no mind, I rush through making him oatmeal with fresh blueberries. I hear him flipping pages and assume he's reading through the results. He makes no comment, though.

He meets my eyes when I bring his bowl to him. All that coldness he wears like a crown melts away the moment I present his food. Fear flashes in his eyes like molten gold, and he reaches for my chin. Just as quickly, he schools himself back to the aloof man I'm so familiar with.

Raising my chin with his fingers, he examines the faint marks on my neck that he left last night. I didn't cover them up, but I hadn't planned on discussing them either.

"I'm fine," I say with a mix of wanting to placate him and be defiant all the same. He doesn't deserve to know how I really feel. He hasn't earned that.

"I didn't ask."

Ignoring that, I go back to my breakfast and the tests I hadn't yet gotten to.

If he was at all concerned, it would be my sore ass he'd inspect. It's still tender this morning. The hot water in the shower stung. The fucked-up part is that I like it, because it's a lasting reminder of what he gave me.

"We'll want to up your vitamin D. It's low."

"Fine," he agrees, but he doesn't sound pleased about it. I'm sure it's me causing him displeasure, not his test results.

We both let the conversation die throughout the rest of the meal.

"What time are we working out today?" I ask while I clean up.

"I have work today. I'll be back by four."

"Okay."

I don't know exactly what Noah does, other than it's something about consulting for the New Orleans' Saints. He has offered no information about his life, and I haven't asked. The reverse is true, as well. He thinks he knows me, but he has no clue.

Noah leaves for the day and I decide to use the time to explore the French Quarter. I need to shop for groceries now that I have a list of foods to eliminate from his diet. I can do that while I'm out, too.

I end up at Jackson Square first. It's a cool morning. At least it isn't raining. A few days ago, I splurged on a long cardigan from a secondhand consignment shop near Noah's condo. I'm thankful for it now as I wrap it around me more tightly to ward off the dewy chill.

Tourists filter in and out of St. Louis Cathedral and I watch for a handful of moments, imagining the beauty inside. I don't enter, however. My general disdain for religion overshadows my fascination with beautiful old churches. A side effect of my father's 'teachings'.

Shaking thoughts of him away, I wander further through the streets. They are busy and crowded, even this early.

Despite my aversion to all things religious, I peruse the window of a Voodoo shop. The display is a menagerie of beautiful, yet dark, pieces. Carvings, figurines, candles, dolls. All mysteriously enticing in their own ways.

"You can come in if you like, Mama," a deep voice says from the doorway.

Looking away from the window, I take in the tall, pretty man. It is the perfect word to describe him. He's androgenous—bronze skin, dark eyes, shoulder-length hair styled in an artfully messy way. All on top of lean but masculine body.

"Looks like you could use some healing. Come in, let me help."

"Oh no, I'm okay."

"You're not," the stranger says. "But you can be."

He turns, walking back into the shop, and after a brief hesitation, I follow.

"What's your name, beautiful?"

"Lorelai," I answer as I weave through the bodies of shoppers filling the space.

"Pretty name for a pretty lady." He assesses me, eyes roving up and down my body. "I'm Alim. It literally means knowledgeable, so no arguing with me, okay?"

His smile is infectious, and I return it easily.

"Does that work on all the women?"

"No, women see right through my bullshit. The men though… they're another story," he says with a cheeky wink. "Let's get you fixed up."

"What do you mean?" I ask while watching him flit through the store, picking up various items.

"Beautiful, you are a hot mess. You are not happy, nor are you lucky. And you're missing some much-needed love in your life. I can help you balance all of that."

"How could you possibly know all that at a glance?"

"It's what I do." He shrugs. "My grandmama was a voodoo priestess and taught me everything I know. Though a surprising amount of it is instinct. If you believe in auras, it's a little like that. When I look at someone, there's an air around them I can read. Some are easier than others. You're like an open book."

"Really?" I ask, skeptical at the idea.

"Honest," he says while dropping a handful of items on the counter. "Voodoo is all about healing, despite what the movies show you. It's a lot of homeopathic practices and ritual habits to bring balance. This oil here," he says, raising a small vial, "you place a few drops on you each day. Temples, behind the ears, wrists, places you'll smell it, okay? You're going to anoint yourself with it."

I nod so he knows I'm following along. It feels far too reminiscent of my childhood, however.

"Two candles. Blue for good health and peace. Green for luck. Burn them for a few minutes every day and just be with them, you understand? Like meditation, if you will."

"Okay."

"You start there. If things don't improve, we'll make you a gris-gris."

I don't know what that means, but I'm leery of it. Of all of it, honestly. A couple of candles and some perfume can't do much harm, so I go with it and wish Alim a good day on my way out.

After picking up groceries, I return home—or whatever Noah's place is—and get a quick workout in, a shower, and a few minutes with my candles. Which is more me just looking at them and far less actually burning them.

I don't go that far.

They're just nice smelling globs of wax. I'm reading too much into this.

It feels silly at first, but after a few minutes, a calm I haven't felt in years takes over me. Maybe it's just the power of suggestion. I want it to work, therefore it does. I don't know, but I'll take some peace however I can get it while also completely ignoring the way the religious aspects make me cringe.

At this point in my life, it's time for me to take control of something. Even if it's just some stupid candles and a fruity smelling oil. They only have the power I give to them, and I'm only allowing them to give me balance.

With my better attitude, I prep vegetables for soup. A knock on the door interrupts me. If it was against the rules for me to answer the door, I assume he would have told me. It's just after four. Maybe it's Noah, and he forgot his keys. Unlikely, considering how anal he is, but I suppose it could happen.

I open the door to June Mckenna. She balks when she sees me. And yeah, I get it, because I do the same.

"Sorry, I was looking for Noah," she says in a confused daze.

"He's not back from work yet."

"Are... are you staying here?"

"He didn't tell you?" I'm just as confused by all this as she is. It's my understanding that the two of them have become fast friends.

"No." She laughs uncomfortably. "No, he sure as hell did not tell me."

"It's temporary. Just while I help him with his hip." June doesn't need all my life details. I guess that isn't very fair since I know quite a bit of hers.

"I see. Well, I was just dropping this off for him. Can you make sure he gets it?" She holds out a small package, wrapped in brown kraft paper and tied with a perfect red bow.

"Of course," I answer, taking it from her outstretched hand.

Both of us stare at each other awkwardly for a moment before she turns to leave. I don't know what to say to the wife of the man I was fucking any more than she knows what to say to her husband's ex-sidepiece.

"Hey, June," I call, sheepishly.

She turns to look back at me, one brow raised.

"I know it doesn't mean much. Especially after everything I've done. But... I really am sorry."

Her eyes narrow.

"Don't placate me, Lorelai, by saying something you don't mean."

"I do," I answer with all honesty.

"Was I a consideration at all when you made your deal with Drew?"

I wince because this isn't something I can give her. She wants to know that I agonized over what we were doing to the sweet wife waiting at home. That was Drew's role, not mine.

"You weren't a factor for me at all, June. Though, I don't like that I was part of the reason for your pain. I haven't been a good person and while there are reasons for that, I never attempted to change. So, that's on me. I'd like you to know that I'm not proud of what I've done, and I never wanted to steal him away from you. What I said the other night was bullshit; I didn't mean it. Anyway, I am sorry, not that I expect you to ever forgive me or anything..." I trail off, lacking any more words to say. There is nothing I can say to her. My side of the story doesn't change anything.

I'll always be the woman that nearly ruined her marriage.

"Are you trying to be a better person now?"

"As hard as I can."

"Good for you, Lorelai," she says, albeit somewhat snidely, before walking away. I shut the door, more in awe of the woman than ever. If I were her, I would have punched me again.

How did my life get so weird?

Noah walks in a few minutes after June leaves.

"Meet me in the gym in ten minutes," he barks.

I beat him in there and am stretching when he walks in. Since that first day, he's been wearing more clothes. Shorts or sweats paired with t-shirts. Today, he's back to the too small shorty-shorts and nothing else.

As if he hadn't tortured my body enough last night.

Noah runs through the series of stretches I've had him do before every workout while I stay on my own side of the room.

"Do you want to fill me in on some of the reasons you are such a bad person?"

His question takes me off guard. Partly because he obviously overheard my conversation with June. Partly because Noah doesn't show interest in me. Not like that.

"You don't want to know me, Noah."

"At one time, I thought I did."

"At one time, I wanted you to."

"Wanted me to know you or wanted me to believe I did," he asks, pausing in his stretch.

"Can't it be both?"

"I suppose it can," he says, then lets the subject drop.

We finish the workout, and I'm halfway done with his massage before he brings it up again.

"I'd like to, I think."

"Like to what?"

"Know more about you."

Thankfully, he's on his stomach so he can't see my emotions as my fingers stumble along his thigh.

If I could choose just one gift for this life to give me, it would be Noah knowing me. Truly and honestly knowing me, understanding me… and loving me despite it all.

That's not what is on offer here. I'm an idiot, but I'm smart enough to know that.

"I'll pass, Noah. You have enough ammunition to fire at me. I don't need to reload the gun and hand it to you."

8
LORELAI

Breakfast with Noah the next morning is more chipper than usual. It's unnerving. I'm so used to his controlled grumpiness; I do a double take at his smiling face. And what a handsome face it is. He's good-looking regardless of his expressions. With his classically cut jaw, sparkling eyes, and wavy dark golden hair, he's fairytale worthy.

Noah is a living, breathing Prince Charming. In looks only, of course. His personality is closer to Ursula the Sea Witch.

"We'll have company tonight," he says with a cheerfulness that matches his stupid smile.

"Why?"

"It's Fat Tuesday, Lorelai. Plan on no sleep for the rest of the week. It's going to be loud."

"Mardi Gras?"

"Yes." He looks at me like I've lost my mind. "Didn't you notice yesterday while you were out?"

"Notice what? I've never been here before. For all I know, it's always like this."

"It's not."

"Good to know, I guess," I say, shrugging away his weird disdain. It's not like I'll be here forever. A handful of weeks is all.

While I noticed the streets flooded with people, my mind just wasn't on why. It's a big tourist destination, and for all I know, this is just leftover from the Superbowl. "How many people are coming over?"

"Only a few." His response is cryptic, and he's not looking at me.

"Noah, who is coming?"

"My brother. And a few others."

"Noah." He doesn't have to answer. I already understand. "I'll just stay in my room."

"You most certainly will not," he says through thin lips.

"It's for the best," I protest.

"Lorelai." His grim expression bears down on me.

"Don't make do this," I manage to whisper. The last thing June McKenna needs is the constant reminder of me. The last thing I need is the constant reminder of what I've done to her.

"What's best is for you to face the consequences of your actions. You'll not hide, you'll be polite and entertaining. If you're good, you'll be rewarded."

"Fuck you, Noah."

I forgo breakfast and retreat to my bedroom to debate if I've made enough money to accomplish what I need. The simple answer is no. My mom isn't employable. Once I move her out of where I currently have her hidden away, all expenses will be on me. Which means I need enough to secure us housing, furnishings, clothing, and food until I can get a reliable job. With Olivia in tow, that's three mouths to feed. Even with the exorbitant amount Noah is paying me, I need more than a couple weeks' wages.

Besides, I'm not sure he'd even agree to letting me out of the contract this early.

I need more time. A couple of months would give me enough financial padding to get us set up somewhere safe.

Noah enters my room without knocking, interrupting my panicked fretting.

"Don't walk away from me, Lorelai," he rasps.

"Can you please knock next time? I could have been naked."

"I don't knock in my own home. There isn't a single room for you to hide in here. Everything in this place belongs to me. Including you, naked or not."

Noah's jaw is tight, so tight I swear I can hear his teeth crack. I'm not sure why me simply walking away from him has him on the edge of his temper, but that's where he is. Like the other night, I wonder if he wants to fuck me or kill me.

Probably both.

"You don't own me, Noah. No amount of money you pay me gives you ownership. And no amount of money gives you the right to demand I smile and play nice while you make every attempt to humiliate me."

He takes one long stride that places him mere inches away. Grabbing the back of my skull, he hauls me over the short distance so we're heaving chest to heaving chest. Both of our tempers riding the fine line between lust and hate.

"Care to prove that?" he asks, and my eyes narrow on his. But it's his mouth I want to see, the one blowing a soft, minty breeze over my face, making me want to taste him. To lick up the long line of his throat, feel the scrape of his bristly chin, until we're tangling tongues and limbs.

"How?" I push the shaky word toward him.

"Ten thousand dollars. All you have to do is be polite throughout the entire evening."

"Twenty thousand and I only have to stay out there for two hours," I counteroffer. It's a lot of money. Enough to give me a head start away from all of this, if I can convince him to let me go.

"No." He laughs, and fuck him for being so sexy at it that I'm noticeably wet. "Fifteen. You stay for four hours, and you wear what I tell you to."

Fuck it, I'm doing it. Screw Noah and all his rules. I'm making my own.

Raising to my toes, I start at the base of his throat where his shirt's top two buttons are undone. Slowly, I drag my tongue up, feeling the hard swallow he takes underneath it. The triumph of his reaction sends an excited thrill through my core. I keep going until I'm just below his lips.

"Twenty, and you can have all those things. I'll be your bought and paid for punching bag. I'll be your good little girl that you dress up like a high-class whore. Whatever you want me to be, Mr. Anders," I purr.

Noah's mouth opens to argue or agree; I don't give him the chance for either, thrusting my tongue in to take what I want. What I've earned. I've followed all his rules, and the only reward he's given me is one angry orgasm that was given with more hate than pleasure.

All thoughts of swearing off men and orgasms fly away. There are no other men, only Noah. No other can compare, no other ever has.

He could be my everything, but I'll always be his nothing.

He responds by tightening a fist in my hair, his other hand cupping an ass cheek to bring me up closer to his level as he meets my hungry kiss with equal passion. My walls crumble at how good it feels, how long it's been since I've felt this type of intimacy.

Drew didn't kiss me, aside from a goodbye peck to the forehead or a cheek. He thought it too much of a betrayal to his wife. Fucking me wasn't intimacy. I didn't really understand. Until now.

Because this is different; it's more than just getting off on another person's body. It's more than an alpha controlling his brat. Those things don't put you on equal footing, kissing does. It's giving and taking in a well-balanced dance.

Noah makes me want to give and give and give with a desperate desire to take just as much.

It's terrifyingly heady.

Releasing my hair, his other hand palms my bottom, pulling my short skirt up enough that I can wrap my legs around his waist. The feel of his hardening dick against me has me grinding like the wanton thing he thinks me to be.

I am, though. For him, I am. I always was, and moments like this fill me with a deep, biting longing for what we once had.

Noah steps toward the bed, only to drop me down with a bounce, my hair cascading to hide my view of him. I brush it away quickly and watch as he deliberates his next move. Holding my breath in anticipation of whatever it is. The longer the moment stretches, the more I know he'll turn around and leave. Just walk out on whatever this is between us.

For him, it would be taking a treasonous taste. For me, it would be one last touch of something I gave up. I want this more than he does. I want it too much. In my experience, the things I want with such greed are the things forever out of my reach.

My eyes shut tight against it; I can't watch him walk away. Even if it's all I deserve.

"Are you frightened of me, Lorelai?" Noah asks with a dark edge in his tone.

"Yes," I breathe, but not for the reasons he thinks.

"Good, you should be."

The delicate scrap of white silk, the thin barrier between us, gets ripped away with the speedy efficiency of his capable fingers. I gasp as cool air chills my sensitive folds.

"The things you make me want," Noah growls before his head dives and his tongue plunges in.

"Noah," I yell, half startled by the intensity with which he's devouring me. His tongue flicks my clit and traces my folds in between sucks and thrusts. Planting my heels on the bed to either side of shoulders, I open wide as I grind up into his talented mouth.

It's been so long, he has no idea.

This is another thing Drew never did. What we had was about him getting release and me getting punishment. My pleasure was never a priority.

Noah reaches up to my tummy, pushing his palm down, then moving it farther up to my breast; my light camisole bunching and tangling with his fingers.

"Fuck," he says as his hand tightens. Raising up off me, he uses both fists to tear it apart, exposing my lacy bralette below. "Take it off. Now."

I scramble to a sitting position and yank it over my head while he unbuttons his shirt and drags it off, gracing me with those impressively cut muscles that torture me every day in the gym.

"Flip over."

"I want to see you."

"Flip," he says icily.

As soon as I do, Noah grabs my hips and pulls me into the position he wants. Ass high in the air, legs spread, his hand pushes my head and shoulders roughly into the messy bedcovers.

"Why do you push me, Lorelai?" he asks. I'm barely able to hear it over the loud smack of his spank. I yelp as I sway forward, but hurry to right myself. Prepared for more.

"I like how you react when I do."

"You like to piss me off." Another swat lands in the same place as the last, this one harder than the first.

"Of course."

"Why?" Smack.

"Because it turns you on, Noah."

Smack, smack, smack.

"Such a slut you are."

His hands knead both cheeks, one with only the marks from last night, the other what I imagine is an angry red. One pleasure, one pain. He clenches his fingers into my flesh and pulls them apart without gentleness.

Expecting the warmth from his mouth to spread back over my pussy, I moan with pleasure, when instead, it hits the hole of my ass. Noah's tongue swirls around before lapping it a few times. I'm mewling from the sensation.

I've always been an ass lady. It's the most erogenous part of my body. I think he must remember when he stiffens his tongue and pushes in.

"Oh god," I cry out, and he moves deeper. In and out and over again. Every few seconds, he delivers another swat and I climb closer to losing my mind. To losing all control. To losing all pride and begging this man to keep me forever. *Just keep me for real.*

"You can make yourself come, Lorelai," he says before continuing his wizarding ways on my ass in earnest.

I make no move to do it, even though he's allowed it. Staying focused on the pleasure he gives me instead. It's all I want, all I need. Only what he provides me or what I can provide him.

After a few more moments, he backs off. "I need to come. Give me that mouth," he says, then bites the globe he's already made so tender.

Ignoring the pain, I flip over. Lying on my back, I throw my head off the side of the bed between his legs. His pants are still on, but he undoes them enough to pull his heavy cock out. The bed is high, the perfect height for me to open and lick at his sack as it hangs out just above my mouth.

"Yes," he hisses, grabbing his dick. He points it downward, and without hesitation, fucks the shit out of my throat.

Gagging, choking, giving him whatever I can with my tongue and the suction of my cheeks, I writhe while he takes what he needs. My hips rise and fall as if the air itself is enough to get me off. It's not, of course, not nearly.

Noah angles over me, his hips thrusting in time with mine, and I know he's close. I feel it in the twitch of his cock, the tightening of his thighs that my hands cling to like a lifeline. If I can just hold on, he'll ask me to stay.

It's a stupid thought and I'm a stupid woman.

As if he hears the words in my head, he delivers my punishment for them as another spanking. This one to my cunt; his soft fingers feeling nothing of the sort as they sting against my clit. Once, twice, and then he blows.

With a feral roar, he fills my throat faster than I can swallow. A firm hand reaches behind my neck, angling my head higher, making it only slightly easier to choke his cum down. He takes a step back, allowing me to gain more air through my nose as I sputter.

It takes a minute, but I get through it and open my eyes to find he hasn't softened in the least. One of his hands stroking up and down his long length, the other still holding my head.

"Jesus, you're amazing," I say, pushing him farther away so I can all but fall off the bed to the floor at his feet. I grip his hips and bring him to me, cleaning the rest of his first load off him before one of my hands takes up the rhythm he was just keeping himself.

"You want more, Lorelai."

"Yes, I want it all," I agree.

"Stick that tongue out."

I do, and within seconds, Noah is coming again. The first few spurts erupt in my mouth, then he angles down to my chest and throat. I'm in utter shock at just how much he had in him. I swallowed most, yet it stains everything from my lips to my nipples.

Noah watches me intently as I snake out my tongue to lick what remnants I can reach. And as I stare back up at him, I see when his high fades and the cold brute returns. Steeling myself for it, I don't move as I wait for whatever he has planned.

"Do I taste better than Drew?"

Every cell in my body wants to howl in rage while my heart wants to wither and die inside me. With all my might, I fight the desire to sag my shoulders and curl up into a ball to hide.

I almost lie. Instinct and self-preservation urge me to tell him how he'll always be second rate. That's what the Lorelai he wants me to be would do, after all.

"Yes, Noah," I say, not even trying to keep the emotions out of my shaking voice. The attempt would be futile. "Your taste has lingered with me since the start. On our third date. After you took me to see the movie *Get Out*. You drove us back to your dorm, carried me up to your room where we ended up naked together for the first time. I had only been with two other guys before that, besides Drew. The others were boys really. I'd never felt the way you made me feel. Cherished and cared for, like I was more than just a body you could use. I've never forgotten. You've always been the best thing I've ever had in my mouth."

He clasps a hand around my chin, firmly holding me in place as he studies my face for the game. Or for the lie. He won't find it. Today, I'm all truth.

"You don't remember," I muse sadly. I remember everything about us. "You've hated me so long you can't remember what it was you ever loved about me. But I know you did. I remember how you'd never eat your entire meal, so that there would be plenty for me to take for leftovers because you knew my budget was tight and you worried I didn't eat when I wasn't with you. Or the way you used to hide your bruises and sore muscles from me because you didn't want me to think that you'd invited me over just to tend to you. I can still feel the warmth of your hand holding mine. I remember all the little things about us, even if you've forgotten them all."

The truth of it is all over his face, making my already fractured heart skip a few beats in mourning as Noah pushes my face away and walks out.

9
NOAH

Lorelai spent most of the day out roaming the city. I'd have worried about her in such a crowd, except unbeknownst to her, I placed a tracking app on her phone.

Yes, I'm that man now. Apparently. I'm not proud of it, but I love knowing where she is more than I love my pride.

She steadily wandered for several hours, only stopping for any length of time at one location. Some gimmicky, voodoo tourist trap shop a few blocks away. There, she lingered for over an hour.

Likely, she bought spells to curse me and dolls in my effigy to burn in the witching hour.

I wouldn't blame her. I was particularly insulting again this morning. Something cruel possesses me each time I smell her arousal. It's a purely immoral impulse to wring her gorgeous neck whenever she's laid bare to me. Stemming from the acute pain I still feel from the day she took herself away from me and ran to Drew, without so much as an explanation or even a simple apology.

That's why she gets pain and suffering now. It's all an attempt to give her a taste of what she's given me for years. Except today she delivered me the unexpected. I thought I'd get the vicious wild cat version of her, but she showed me her gentle, nostalgic side instead.

Someone who could care. Who maybe knows what love is. Or was once upon a time.

I love the unexpected.

And for that, I'll make her pay twice over.

It's not that I've forgotten what we had. It's that I remember it all too well, including the trauma of its ending.

I set her clothing out for her while she was gone, and wait for her tantrum. She arrives home and enters her room. No fit comes. She quietly makes her way to the bathroom, where I hear the shower start.

Money quells a lot of her childish behavior, it seems. I would have agreed to more. I should pay her more for what I plan to put her through. Twenty grand seems like a steal, and money isn't much of an issue for me.

Pretending guilt isn't stabbing me in the gut, I finish dressing for the evening just as the caterers arrive. I direct them to where they can set up, then pour myself a generous amount of expensive whiskey. A balm for the night of sorts. I need it with Lorelai nearby.

Guests arrive before Lorelai appears. First, my brother, Connor, accompanied by June's best friend, Leighton. Their relationship has grown into… well, I'm not entirely sure. Connor is not the type to stick with one woman for long, and from my understanding, neither is Leighton. Regardless, they've seen plenty of each other these past months.

Next to arrive is Pope. He's a friend, if I had to label him, from Lupus et Agnus, the sex club I pay ridiculous amounts of money to be a member of. Pope is an imposing figure, all dark features and hard edges. Like me, he's dressed impeccably in a three-piece suit. Unlike me, his skin is splattered with an array of ink. One tattoo climbs up his neck from below his shirt collar, several fingers are dotted with various words and shapes. He looks like what you'd imagine a mafia hitman might look like. In truth, he's a very successful financial planner.

I invited him for a single purpose, one of which he is aware.

Torment the sharpest thorn in my side.

He's accompanied by Mylene, though she's here for me, not him. She, too, is an acquaintance from the club and is here to be my companion for the night. She's a regular playmate for me, a favorite of mine. Though we mostly meet at the club, or her house. She's never been invited here before tonight. I greet him with a handshake and her with a kiss to the nape, setting the tone for the evening.

My parents arrive, gathering on the balcony with the rest of us. Just as a knock on the door signals my last guests have arrived, Lorelai steps out of her bedroom, looking exactly like she described.

A high-class whore. Barely covered by an awful shiny red dress that's so short it barely covers her ass cheeks. It's sleeveless and missing bits and pieces on the sides, leaving little more than a thin strip to cover her breasts.

The damn thing cost me several thousand dollars. Absolutely ridiculous. But worth the sheer look of discomfort she dons with it.

From the corner, she scans the small crowd of guests, and I see how she shifts from uncomfortable to defiant. Her shields arming up for the inevitable battle. There's a slight crinkle at the corners of her eyes when she notices Drew and June enter. Small enough that most wouldn't see it, but I do, and it makes me smile.

June, as always, looks beautiful. She's perfected the art of showing off her battle wounds but still looking classy. The comparison only makes Lorelai look worse tonight. Drew ignores Lorelai completely as he leads his wife toward me. June gives her a small, albeit cold, nod in greeting.

That woman wouldn't hurt a bear as it'd maul her to death. June McKenna is all kindness and heart. Luckily for her husband. Otherwise, I dare say he'd be embroiled in one hell of a divorce right now.

"Anders," Drew says in greeting. I don't think he's ever once called me by my first name. Well, maybe during the threesome we had with his wife, but that surely doesn't count. "June said the bitch was staying here. Can't say I understand."

"Drew," June admonishes, making him roll his eyes at me before offering his wife an apologetic smile.

"It's temporary. I'll say one positive thing about her. She's an amazing physical therapist."

"That's what she's doing here?" Drew asks with a raised brow.

"Among other things," I answer vaguely.

June gasps at my innuendo, her face contorting in a mix of emotions I can't quite read.

"Hey," I placate, cupping her cheek. "She'll be gone before you know it. I won't let her hurt you."

"That's not my concern, Noah."

"What then?"

"I'm worried about you."

"No need, my sweet June," I say, then press a kiss on her forehead that has her husband pushing me away.

"Find your own woman, Lothario."

"I'd rather steal yours," I tease, giving him a wink. Drew grins while also wrapping a protective arm around June. Drew and I have become friends, thanks to June. He knows my intensions for June aren't romantic. I only want her happy and healthy.

We shared a night together, the three of us, not so long ago. I enjoyed it more than I expected, and it's done a wonderful job at growing trust between the two of them. Sometimes it's the most unconventional methods that work the best.

Speaking of...

"Lorelai," I call, walking toward her. "Come meet my guests."

She schools her features.

"Of course," she says with a smile that almost looks believable.

"Mom, Dad, this is Lorelai Simmons," I introduce her.

"Nice to meet you, Lorelai," my dad says somewhat dismissively although he amicably shakes her hand. "Noah says his hip is feeling much better, thanks to you."

"I'm happy to be helping him heal, Mr. Anders." Her tone is genuine, making him give her a double take.

"Call me Calvin."

Lorelai gives him a nod, appearing pleased enough with the interaction. Until she meets my mother's eyes. I get mine from her, molten brown, my father has always called them. He likes to tease my mother that he always knows when he's in trouble because her eyes erupt in color.

Just like right now. Mom remembers Lorelai. We had lunch together once when my mother was visiting me in California. She also remembers what Lorelai did. Another thing I get from my mother is how long I hold a grudge.

"Lorelai," she says coolly, looking Lorelai up and down.

"Mrs. Anders, it's nice to see you again."

"Hmm."

"Come on, Grace, let's go throw some beads," my father says as he leads her to the balcony. He doesn't like a scene.

"Who's next?" Lorelai asks with a pleasantry that I know she doesn't mean. Kudos for the effort, however.

"Connor, Leighton, this is Lorelai, my physical therapist."

"Is that what we're calling it these days?" Leighton asks with a laugh and walks over to the bar cabinet to pour herself a drink.

"Hello, Lorelai. It's nice to meet you."

"You too, Connor. I've heard tons of stories. I'm glad to have a face to place in all of them now."

"Me too," he says with a curiously raised brow.

Lorelai smiles at him, probably in gratitude for not being cruel, then turns on her high heel to head over to the last two guests. Mylene immediately wraps her arms around me and gives me a quick, but deep, kiss.

"Hi, Noah," she says near my ear, loud enough for Lorelai to hear.

"You look delectable tonight, Mylene."

"I'll let you taste later."

"I can't fucking wait," I say. "Lorelai, meet Mylene and Pope."

"Hello, beautiful," Pope says in the deep, raspy voice he uses while playing at Lupus et Agnus.

"Hello, Mr. Pope."

"Just Pope is fine."

"Is it?" she asks, bringing out a bark of his laughter. Pope is a Dom, and Lorelai has instantly picked up on that. "Nice to meet you, Mylene."

"Is it?" she throws back at Lorelai.

"Of course. Any fuck buddy of Noah's is a friend of mine," she says with a plastic grin.

"I'd say the same, but I know he's not fucking you."

Only one thing gives away Lorelai's raised hackles at Mylene's retort. The slight darkening of her irises.

"Lorelai," I warn.

"Sorry, I promised good behavior tonight, didn't I?" She pouts.

I sigh. If nothing else, she keeps me on my toes.

Grabbing Mylene's hand, I lead her to the balcony, leaving Pope to deal with my live-in brat.

A couple of hours later, everyone has a pleasant buzz happening and laughter flows as easily as the booze. It's loud, colorful, and fun watching what the crowd down below will do for us to toss them some cheap beads.

My parents, thankfully, aren't easily scandalized by the copious show of bare breasts on the street level. In fact, I think if my mom has any more vodka, she'd bare hers as well.

Something I never need to see.

I haven't been back inside since coming out here with Mylene. The catering staff is doing well in their task of passing around food and refilling drinks. Besides, the affectionate brunette on my arm has done a great job of keeping me occupied. As has the company. Drew and I get along well, surprisingly. Though I suppose we have a lot in common.

And, as always, the banter between June and Leighton is a good show. Leighton is very outspoken and even more outgoing. A complete clash with my brother now that I think about it. They get along great, regardless.

Because of all this, I realize I haven't seen my pet in some time.

"I'll be back," I say absently, then go in search of Lorelai.

She isn't in the kitchen or living area. Peeking into her room, I find it empty as well. It's almost silent as I walk down the hall, past the office and gym, toward my room. I can hear the crowds outside, but not a peep from anywhere inside.

Hesitating at the door, I think about what I might see if I enter. What I want to see, what I don't, what I'm terrified of. I baited her into this, but deep down, I don't want her to bite.

Grasping the doorjamb with both hands, I fight the guilt and the hatred that twirls like a hurricane inside my gut. If she's in there, fucking Pope, that will just prove that she's what I suspect she is.

A woman who will use me as her cash cow while she fucks her way through the city.

When I open the door, Lorelai is standing right in front of it. Her eyes dilated, her hair, which had been artfully styled, now askew. Pope stands only feet away from her.

"All this sexual tension needs to stop. I only like it when I'm part of it," I say. Pope laughs. Lorelai does not.

"He's all yours," she says, hurt flashing on her face as she pushes past me.

Obviously, I've missed something.

"Everything kosher, Pope?"

"All good, Noah. Just trying to get a handle on your project."

I'm about to question him on what went down when the caterer interrupts with a question. Pope slips away as I handle it. When I step back out on the balcony, he's in a deep conversation with my father about investment opportunities.

I find Lorelai in the dark shadows of the opposite corner.

"What happened?" I ask, stepping to her.

She doesn't turn from watching the crowd down below. Music loudly wafts all around us, mixed with excited chatter and laughter. It's the biggest party of the year, with everyone having a wonderful time. Except her.

Lorelai's profile is a mask of indifference from the bright sequined ones donned by all the revelers. Hers isn't one of celebration, it's one of resignation. Her body trembles from the chilly wind, and I feel it in my bones, though I'm comfortably warm.

Stepping closer, I lean down to her, ghosting my words on the shell of her ear.

"What happened?"

"Nothing you need to concern yourself over."

"That's for me to decide."

"Isn't everything?" she asks, finally shifting so she can pierce me with an angry stare.

I huff, blowing down the long line of her delicate neck so fully exposed. "Here, put my jacket on. You must be freezing."

"No," she says, firmly. "This is what you wanted. Own it."

"Lorelai." I'm about to give her another direct command, or bribe her with money if I must. Whatever it takes to make her see reason. I wanted her exposed, not frozen. But another booming voice sounds behind us, causing me to turn and her to cower further into the dark.

"You will have songs as in the night when you keep the festival, and gladness of the heart as when one marches to the sound of a flute," Pope recites loudly as a group of raucous flutists march by below.

Lorelai grimaces at his words, but it vanishes quickly as, once again, she quickly rebuilds her defenses. Goosebumps break out on her arms as another soft gust of cool wind blows around us.

"Lorelai, put the jacket on," I say, handing it to her. I feel the attention of my guests shift to us, and though I try to soften my tone, I'm not successful. "Now."

Her eyes don't leave mine as she reaches for it and pushes her arms into the sleeves.

"Thank you, Daddy," she says in the sweetest voice she can manage and with just enough of an innocent pout to sound both contrite and shocking.

My mother gasps, my father chokes on his whiskey, and Connor bursts out in loud laughter.

Fuck me.

10

LORELAI

Noah pretends to avoid me for the rest of the night. But I see how he tracks me, always knowing where I am, what I'm doing, who I'm doing it with.

Pope is a constant. Never leaving me for too long, constantly offering to get me food that the caterers are handling fine without his help. Or offering to fetch me a drink. I'm not drinking tonight, though.

I'm messy enough sober.

Pope and I had been having friendly enough conversation earlier. Though he stood too close and looked too intensely at me. Attentive men don't scare me. I've lived with that forever and have become adept at avoidance and escape. And I had escaped him for a short time, speaking to Connor, until Leighton pulled him away.

I tried to use the restroom. As the main one was occupied, I made my way into Noah's en-suite. That's where Pope cornered me again.

"But if he brings a lamb as his offering for a sin offering, he shall bring it, a female without defect," he'd said as soon as I stepped out of the restroom.

I froze instantly. That had been one of my father's favorite biblical quotes. He used it to manipulate followers to offer their most beautiful daughters as his next bride.

He used it to offer me up as someone else's next bride.

I hate that fucking verse.

Pope's voice isn't the one I heard in my head; it was my father's. The cleric's. The devil's. I'd time warped back to that day. Twelve years old, dressed in a virginal white baby doll dress two sizes too small. He made me stand on a round pedestal in the center of the Offering Room while grown men came to inspect me.

It went on for hours. I obeyed every order. The most important ones had come from the cleric himself when the day had started.

Do what they say. Don't tell them no. Don't cry. Smile.

Smile as they sexualize you. I didn't understand it then, not fully. I knew I hated every minute. But I didn't understand what was really happening.

It was an auction. I was being sold like prize cattle.

Pope's voice took me back there. When he snapped my name at me, I found I was crouching on the floor of Noah's room, my hands covering my ears, shutting out the dead booming voice of my father.

I was trying to make a speedy escape when Noah walked in and mistook the scene for something more sordid.

Noah may feign indifference to me, but something he saw in me has him concerned. It feels like a win. But I refuse to look at it that way. Maybe it's a point in my favor, but the game is still on. The asshole didn't even notice I hadn't come during our play time earlier. Now he's cozied up with Drew, Connor, and Mylene. It's not the same woman he brought home to fuck before. For all the shit he gives me, he sure offers his own dick around freely.

Even with Noah's suit coat, I'm chilled. Not because of the temperature, but from the anxiety of the situation. I'm on edge in all the worst ways, feeling like there is a threat in every direction. Anyone of Noah's guests could come at me. Most have reason. I'm fully exposed without a safe place to retreat to.

It's the worst feeling. I'm sure that was Noah's intent. The man who once loved me is now so full of hate for me. It would be enough to break my heart, if it was whole to begin with. But it hasn't been that in a long while.

Deciding to find a cup of coffee, I head for the kitchen, only to run into June and Leighton on my way. Even though I've done my best to stay out of her orbit tonight, this was inevitable.

"I don't know why Noah wants you here. That's his business, but at least you could dress like you aren't trying to lure every dick within a two-mile radius into your hoo-ha."

"Leighton, just pretend she isn't here. I do," June responds to her best friend who's eyeing me like I'm little more than a speck of dirt.

This is a crossroads for me. One direction leads to a battle of egos. The other to a destination I have visited little in my lifetime. The first is much more tempting, and that's exactly why it's not my choice now.

I need to grow the fuck up. No time like the present to get started.

"There's a lesson hidden somewhere in this high-priced piece of fabric. Noah probably expected me to find it straight away, but I guess he underestimated my blondness when he told me to wear it tonight." Giving a small shrug with my contrite words, I circle past Leighton to the coffeepot and fill a cup.

Of course, I know what he's trying to do, but if there is a list of people I owe, June tops it. I can play dumb for her sake.

Jealousy bubbles up inside me as I watch Leighton take a step closer to June. Because I've had no one stand up for me the way Leighton is so ready to do for June. Drew tried to once, when I fed him a lie about Noah. But that can't possibly count because it was all based on bullshit. I manipulated him into giving a shit. He didn't have my back because we had such an incredible friendship. Or because he cared deeply about me.

June has that with her friend. She has it with Drew. And now Noah, too.

I envy her. This woman whose life I helped destroy… even for just a short time. Even though she's gotten it back, with interest, I'm aware of how hard of a time it was for her.

It reinforces the belief that I shouldn't be here, and if I saw another way, I wouldn't be strutting in front of her with false bravado. I wouldn't be living in this condo, trying hard not to care too much for Noah. I'd leave, let them be happy without the reminder of me.

If only I could.

"Noah's playing the fashion fairy again, I see," June says.

"Again?"

"Again." June's answer is vague, and the hit lands. She wants me to wonder what she means. And fuck me, I do. My mind immediately questions if he undressed her before he dressed her. The moment she sees that my mind went exactly where she wanted it, a smug smile teases her mouth. Her chin raises, and she takes her friend's hand to lead her away. Leighton glares at me the whole way.

I stare after them, realizing that I like June. Which only makes me hate myself more. I follow them outside, feeling a little dazed by it all.

Pope stands alone at the other end of the balcony, thoroughly engrossed by the goings on of the crowd on the street. Since I don't fit in with Noah's group, and his mother clearly doesn't like me, I step next to the sexy, tattooed man who breathes scripture that makes my skin crawl.

It's not his fault, and I learned a long time ago that not all religious folks are cultist fanatics into pedophilia and complete control. I'll give the man a chance, but keep a distance, too.

"Why the scriptures?" I ask when I settle my arms on the railing beside him, peering down to wonder what has him so rapt.

"I am the son of a preacher man," he says, turning to smile at me. He's incredibly handsome. Noah's opposite in so many ways. His hair is an inky blue-black that falls messily to his chin. There's an artful black dove tattoo stretching across the front of his neck. I lean forward a little to get a better look. I've always wanted to get a tattoo but haven't yet determined what I want enough to permanently have it stain my skin.

"Same here."

"Is that why you had your meltdown earlier?" He says the words with a casual concern, but there is something about how he says it that has me believing he won't approve of me skirting the question.

"Yes. Terrible memories wrapped up in that quote. It wasn't personal."

"I took no offense." He shrugs. "What denomination?"

"His own." I laugh sardonically. "He claimed it was a purer form of Mormonism."

"Fundamentalists?"

"Something like that, certainly just as extreme." I don't know why I'm opening to this complete stranger. Or maybe that is why. Because he's a stranger. I don't care what he thinks or if he judges. I'm not afraid to put it behind me for a brief conversation with him. Pope isn't part of my life. I don't want him as part of my future. He doesn't get to know the holds my father still has on me, even from the grave. He can't psychoanalyze me the way Noah can.

"That must have been hard. Strange, to say the least," he says, clearly opening the door wider for me to walk through.

"I didn't know any different until I moved away. That's when I realized how bizarre my life had been up to that point."

"You aren't a believer anymore, then," he states.

"I don't think I ever was. I'd call it something more like brainwash or indoctrination. Which I'd say all religion is when it's being forced on you from birth."

"You're saying my parents indoctrinated me?" His brows raise, but I see the glint of amusement. He's entertained by my train of thought.

"Didn't they? If there's a better name for parents forcing their own beliefs on their children, I don't know what it is. Except maybe grooming."

"I actually agree with you." He laughs lightly. "You are, however, the first person I've ever met that has voiced that opinion."

"You should get out more," I snark, and his humor turns to something else entirely.

"You should watch your tone."

"Oh, I already have one Dom Daddy in my life, Pope. I'm not looking for another."

"Does Noah plan to keep you?" Pope's voice is dangerous, and it sends a chill up my spine as he turns his body toward me, his gaze dancing down my body like it's done several times tonight. I'm sure he knows the answer already, and I'm not buying that he'd like to 'keep' me anymore than Noah does.

But I also don't know all the rules of whatever game is being played.

"Hell no, I don't think he can run me out of town quickly enough." I try to laugh off the ominous feeling he invokes. Pope is handsome, but I feel he's the preachy type of sadist, and I don't need that in my world. "You didn't leave the sermon behind when you aged out," I ask, trying to change the subject away from me.

"I left the religion. The words stayed, but I apply them differently now."

"What does that mean?"

"It means, little lamb, that they only have the meaning I give them. I've taken the power of the words back."

I'm mostly quiet after that, ruminating over his words. Pope tries to engage me in more conversation, but I can't invest.

He mentions the club he and Noah belong to. I recognize the name Lupus et Agnes from the contract and wonder what exactly Noah would expect of me at such a place for fifty thousand dollars. Nothing good, but I can't dwell on that just now.

Partly because Pope's statement about power has me thinking about my own life and how I've never felt like I've had power in any situation.

Partly because I keep catching sight of Noah and June.

There is something more between them than innocent friendship. It's a familiar easiness that I have only ever seen born from intimacy. Drew isn't wary of it; he doesn't block it. In fact, he has a bit, too. If I had to bet on it, I'd place money on the idea that they've all been together. Sexually. A hurt of some sort worms its way into my soul.

I didn't seek the arrangement Drew and I had. When he offered it, I agreed with the same apprehension he had.

Drew's a bigger villain than me in this situation. Yet there he is, forgiven and loved. Accepted. While I'm here. Alone. Watching from the sidelines, wishing I had a team of my own.

Fuck this.

I offer some pleasantry to Pope and rush to my room. Tossing the dress on the floor, I dig out my well-worn leggings and tee featuring one of her favorite rappers. I need something familiar and my own.

More than anything, I need someone to talk to. But that person doesn't exist. The only friend I've had in recent years is outside, standing next to his wife. There's been no one else. Nobody that I've felt a trusted connection with that would let me put the most vulnerable parts of myself on display.

The loneliness vines its way around me. Ever suffocating. In a city full of revelers, I feel more isolated than ever.

Crawling into bed, I do my best to block out the noise and let sleep come. My nightmares can't be any worse than my reality.

I wake to banging. And it's not fists. By the sounds of it... Noah and Mylene are fucking up against my bedroom door.

She's crying out in pleasure as he praises her tight pussy and calls her his good girl.

I'm such a glutton for punishment that I sneak to the door to hear better. Every grunt, each breathy moan paints the scene on the other side of the door. How she's bracing her hands up against the dark, wood surface, while he fucks her from behind. His hands gripping her ample breasts. Her telling him how good his cock feels.

She's not lying. I know because I remember. I remember it all.

I want it back. I want Noah back. What we had was special, I'm sure of it.

On the flip side, I'm angry with myself for wanting him despite how horrid he is to me.

Grief and hatred turn inside of me, a hurricane of emotion growing larger and larger. Hate for myself, for my father, and his abuse. For my mother and how she didn't save me. Hate for Drew for pulling me in, then cutting me off. For Noah, because I want him to understand. Or to just not despise me.

It all comes back to me.

Scrambling away from the door, I don't stop until I'm in the opposite corner of the room. Staring at my pale reflection in the gilded mirror above the dresser.

Even distraught, I'm beautiful. The perfect daughter my father had dreamed of. The one that would bring him the greatest price, the biggest offer. With white silky hair and watery eyes, the men would fall at her feet.

The outer image doesn't match what I feel.

Ugly. Dirty. Vile. Unwanted and unlovable.

With a pair of scissors sitting in a penholder on the surface in front of me, I go about fixing the situation. Stoic and dry-eyed, I let lock after lock flutter to the floor. Each one landing with a heavy thud to the tune of the only man I ever loved fucking another woman on the other side of my closed door.

11
NOAH

I don't manage to stumble out of bed until nearly one o'clock in the afternoon. Too much whiskey wiped me out. Or rather Mylene did.

Damn, that woman can fuck. We're not very compatible, honestly. She's bossier than I like, always trying to top from the bottom. But she's a good time, regardless.

Replaying how I spent my night, I don't immediately pick up on the change upon entering the kitchen.

The atmosphere is as different as Lorelai's new hair. What was a mass of full, wavy length reaching damn near to her ass, is now bluntly cropped to her chin. Her demeanor, normally sassy and a bit playful, now feels depressed as she stands with her back to me, staring out the window.

She must know I'm standing here, but she makes no acknowledgment.

"Lorelai?"

"You missed breakfast. I put a plate in the refrigerator for you. I added lunch when you missed that, as well," she says without bite, still facing the window so I can't read her face.

"Turn around, Lorelai."

We both balk at the gentleness I use, the softness I shouldn't be feeling. Except something isn't right here. She's wounded. While I know why, vague images of how I spent the early hours of this morning flash in my mind… this feels different. I expected another small battle with her this morning. Instead, it seems she's given up. She's defeated.

Yet I'm the one feeling the loss.

Of course, she ignores my prompt.

"Lorelai, turn around. I'll make you if I must." I step closer to her, and she finally shifts to face me. The haircut is uneven, the fine hairs falling haphazardly around her heart-shaped face. Twisting some around a finger, I ask, "What is this?"

Her eyes snap to mine, and I swear I feel her sadness in my heart, like it's my own to carry. A deep, dark foreboding feeling flushes through me, and I wonder if I'll ever see light again.

What the fuck?

"Penance," she whispers.

"For what?"

"For so much," she says to the air between us. She's so vacant. Her expression and her voice, both devoid of emotion.

"Can you be more specific?"

"Not without a lot of time," she says, shrugging one shoulder up, seeming to shake herself out of whatever place she was. It certainly wasn't here with me.

"I don't have that right now. There's somewhere I need to be." I have an appointment with my realtor to view a house. I've been looking for the perfect one for damn near two years. June is meeting me there and we're having dinner after with her brother and Leighton.

Though, admittedly, I'm nervous leaving her like this. I never took her for someone who could self-harm, but as she's been telling me, I don't know her at all anymore.

"I'll be fine," she tells me, but it smells like a lie.

"We'll talk when I get back."

"No need," she answers, her voice still dull.

"We'll talk when I get back," I repeat. "You'll be okay until then?"

With a slight nod, she moves past me and into her room, shutting the door with a soft click. Leaving me to stare after her, or stare at the scene of the crime that I think caused all this.

The house is everything I'd hoped for, and more. Not wanting to take on a project, I've been looking for an updated version of an old property. Still wanting all the character, but with all the modern-day conveniences. It's a historical property. A Greek Revival designed by some famous men back in the mid-1800s. Yet it's been lovingly restored and renovated. Even with so many feminine touches and colors, true to its time period, it's perfect. Albeit, too large for just me, at nearly 7,000 square feet and six bedrooms.

I'm buying this house.

June fell in love with it immediately. It helps that it sits only five blocks from the house Drew bought her.

My only concern is that when I stepped into the kitchen, much lighter than my condo as the sun shone bright through the many windows, it was Lorelai I pictured utilizing the space. Her handing me my morning cup of coffee and bowl of oatmeal, hair piled up messily, as she danced around to that awful rap music she's been listening to more and more.

"Grumpy is your everyday go-to, Noah, but today you're down right dower. What gives?"

I smile at Leighton as I attempt to shake away the confused feelings overriding what should be a great day. I found myself a fucking house, finally.

"A little lost in thought, nothing to be concerned about."

"Noah," June admonishes.

"What?"

"You don't lie, but that didn't sound like the truth. What's going on?"

"Can't a guy be hungover after a long night? You said you didn't get home until nearly four in the morning," Reed asks his sister. He flew in today, after only being back in Seattle for a week. Connor and I are close, but not like Reed is with June and Drew. They're inseparable. Family in a deeper sense of the word.

I wonder what it's like. To have such a sense of security with another person. June and I have become incredibly close, and I know with certainty that I'd do damn near anything for her, and I think she feels the same.

But it isn't the same. It isn't family. Though it's likely a normal reaction to a bachelor buying his first actual home, I have a longing for a family that has never been present before. I want to fill those bedrooms with babies. Kids that will grow up knowing I'm their security.

I want to provide for more than just myself.

"Cyborgs can't get drunk, let alone hungover. If you knew Noah at all, you'd know he's not human," Leighton argues to Reed.

"That's the dumbest thing I've ever heard you say," Reed retorts.

Leighton blinks at the cruelty in his tone. Bickering with Reed is a given, but I don't think she expected him to be hurtful. I can't help but think my brother's constant presence in her life these past weeks is wearing on the poor man. But hey, he should man up and take his woman before someone else does.

As they continue to argue lightly, I feel June studying me.

"I am perfectly well, June. No hangover. No fried circuits."

"They're not paying attention." She waves toward her brother and friend. "You can tell me the truth. No lies, remember?"

"It's not a lie. I'm fine," I reassure her, knowing I need to give her more even though I don't want to. "I think I may have broken Lorelai, however."

"Elaborate," she commands.

"She wasn't herself this morning is all. Quiet, depressed even. She cut off all her hair sometime in the middle of the night." I grimace, because yeah, that can't be good. It's downright bad.

"Noah," June gasps in concern.

"I will never understand how you can give a shred of sympathy to that woman."

"The majority of my concern is for you, and what you're becoming with her in your house. After all, she's still a living human being, Noah. She's been through something. Drew says it's awful. Maybe she needs actual help and not more problems piled on her. Healthy grown women don't just lop off their hair on a whim, you know?"

"She's anything but healthy, June. You, of all people, know that," I say. But I know June is right. "It's severe, isn't it?"

I can't help but worry about Lorelai's current state of mind. My take-no-prisoners attitude with her was a bluff born from heartbreak that never fully healed. I thought I'd get some sort of closure taking her in and making her suffer.

It's only made me feel worse, because I don't think she's what I've been accusing her of being. If I'd truly tried to look, I would have seen it earlier. The signs are all there in the way she takes care of me. Even in the way she spoke with June that day I eavesdropped as June stopped by. I heard the truth in Lorelai's words. Or last night, when I paraded her around like my live-in plaything and she bore it all with her chin held high, all while being pleasant, polite, and at times even charming. She did that for me as much as she did it for herself.

While I focused on embarrassing her, she concerned herself with not embarrassing me.

I'm an asshole of epic proportions.

Lorelai wasn't wrong about what she remembered. I did try to hide my aches and pains because she was always so concerned about them. Or rather, me. Worrying about her came naturally to me. I wanted to take care of her, but her pride only let me go so far. So, I pretended to always be too full to finish my plate so I could force half of my meals onto her.

In hindsight, it was stupidly obvious. I was a high-level athlete; I never had a small appetite after grueling workouts and games.

She knew me better than I knew her. She still does.

And I threw it in her face by fucking Mylene up against her bedroom door.

"What did you do?" June asks, probably seeing the guilt on my face.

"Nothing that I should be proud of."

"Fix this, Noah. Before it's too late. Before you become someone you're not."

"It may be too late for that."

"Can we move away from all this moodiness and straight into the details of this house you looked at," Leighton asks. "By June's excitement, I assume it's some old, creepy, haunted mansion."

"It better not have ghosts, because I'm making an offer."

"You are?" June asks, the concern around her eyes now replaced with happiness.

"I am. It's too big for me, but I can't pass it up. All that old world style, and that pond alone is enough to fall in love with. It feels like home already."

The entire lot was landscaped with care. There's a small pool, a courtyard with an Alhambra fountain, and the most gorgeous lotus pond, all surrounded by beautiful mature plant life. I can't wait to sit out there with a glass of whiskey every night and just relax.

Again, my mind conjures images of towheaded children splashing their tiny hands in the water or cozying up on my lap for me to read them their favorite story. I don't know where this need for a family of my own has come from, but now that it's here, it's hard to outrun.

My mother, like most, I assume, has been pressuring Connor and I for years to settle down. She's past ready to be a grandmother. I had hoped Connor would be the one to give in. He seems comfortable with Leighton, but neither of their hearts are in that relationship. I don't see him falling for anyone else soon, either.

Not that what my mother desires is a factor in my life planning. It's not. Of course, I'd love nothing more than to make her happy. But I won't marry and breed just because she wants me to. I like my bachelor life and I'm only giving it up for a love that consumes me wholly.

For as much as I love to study other people, I'm currently avoiding self-reflection at all costs. Obviously.

Regardless of what ridiculous images are playing in my mind right now, I know I don't love Lorelai. I can't. Because I don't know her at all.

Conversation moves from my soon-to-be new home to the reason we decided tonight was a good night for dinner. It's the first night June and Drew are spending apart since getting back together. He'll be gone for barely more than two nights. June could have gone with him.

She and I became friends from co-hosting some pre-Superbowl programming for ESPN. They've asked the two of us to continue working with them, but the details are still being negotiated and she isn't working on anything else just now, instead deciding to concentrate on her new house here in New Orleans until they travel back to Seattle for the start of the next football season.

But she says they need this test. Drew hated the idea. He also knows he can't make the decision for her. Reed was called, and between him and Leighton, they'll be a solid support system for her if her anxiety gets the better of her.

She's done well spending the day with me; I've seen no signs of distress.

"Your house doesn't have any furniture yet, Reed. Drew and I made up a spare room for you at our house," June tells her brother who is determined to spend the night at his house.

Drew bought June a house here, and one next door that had been converted into a duplex. One side for her brother, one side for her best friend. Reed hasn't officially agreed to move here. Yet. It's coming, though.

"Your house is full of ghosts. Fuck that. I'd rather sleep on the hard floor."

"Pussy," Leighton chimes.

"Yep, I am that. Pussies are strong. Have you seen what they do when they give birth? Then they just bounce back, good as new. That's me."

"Strong pussies aren't afraid of things they can't see," she retorts.

"You go stay with her, then. I'll take your bed," Reed says.

Leighton flushes. I must say, I'm enjoying it. This woman lets little faze her. In fact, I think today is the first time I've seen her normally confident, easy-going demeanor jostled. I watch in awe as Reed keeps it up and we finish our meals.

Before we part ways, June pulls me aside.

"I know you made her dress that way last night." For the first time in our short relationship, I'm the one that has wounded June. It's a weight I never expected to carry.

"Making her uncomfortable was the goal, not you. I do apologize for that. Thinking clearly is difficult with her around," I say, wrapping my arms around this woman who've I come to care for so quickly.

"I know you well enough to know you're trying to fix her somehow. Like you did me. I also know you're out for some sort of revenge. But at what cost?"

"I've yet to figure that out. I'll promise to work through it if you promise to take it easy the next two nights. Call if you need help."

"I will, Noah. But you have to ask for help if you need it, too."

June's words play through me as I walk back toward my condo. June doesn't need to hear that Lorelai takes care of me well. She doesn't need to know that my body feels better than it has in years. I certainly can't tell her that for as much grief Lorelai's constant reminder is, I also find myself enjoying her company daily.

For the sake of my friendship with June and Drew, I do need to get rid of Lorelai.

For the sake of whatever soul I have left, I can't do that until I know what's truly happening with her. Lorelai may be a monster, but I won't be.

Only, maybe I already am.

Whatever I am or have become, tonight I get the truth. The full story. Why Lorelai played me in college, why she became Drew's mistress, who's on the other end of all these quiet phone calls she makes.

All of it.

Except, arriving home, Lorelai is nowhere to be found. I pour myself a whiskey and take it out to the balcony. The music from the city is loud again tonight, as is the revelry. Neither stirs any emotion out of me as I settle my arms against the railing and take it in while the warm burn of the amber liquid coats my throat.

Lorelai still isn't home when I finish. Pulling up the app I use to track her with, my blood runs cold. The small blue dot that indicates her phone is in the last place I expected it to be. Tracing back through the history, I find she left here shortly after me. Made her way to that same ridiculous tourist trap she's been frequenting where she stayed for almost two hours.

From there, she went straight to the airport.

It's not her number I dial when feeling returns to my fingers from gripping my phone tightly in anger.

"Anders. Is June all right?"

"Tell me the truth, Drew, or so help me I will fucking murder you."

"What the fuck are you talking about, Noah?"

"Is she coming to meet you?"

"June? No, she's staying home. You know this. What the hell is going on?"

"Not June. Lorelai. Is she fucking flying to you?" My voice rises, uncontrollably.

"No. And fuck you for even thinking it. I don't know where she is, and she sure as hell doesn't know where I am. She is your problem now, Noah. And if you've done anything to make June more anxious, it's you who needs to be worried about being murdered."

"Fuck," I yell. "Where the fuck could she have gone?"

"Honestly, I'm past caring, man. But likely she's running away from you and whatever that stunt was you pulled last night."

"You're probably right. I'm sorry for jumping to assumptions."

"Fuck you, and don't scare my wife with this bullshit," Drew says before hanging up on me.

I pour another whiskey and take my place back at the balcony, staring at the dot that hasn't moved on app. It's getting late, nearing eight o'clock. Wherever she's going at this hour must be important to her.

Why don't I feel happy that she's left? I should be. She didn't ask for her money, she's out of my hair, and she can't make June uncomfortable if she's long gone.

Happiness isn't what I'm feeling. It isn't sorrow either.

Anger is what I feel. Because I haven't gotten my answers, nor my pound of flesh.

About to call her, I startle when my phone buzzes in my hand with an incoming call. I don't see who it is though, as I watch the cell slip through my fingers and crash onto the pavement below. I'm sure it shattered and died when it landed. But if it hadn't, the angry, and likely drunk, dude that it almost hit in the head takes care of the job when he picks it up and throws it at a brick wall.

Fuck.

12
LORELAI

The last forty-eight hours have been the longest of my life. I'd be dead on my feet if Olivia didn't need me to keep moving.

After Noah left the other morning, I'd walked to Alim's shop to visit. I couldn't stand being alone with my own thoughts for another minute. Sad as it is, he's the closest thing I have to a friend. I've been making a habit of stopping by the store when out on errands, which has been nearly every day. He always seems happy to see me and doesn't mind if I loiter so we can chat in between customers. In fact, he encourages it.

He's taken an interest in my well-being. I can't help but cling to that since it is such a foreign thing in my life.

I'd been about to walk back home when Giving Hope called. They're the organization that's been housing my mother and Olivia. Drew donated enough money to them to secure my mother a six-month stay. Something I couldn't do because it took everything I had to pay off the guard at the ranch that helped sneak them out.

It was all for nothing, it turns out. I shouldn't think that. It wasn't for nothing. I got Olivia out and that's most important.

But my mother returned. Leaving Olivia alone at Giving Hope with nothing more than a document turning her over to my care. I'm so mad at my mother. More so, I'm disappointed. I gave everything to give her the chance to be free, to live a real life. With me and with Olivia. It still wasn't enough.

The past two days were a rush of getting to Olivia before Giving Hope would have to call child services. Then I had to meet with a judge to approve the guardianship paperwork my mother had written up. Luckily, the judge is someone sympathetic to the charity's cause.

Now here I am, exhausted, wearing the same clothes I had on two days ago. And hauling the dead weight of a thoroughly passed-out four year old into Noah's condo. I've tried to call him so many times, each one going straight to voicemail. I left messages. I texted.

All went without reply, meaning I don't know what reaction I'll get as I struggle through his front door.

Turns out, I don't get any. The place is dark and quiet. As still as a tomb.

I drop Olivia's small suitcase inside the door of my room and settle her onto the bed as quietly as I can. Not that it would matter, she's beat. It's been a traumatic couple of days for her, too. Starting with the knowledge that her mother left her and ending with her very first plane ride.

Once I have her settled, I grab fresh clothes and slip into the bathroom for a long, overdue shower.

There's been no time to think since I boarded the plane to Utah. Obviously, I need to readjust all my plans, but I'm not sure where to even start. I'd thought I'd have my mother to look after Olivia every day while I worked. Now, I'll need childcare wherever we end up. For a girl who's never experienced the gentile life, who's going to be awkward and shy and untrusting of everything.

Damn it, Mom.

I'll make it work, though. I'll find a way. For that innocent little girl in my bed. I'll fucking find a way. Not letting her experiences be the same as mine is my top priority. She'll have in me what I never had in anyone.

Or I'll die trying, anyway.

Which is an entirely other issue. The lawyer for Giving Hope suggested I set up chain of custody for Olivia in case anything happens to me. But there is only me, and that's terrifying. I'm young and healthy, sure. Anything can happen though and there's no other kin to take care of her.

Showering is a surprisingly quicker task when your hair is over a foot shorter. I should have done this a long time ago. Even if it needs a professional to clean it up. The melancholy I felt that night is gone, replaced by the urgency of getting Olivia into a safe environment. All the issues I had are still there, of course, just buried under another layer of things to stress about.

There's no time to wonder how Drew gained such forgiveness, or for how long I'll be labeled a home-wrecking whore. It is what it is, and I have more pressing issues than my reputation.

I'm out of the shower in no time, and just as I exit the bathroom feeling much better after the long trip, Noah stumbles in the front door.

He looks like shit. Something I never thought I'd say. His clothes are askew, shirt half untucked, and his hair disheveled. Eyes bloodshot, like he hasn't slept in days either.

He stops short when he sees me. Then just as quickly beelines toward me, crowding my space until I'm backed up against the wall.

"Where the fuck have you been?" he growls, and I grimace at how he smells. Booze and sex. Two things that are only attractive together when you've been a part of them.

"You wreak of sex, Noah. Go clean yourself up." It's four in the afternoon. He must have had one hell of a night. I don't allow myself to imagine with what or who. It will only bring me more hurt, and I've had enough of that to last me a while.

"Answer my fucking question."

"I was in Utah, like I told you when I texted and left voicemails. Did you even look at your phone for two days?" Jesus, what the fuck has he been up to?

"My phone broke," he spits at me, like it's my fault. "Who were you with?"

He's practically yelling now and it's enough to wake Olivia up. I hear the soft putter of her feet before her voice reaches us.

"Lie-lie?" she questions. Never quite being able to pronounce my name correctly, this is what we've settled on.

Pushing past Noah, I crouch in front of her. Tiny fists rub at her red-rimmed eyes.

"Shh, it's okay, Livi. Let's get you back to bed."

Her tiny hands lower from her face and she wraps them around my neck so I can lift her up.

"Who's that man," she whispers in my ear.

"That's Mr. Noah. You can meet him after you have a good nap."

"He looks scary."

"He's not, Livi. I promised nobody would hurt you, remember?"

Olivia, nods and she's back asleep before I even place her back on the bed.

Noah's still in the kitchen. With a mug in his hand.

"Is she his?"

"What?" I ask, confused.

"If you lie to me right now, I will end you in every way I can. Do you understand?"

"Fuck, Noah. Yes, you will end me. But what are you even asking me?"

"Is she Drew's?"

Noah Anders finds new ways to break my heart every day.

I'm not sure I can take any more of it. There's only so much left beating inside of me as it is. As utterly spent as I am, I can't find any strength to will the hurt away.

"She's my sister, Noah. As of yesterday, I'm now her legal guardian. She's four, you asshole. I wasn't fucking anyone, let alone Drew during the time she was conceived."

"Bullshit." He sneers. He's gained color back, so while I think he believes me about Olivia's parentage, the comment must be aimed at my sex life.

I'm done with accusations, however.

"It's the truth, Noah. You want to know what happened after I left you? You think Drew and I had a relationship, but that couldn't be further from the truth. We didn't. We did have sex a few more times and I hated myself for it. He didn't mind when my interest waned because he never lacked for women willing to crawl into his bed. It was never about sex for me, anyway. Not with anyone but you. I rarely date. I have sex even less often."

"Again, I call bullshit." He laughs and sets his mug on the counter. "You were at a private, exclusive sex club. Why would you have membership if you weren't getting laid?"

He'll want all my secrets now. I can't give him only part of them; he'd never settle for that.

A part of me still wants to confide in him, that same part that wanted to all those years ago. But the other part of me is still here, too. The piece of me that knows he won't let go if he knows. I don't want his pity; I don't want his sympathy. And I still don't want to drag him down.

He has a life here. He has family and people he loves. People that will never accept me and the horrible things I've done. But I can't give him nothing, either. Noah is too stubborn and strong-willed to accept that. He's too vengeful to give me my money without me giving him something in return.

He's left me with few choices.

"I went for punishment. Not sex." I inhale a deep breath to try to settle my nerves.

"What type of punishment?" The words are soft and slow. Almost as if he's afraid to put them out there. I know I'm scared of it.

"You know, Noah." He must, because I'd asked it of him at the beginning of our ending. I'd pinned so much hope on the idea that Noah would enjoy what I asked him to do to me that night. It was all wrong, of course. There should have been conversation, explanations on my part. Maybe if I'd approached it differently, the end result wouldn't be what it was.

Me terrified at what I'd done, at what I'd have to do. And Noah terrified of what he'd done to me. I tried to convince him that I wasn't only okay, but that I was better than that. That he'd given me a relief I hadn't had since I was on the ranch.

He didn't believe me, because he didn't understand. I didn't make him understand because the last thing I ever wanted to be was a burden to him.

"Why?"

"Because it's what I know. It's what culls my hazardous thoughts.

What rights my wrongs." How do I tell him that it's how I was raised, and I've never been able to leave it behind? Anything I did that my father saw as infraction, no matter how minor, was followed by the *rod*. Proverbs 13:24 was another favorite of his. It was my father's excuse to beat his children in the name of love.

I know it's fucked up. I know *I'm* fucked up. But I don't know how to stop, and it works. As much as I wish it didn't, it does.

"Why, Lorelai?" I hear it now. The pain, the fucking pity. Already present when he doesn't even know the half of it.

Whatever thin thread was holding me together snaps. I can't take the pity; I won't. No matter how small a person I am, I refuse to be seen as pitiful. And I refuse to give him more fuel that he can use to flame the fires of his hatred for me.

"You want to know me, Noah? You want me splayed open, heart to head, so all my secrets and nightmares spill out at your feet? You have to fucking *earn* that."

Noah blinks several times, taken aback by that. Because of course he thinks all he needs to do is demand it of me and I'll bend to his will.

The sad truth is, I would, if he'd only show me the smallest amount of care. Anything other than the monetary bullshit he throws at me. Money doesn't matter to him; he's never been without it. All I would need to open up to him is the smallest sign of kindness.

But I'll never ask for that. Never show him how much I crave it.

How I'd beg for the scraps of friendship, if only he'd let a few drop within my reach.

I've always believed Noah was the other half of my soul. Something otherworldly connected us, his heart called to mine and that's why I was so obsessed with him. Because we were destined somehow.

Fate made me believe it, but that bitch lies. Noah can't have ever felt that same way about me. If he had, every time he was with another person, he'd have felt what I felt when another man touched me. Every time I let a stranger spank my ass raw.

It all felt like a betrayal after Noah. My body is his. My heart is his. My hell-bound soul is his. Even if he doesn't feel it, too. Even if I hate him for sharing himself with so many others.

I've had sex with six men ever, only two were repeats. Who knows what his head count is? But I'm the slut, the whore, the trash.

Unworthy and unlovable.

"I didn't have anywhere else to bring her," I say on a heavy sigh. "I'll find a place as soon as I can, if you'll give me access to the other account. We'll be out of your hair in no time."

He stays unmoving, staring at me like he knows me less and less with every passing second. All at once, I feel the weight of my life, and it's so much. So heavy that I feel like I could sleep on my feet if I'd only close my eyes.

Leaving him there, I curl up on the sofa, pulling a throw blanket over me succumbing to sleep.

13

NOAH

For someone who requires as much control in life as I do, my world has become a goddamned cyclone of recklessness.

It would be easy to blame Lorelai. But as I watch her sleep deeply on my couch, I know that would be a lie. I did the heavy lifting that put me here in the middle of this minefield. Passing ownership of my mistakes on to someone else has never been my go-to. I won't start now.

Lorelai has been easy while staying here. The only exceptions are when I've pushed her over the edge or allowed my own anger to do it to myself.

After she fell asleep, I took her advice and cleaned myself up. The past two days I was on a drunken bender to pay her back for a sin she never even committed. I was convinced she ran away from me.

Alim didn't ease my fears any.

That's who I spent the past two days with. Because when I couldn't find her, I retraced what I knew about her day. It was too late to get a replacement phone and I don't have her number memorized. My search led me to him. Then drinks to loosen his tongue up.

When I got him talking about this new friend he'd made, I'd thought I struck gold. He described her as the woman with the saddest eyes he'd ever seen. The one who only needed a friend and a little affection.

Something he'd been happy to offer, because he liked looking at her. She made him smile, and he could sense something deeper about her. Something long buried.

He felt how much she'd be willing to sacrifice for other people, and he felt that same thing in me. So, I fucked him. More than once. More than twice. All while pretending she was there, huddled in a corner, tears falling out of those sad eyes while I stole away the only friend she had.

I didn't expect to find her here when I came home. Never expected to see her again, but that was probably the whiskey talking.

Now I think I've become the worst version of myself, reduced to the shittiest parts. I've lost the man June likes, the one Drew respects. Hell, even the one Alim wanted on top of him.

The only thing I've sacrificed is my own friendships in the name of revenge. That includes Lorelai, though friends isn't what we are. We are tangled, that's for sure.

Movement catches my eye from the shadows on the other side of the room. Livi stands there, perfectly still and silent. Eyes wide like prey who watches for the predator to pounce.

Me. I'm who she sees as a predator. This frail, little slip of a girl with more hair than any child should have to carry on their tiny heads. It's the same color as her sister's, as are her eyes. I imagine Lorelai looked just like her at that age.

If I'd knew her then, would we be as destined as June and Drew?

"You can come in, baby girl. Your sister is here napping on the couch," I say as non-threatening as I can sound.

She raises onto her bare toes to peer over the sofa, ensuring I'm not lying to her.

Slowly she moves toward us, hesitating when she gets closer.

"I think she should sleep," she says. "The airplane made me sleepy, too."

"They tend to do that. Are you hungry?"

Her gaze bounces from studying her sister to me, and she nods.

"Come with me, let's see what we can manage."

I lead her to the kitchen and open the refrigerator.

"How many people?" she asks, pushing in front of me and moving contents around on the shelves she can reach.

"How many people for what?"

"How many people are we feeding?"

"Why don't we just worry about you and me? We can make something for your sister when she wakes up."

"Okay."

I watch as this toddler pulls ingredients out of my refrigerator like she's a sous chef, moving all the items to the counter next to the stove.

"What are we making, Livi?"

"You know my name?" she asks, pausing in her task.

"I heard Lorelai call you that earlier. Is it short for Olivia?"

She nods.

"My name is Noah." I reach out my hand to her, intending to shake it, but she high-fives it instead and gives me a big toothy grin. Her front teeth are slightly oversized compared to the rest and it's maybe the only flaw this child has.

She'll grow up to be as stunning as Lorelai.

She grabs a tomato before closing the refrigerator.

"I can make an omelet."

"How about I make it and you walk me through the steps? Teach me how." Of course, I know how to make an omelet. But in what universe have I stepped into where a four year old is so comfortably capable with such a task?

Where did this girl come from? I could ask her. Pry for the answers I intended to get from Lorelai earlier. But her words replay over and over.

You have to fucking earn that.

I've done anything but that since hauling Lorelai into my den of torture a couple weeks ago. I won't lower myself to manipulating a child instead of putting in the work myself.

I'm an asshole, not a monster.

Instead, I pull a chair over to the counter for Olivia to stand on, and I let this tiny human guide me through each step with surprising detail and patience. Instructing me on the proper technique to slice the meat and vegetables. Telling me which, and how much of each seasoning to add to the eggs. Within minutes, we're sitting down at the table sharing the best Denver omelet I've ever eaten.

Again, I wonder where she's from and how she knows the things she does. Why does she have these skills?

It's a likely assumption that she's been with Lorelai's mother, but where is she? What's wrong with her that she needed to teach a toddler to cook? I have a million questions and no answers.

It only makes me more determined to crack open Lorelai's head and sift through the contents.

"Lie-lie said when we came to live with her, I'd get my own bedroom," Olivia says. Her has demeanor completely changed from the in-charge little boss lady to something more expected of her age. She's wistful at the idea.

Me? I'm curious as to who 'we' is.

"You've never had your own room before?"

"No, sir."

"Oh, none of that, little one. It's just Noah, okay?"

"Okay, Just Noah." She giggles, and fuck if it isn't contagious. Her entire body moves with the action. I laugh right along with her, which only makes her laugh more, and she spits a little egg back out onto her plate with an adorable snort.

"Olivia?" Lorelai calls, walking through the kitchen to find us.

"Sorry, sorry. I lost my manners," Olivia says. Her spine straightens and her chin dips down. Gone is the happiness, replaced by fear.

"Hey, Livi," Lorelai soothes, her hand coming to cup the child's cheek. "You are not in trouble. I don't care about those rules, remember? We talked about this."

Olivia side-eyes me.

"I don't know what rules you two are talking about, but you sure didn't break any of mine," I tell her, and snort in imitation of her laughter. She smiles, and one of her legs starts to swing under her chair.

"Omelets, huh?" Lorelai asks, giving me a glare. I shrug.

"I taught Noah how to make them," Olivia answers with pride.

"That was very nice of you. But eggs make Noah's body sick sometimes, so next time let's teach him to make oatmeal. Deal?"

"You didn't tell me!" Olivia's lower lip juts out in a pout.

I match it with my own. "I'm sorry, I really missed eggs. They're delicious," I say, before forking another bite into my mouth.

"Well, if you get a tummy ache, don't blame me." Olivia's voice turns stern.

"I promise," I tell her, making a crossing motion over my heart. Pushing my plate toward Lorelai, I tell her to eat.

"It's fine, I can make something for myself."

"Eat, Lorelai. You like exhausted. Refuel."

"What's refuel?" Olivia asks me.

"It's like when you put gas in a car, you fill up the tank so the car can go farther. Food is like that for people," I answer.

"If I eat lots of food I won't have to sleep anymore?"

"No. That's not quite how bodies work. We need fuel *and* rest."

"I don't like nap times," she says, and something about that makes Lorelai's eyes turn grim. As if a memory pulled her away. She's lost to it for only a moment, though.

"There will be a lot of changes now that you're with me. It's going to be a lot to learn, and we'll have to adjust to new things. We'll see if we can cut out those naps, but it might mean you have to go to bed earlier at night, or sleep later in the morning," Lorelai says, and I'm struck with how at ease she is with her young charge.

We dated for almost a year, and I never once heard of her hanging around with kids. She didn't talk about family, never visited any while I knew her. She'd said she didn't have much, but maybe that's wrong. Because she certainly seems comfortable around them.

"Okay. In my own bedroom, right?"

"Oh, Livi." Lorelai sighs. "I'm sorry. I promised you that and I mean to keep it. Once we have our very own place, you'll have a room of your own. But this is Noah's home and we're only staying here for a little while."

They stare at each other, each with those crazy silver eyes, both filled with a sadness I can't comprehend. It's obvious this was important. Not only because Olivia wanted it so badly, but because Lorelai really wanted to give it to her.

Olivia offers a shaky nod, but a single fat tear rolls out of her eye.

"I'm sorry, it won't be long. I promise," Lorelai vows, and presses a kiss to the girl's head. "You finish your dinner; I'm going to get a bath ready for you."

Lorelai does her best to keep it together, to not let us see. But I do. I hear the soft sob she lets out when she thinks she's a safe distance away.

"You really wanted your own room, huh?" I ask.

Olivia nods, sniffles, and takes another bite of her eggs.

"Who did you have to share a room with before?" I shouldn't ask. I should not. However, I can't sit here, watching this tiny child eat her dinner with such sorrow and not discuss it.

"All the daughters," she mumbles dejectedly. "Then with Mama when we went to Giving Hope."

What the hell does any of that mean?

I try to ask questions about other things, inconsequential ones, to distract her. To get that leg bouncing in playful excitement again, but she isn't having it. So I let her be, studying her while she finishes eating and puts her plate away.

She toddles off to find her sister, her shoulders slumped. There is no pep in her step and all I want to do is bring it back, that smile, that infectious laughter.

In mere minutes, this miniature human has turned my life upside down. Just as her sister did years ago.

One thing Olivia said has me headed to my office while Lorelai tends to her new motherly duties.

Giving Hope.

A quick search on my laptop brings up a wealth of information on the charity organization. As I read through it, my muscles burn hot with tension at the same time my blood runs cold.

An hour later, Lorelai steps into the doorway of my office. I haven't moved an inch. Physically, anyway. My mind has run a marathon or two.

"Is she in bed?" I ask.

"Yes, passed right out," she answers. Her fists clench and unclench in nervousness. I do my best to relax, to ease the tension. But all I want to do is rage. "I… I just need a few days. I'll find us somewhere to go."

The fuck you will.

The thought startles me, and though I know I didn't say the words out loud, she retreats a half step as if I'd growled them in her ear.

"Come here, Lorelai." I push back from the desk, allowing space for her to come see what I have pulled up on my screen.

"I should check on Livi," she argues, fear lacing the words.

"She's fine. Come here."

Her body wants to follow my instructions. It's evident in the way she leans forward slightly, leading with her chest. Her fists are tight now, her eyes narrowed. Her mind is what's fighting me.

I will revel the day that head of hers is bleeding out every thought, every memory, into my waiting hands. She may rue it, but it will be my hardest won victory.

"Now, Lorelai. Please."

She hears my thin patience and finally gives in. Silently taking the path on her bare feet, her legs showing under a pair of wide, flowy shorts. The top she wears is one that makes a regular appearance, an old band shirt she arrived here with. It's so worn through that I can tell she wears nothing under it.

Cursing myself for ogling her, now of all times, I avert my gaze from her back to my computer.

Finally, she stands between me and the screen. Her body sags when she sees it. When she knows what I now know. The small amount of it, anyway.

Spinning toward me, she asks, "How?"

"Olivia mentioned." I stand from the chair, boxing her between me and the desk. She doesn't get to flee this conversation. We're past that. I'm done letting her give chase.

"Say it, Lorelai. Tell me."

Her chest rises and falls with heavy, anxious breathing. Eyes closed tight, fists clenched.

She's so rigid, so frightened. It's not what I want.

I want the truth. The whole sordid fucking story.

I hate that she's terrified to tell me. I don't know exactly how I caused that, but I am not proud of it. Taking a step forward, I allow my body heat to mingle with hers and clasp my hands to her cheeks.

"Damnit, Lore. You can tell me. Anything. You can tell me anything."

"Don't act like you're my friend and not my tormenter, Noah. That isn't fair," she says and it's the weakest I've ever heard her sound. Again, a little more guilt stabs through me.

For all the suffering she's caused, if what I suspect is true, she needs help.

"I'm not going to use this against you. How could you think I would do that?"

"How could I not?" she questions, and it sounds more like a sob.

"Open those eyes, and look at me while I say this." I pause for far too long as I wait for her to do what I plead, only continuing once those damn stormy eyes pierce me with accusation. "Let me in. Let me help you. And Olivia. You know I will."

"How do I know that? You just accused me of having Drew's secret baby. You always think the worst things about me first. You don't know me. We don't know each other at all."

"That changes now. We use this as a fresh start to get to know one another," I say, resting my forehead against hers. "Tell me. Please?"

Her gaze darts between my eyes, and her rapid breath hitches a few times before finally, fucking finally, she speaks.

"I was born Abigail Simms. First daughter to Albert Simms. My aunt changed my name after she gained legal guardianship of me when I was twelve and smuggled me out my father's polygamist ranch."

14
LORELAI

"How did your aunt get you out," he asks.

"I'm not sure, but it couldn't have been strictly legal. My father would have never given up parental rights," I answer. I never asked my Aunt Alice the details. Nor did I ask my mother. I assume she forged the documents. Whatever they did, I'm forever grateful for it.

"How many wives does he have?"

Noah's voice makes my skin crawl.

I hate it, I hate it, I hate it.

The careful tone he's using with me screams that I'm damaged and he's treading lightly, not knowing what's going to cause me to implode.

It feels false. As if he's handling me or dealing with me, instead of trying to really know me. He sounds like my father manipulating every conversation to make us all believe he knew what was best for us.

"Lorelai, look at me."

My mouth is dry like the desert. I try to swallow a few times while I blink at him, ensuring it's Noah here in this room with me.

"When I left, he had seven. It was a sacred number. We expected him to stop there. He didn't." I laugh humorously, the words raspy. "When he died, he had four times that."

Noah's eyes widen in a moment of shock before he schools his features back to a neutral state. It's perhaps the worst thing he could do. I need his emotions, not a cold and clinical evaluation of my life.

"Do you know how many siblings you have?"

"One," I snap. But after a few seconds and a long slow breath, I try to explain further. "My mother had five sons before she had me. She wasn't able to conceive after that. Or so we all thought. She'd been sneaking birth control. When she thought she no longer had viable eggs, she quit. Then came Olivia. She's the only sibling I'll ever claim. My brothers can burn in a fiery pit for all eternity."

"Step-siblings?"

"I... I don't know." I sigh. "So many, Noah. I can't save them all."

"Have you been trying to?"

Every fucking day since I left.

Rather, every day since I understood what was happening at the ranch.

While I was there, I recognized moments that were uncomfortable, things that didn't seem right to me even at such a young age. Innocence goes a long way at places like that. Places that prey on such things. We didn't know better because we didn't know any different.

The mothers don't listen to me now—the few I've tried to convince to leave. *Won't* listen. By the time the children are old enough to have free will, they're so entrenched in the teachings, they don't listen either.

I work tirelessly with Giving Hope in any way I can. As well as with an FBI agent who wants to help but has nothing to do it with.

My mother, for all her faults, of which there are many, understood the dangers to her daughters. She refuses to save herself. It's something I must stop concerning myself with, since she's made her choice. I have Olivia now, and I'll do everything to keep her safe and away from that life.

She's all I have. She's *everything*.

With my father gone, they shouldn't be looking for us. He would have. It was insult enough to lose one prize daughter, but two would have him declaring war on the gentiles who harbor us. Uncle Edwin is the new cleric, and he won't spare us the energy. He has prize chattel of his own.

He'll make my mother pay, regardless. She knew that when she decided to go back. Right now, she's likely bound to the whipping post in the heart of the land my 'family' calls home. Naked, dirty, bloody, and alone in her shame for all the congregation to see. Edwin will keep her there for days as she repents, and anyone who wants to partake in his judgment will pick up a yew branch and give her back a few swats.

"No discipline seems pleasant at the time, but painful."

"What?" Noah asks, and I realize I said the verse aloud.

"I'm sorry, I'm still so tired. I should go sleep. Olivia will be up early."

Noah steps even closer, completely invading my space. He's so warm, a bone-deep chill wants to snuggle up and seek refuge. Only, all the hurts, the hurdled insults, and snide remarks bombard, and I can't focus on what I want. Just what I need.

Escape. And the funds that will allow it.

"No. You'll stay here and talk to me."

"Why, Noah? To what end?"

There's no point to any of it. I could tell Noah my life story from my very first memory until this moment right now, and it would change nothing. He'd still see me as Drew's whore, and the woman who betrayed him. I'll never be forgiven by him or by June. If I even tried to earn that, I'd only end up disappointed. Or worse.

"Because maybe I can help. You and Olivia."

"You can help by releasing my money."

"Don't rush this, Lorelai. Let me fucking in," he pleads, but the undercurrent of demand is still so present.

"No." I try to push him back, needing air that doesn't smell like him. "You're not my friend, Noah. We're not anything good, and this isn't a healthy environment. For me, and especially for Olivia."

"Lorelai..."

"No," I repeat with more force. "I won't let her hear the things you say to me. And I sure as hell won't let her wake up to you fucking some random woman just outside her bedroom door. I don't know what else you had planned to put me through. God, I can only guess what horror show you'd expect of me for fifty thousand dollars at your club. What was it going to be, Noah? A gangbang for you to watch? Surely, I'd have loved that being the whore that I am," I rage, a torrent now as every frayed nerve gives in.

As hard as I struggle to get free, Noah's stronger and his arms easily entrap me as he sits in his desk chair, pulling me down with him.

"Shh," he coos in my ear, but I can't calm. Fight or flight kicks in. I want to run.

"Fuck you, Noah. You don't get to comfort me now. It took everything to save her from that life. I'm not keeping her in another shitty environment for a day longer than I have to. I won't let her see me so disrespected, day after day."

Fuck his money.

Fuck his rules.

I want to grab Olivia and flee his judgement and his cruelty. Deserved or not, I have the choice of how much of it I'm willing to take. I'm at my limit.

But his arms tighten like a vise and my crying deepens, overtaking every cell of me. I don't know that I've ever felt so much at once. Despair, determination, fear, and so much love for the small child that doesn't even know the horrors she just escaped.

"I hate you," I sob. I mean it in the moment even if I know it will only be my latest regret when I'm able to finally settle down.

"I deserve that. But I know you don't mean it. I know. I know," he returns, saying it over and over until my mind finally gives way to sleep.

It's mostly dark when I come to. Barely any morning light shines through the slightly parted curtain of the bedroom window.

Not my bedroom window.

Noah's.

I don't know why I'm in here. More so, I don't know why a large, warm palm is settled on my stomach, beneath my shirt. Or how an impossibly comforting body cradles mine from behind. Allowing myself a minute of joy from it is not smart. But I'm already aware I don't make wise choices.

I've missed this. More than he can possibly know. A handful of years of his absence hasn't lessened how I crave his heat, his strength. The protection, even if false, I feel with him so near. He may sling painful words at me, but I know he'd never stand by while I was being physically hurt.

My heart swells with sorrow of knowing none of this can last.

As I try to ease away, Noah stops me by pulling me closer.

"Noah," I whisper, not knowing if he's awake or just moving reflexively in his sleep.

"Stay, Lore," he says sleepily.

I can't.

"Noah," I repeat, louder now to wake him.

"I heard you."

"Then let me up."

"Not yet. I have something to say," he says, and his voice is soft, reminiscent of better times. I try my hardest not to let it seep into my heart.

"I'm listening."

"It's time for a truce."

"I don't trust you, Noah."

"I know." He sighs and rolls me over onto my back. Quickly he moves on top of me, pulling my arms up above my head so we're nose to nose. Eye to eye. Body against body.

I can't.

"I don't trust you much, either," he starts. "We're going to set that aside for now. For that child down the hall that's innocent in all this. I'm going to help you."

I narrow my eyes, and he huffs a heavy breath while bringing his face a hairsbreadth closer to mine.

"For real, this time, Lorelai. No games. No battles. I'm going to support you in your search for stability. I'm asking you to stay as long as you need to. No strings, no bullshit contracts. I'll pay you what I agreed to for as long as you're here. When you're ready, I'll hand it all over."

"No strings?" I'm still skeptical, of course.

"Maybe one. That you talk to me. We have conversations like we're grown adults."

"Grown adults carrying a lot of each other's baggage?"

He smiles a little at that, but nods.

"Like grown adults who once cared a great deal for each other, and lost sight of what's really important," he says before pressing a kiss to the tip of my nose.

It makes me gooey and, goddammit, I can't resist. A little of my wall crumbles in defeat, and I close my eyes to hide my emotions.

I will not cave in to such a tiny remnant of kindness.

"Just talk?"

"Just talk," he agrees. "I can't guarantee it's always going to be happy conversations. But I won't humiliate you or insult you anymore. I never should have taken that route."

I don't know what to say to him, or what I can believe. Noah's never been a liar, though.

"Truce."

"Good girl," he replies.

"You can't say that to me. First rule of our new truce is you can't say that to me." I wanted to make it sound strong, but instead, it comes out pleading and needy.

"If you tell me why, I'll agree to stop."

"I like it too much," I say after I swallow down the lump in my throat. "Praise. It was rarely given when I was a child. If you start to give it to me now, I'll cling to it. It will only make it harder for me when I leave."

Feeling races across his features so quickly I almost don't have the chance to recognize the change. It's forceful, whatever he's thinking. The same as last night in his office, as if I've said something offensive, but I know I haven't.

I wish I could read him as well as I once had.

"Were you an unruly child?"

I shake my head slightly.

"Not unruly. My father terrified me, so I tried to stay under his radar mostly." An impossible task as I got older. "His rules were many, and he'd often add new ones without telling us. If I was his good girl, it usually meant he'd be lenient for a few days."

"Fuck. I'm never using that phrase again," Noah says with no lack of disgust. He hasn't moved from pinning me. While I'm still in my t-shirt and leggings, he stripped down to just a pair of shorts before crawling into bed.

All his bare skin and fresh scent fray my senses as I inhale it, him, deep into my lungs. Hoping it will last me another handful more years without this man in my life.

"Please don't judge me," I whimper. For still needing validation from my abusers or for still hungering for whatever piece of Noah I can get.

"I'm not," he reassures. "There is a lot I want to understand, but I'm not judging. We're going to talk, just like this, every day. Okay?"

I give another shaky nod.

"Okay. Get up, let's get busy. I've missed my workouts the past couple of days," he says, and again something crosses his features that I don't understand.

It seems we're both hiding a lot from each other these days. But I suppose we'll get into all that with these talks of his.

"Lie-lie?"

Noah grins at the quiet voice calling from down the hall.

"I like your new nickname."

"Hush, she struggles with my full name and didn't like calling me Lore," I say, pushing him off and rising. The last thing I need is for Olivia to walk in with a man she barely knows on top of me.

I open the door just as she approaches.

"Good morning, bug, how did you sleep?"

"Good, but I didn't know where you were. You said I won't get my own room here."

Well, shit. I don't know how to explain this.

"I…" I begin, but Noah interrupts me, stepping around the door. Thankfully with some clothes thrown on

"Change of plans, little one. You can have that room all to yourself."

"Noah," I protest.

"We'll make it work. Give her this win," he whispers in my ear as he walks past us both.

Sighing at his underhandedness, I give my sister a good look over. We have a lot of work to do.

"Come on, let's get some breakfast," I say, holding my hand out to her.

She takes it, but also the lead, practically dragging me down the hall. Thankfully, Noah is already brewing a pot of coffee.

"It's oatmeal for you today, Just Noah."

Now, I laugh at his expense.

"Yes, ma'am," he says contritely.

The three of work together until we're all sitting with bowls of banana nut oatmeal in front of us. It's bizarre—Noah's change in attitude. I'm sure Olivia's presence is the catalyst, and I'm happy for it. I wish he could have seen me differently before she came along, but I'll take what I can get. My life no longer has room for pettiness or bitterness. It's not going to be easy, but I'm going to do my best.

For her and for me.

"Livi, do you want to go with me to get our hair cut?"

"You just got your hair cut."

"I did, but I think it needs a little help."

"I like it," she says.

"Me too," Noah says. I can feel him looking at me, but I don't acknowledge it. Something shifted in me that night. I've had no time to really analyze it, and I don't really want to do it now at the breakfast table in front of him.

"Thank you. I like it, too. But it needs a little clean up. I thought you could get your haircut too if you want?"

"Mama said I couldn't," she says and bites at her lower a lip nervously.

"Mama doesn't make that decision anymore. You do."

"I do?"

"You do."

"Can I get it cut like yours?" She drops her spoon and grabs her long strands with both hands. It's down past her waist, much too long, even if it was thin and fine. Which it's not and probably weighs as much as her.

"If that's what you decide. The salon will have picture books with all sorts of hairstyles in it. You don't have to decide until after you look through those."

"What if I don't like it shorter?"

"Then you just let it grow again," Noah says. "And if you decide it gets too long again, you go get another haircut."

"And I won't get in trouble?"

"No, Livi. You'll never be in trouble with me. There may be times when we need to talk about things, because we have something we need to learn, but you'll never be in trouble. Okay?" Maybe this isn't the right way to explain, but I don't know how else to say it. I've never waded in these motherly waters. All I know is that I refuse to let her be afraid of making choices for herself. Or that I'm going to abuse her for any fucking reason.

"Okay," she says, albeit a little skeptically. It's going to take time for her to trust me; she barely knows me after all. We'd never met until the night I got her and my mother out. The night my father died.

15
NOAH

"How about you go brush your teeth? After that, we'll walk to a hair salon I saw the other day," Lorelai suggests.

Olivia nods, but doesn't head off to complete her task until after she's cleaned up her bowl.

"You're good with her," I say.

"I grew up around a lot of children," she says with a shrug. I hadn't really thought of that, but of course it would be true. There are about a million questions I want to ask her. Bombarding her with them all at once isn't the best tactic. Especially when I have her so frazzled to begin with.

I meant what I told her; I'm not going to keep slinging insults at her. Though, I'm still angry and confused as to why she never told me any of this. I wouldn't have run away from it. I laid awake most of the night wondering what I must have done back in college to make her think she couldn't tell me.

That wasn't the only thing keeping me awake. It felt good having her in my bed again. In between all the questions shifting in my brain about her were the ones I had about my own feelings.

Fuck, I've been an asshole to her.

No matter what she's done, she didn't deserve that level of

vengeance from me. I broke her down so far before I allowed myself to see her as human. Flawed, sure. But aren't we all? I sure as hell am. Despite everything I threw at her, the only thing she ever dished back was a little snark.

"This isn't the same as that though, is it?"

"No. This isn't the same at all," she says, and there's hope hidden in the words.

"Will you work out with me after your haircuts?"

"Of course," she agrees without hesitation.

"I meant what I said," I say, reaching out to tug a lock of her hair. My fingers brush her cheek and heat blooms at the spot. "I like it. It suits you."

"Thank you, Noah."

She stacks the remaining bowls and moves to the sink to clean them up. I watch and wonder what these past days could have been like if I'd let go of my hurt long enough to have had a simple conversation with her.

Then I wonder what the last several years could have been like, if she'd done the same with me.

Losing myself in the thoughts, I'm startled when Lorelai comes back in, Olivia in tow.

"We're heading out but shouldn't be too long."

"Sounds good. Have a great time, ladies."

Olivia gives me a little wave, and I can see she's apprehensive.

"Whatever you pick is going to look amazing, little one," I say, hoping to offer some reassurance.

Lorelai wears a sad smile before they turn to leave. I notice Olivia's pink tennis shoes have a hole worn through the back. The clothes she's wearing don't fit well, her shirt too big and pants slightly too small.

I make my way into the guest room once they leave. I shouldn't pry, but this is who I am.

Phineus is my middle name, a horrific mythology reference that my mother put zero thought into. She just loved the name. Really, it should be *Controlling Fucker*.

Noah Controlling Fucker Anders.

Much more fitting.

A small suitcase sits neatly open in the corner of the room. Every item, for which there are few, folded perfectly inside. Rummaging through it, I find what I expected. None of the items appear to have been purchased for Miss Olivia. I'd guess they were what Giving Hope had on hand when she arrived in their care.

It turns my stomach. The whole situation sours my mood. How this child has so little, how Lorelai has so little. I could call Drew and make him tell me what he knows. It's not his lips I want to tell me the story, though. And if I have any hope of Lorelai opening to me, I can't go digging behind her back.

Focusing on what I can do, I lift the suitcase and move it to the closet. I won't have any guest, especially a wayward four-year-old, living out of a suitcase while in my home. If I never see that pouty expression on her face again when she thought she didn't have her own room, it will be worth all efforts I make.

Pushing aside Lorelai's clothes to make room for the few things Olivia has, I pause, examining what's already hanging.

The bile that was already swirling in my gut threatens to force its way up my throat as my gaze hones in on that fucking red dress I made her wear for Mardi Gras.

Who have I become?

Not only did I parade her around in all her bare skin, but I did it in front of June. And my entire family.

Ripping the dress from the hanger, I toss it behind me on the bed. Several more follow. Clothes that, if Lorelai was mine, I'd never want her to wear out in public.

If she were mine, all that creamy, flawless skin would be for me. I wouldn't cover her head to toe and hide her away from the world. But I sure as hell wouldn't force her to display it all either.

I'm not naïve to what Lorelai's, or rather Abigail's, childhood must have been like. I've seen plenty of documentaries depicting the horrors that occur in such cults. I remember not too long ago a Fundamentalist Latter Day Saints, a polygamist sect born from the Mromon religion, homestead being raided. It was all over the news for a few days before everyone's lives returned to their normal status of ignoring such things.

I'm guilty of that, too. I have the means to help people in need, and what do I do with my money instead? Live more lavishly than I need and waste an exorbitant amount on membership to a sex club so I can avoid relationship entanglements.

So I can avoid another broken heart.

I finish my task, putting away Olivia's clothes and tossing out the worst of what I bought for her older sister. I do it all while evaluating the part I've played in this.

It's not my fault that she never let me know her. It is my fault that I refused to look past the worst of her deeds to see what was truly happening.

My rumination doesn't end until Lorelai and Olivia walk back through my door.

Lorelai's hair is only slightly shorter than it was when she left. The haphazardly cut bob, now bluntly styled with precision.

"Miss Olivia, is that you?" I ask with feigned shock at the hairstyle she now wears. Much like her sister's, but a bit longer and without the same sleekness. A child-size version of what Lorelai sports.

"It's still me!" she squeals as she runs toward me. "See?"

"I do see. It looks great. How do you like it?"

"I like it a lot. I look like Lie-lie now."

"You looked like her before, too. Now, you just look more like her."

She beams her toothy smile at me, clearly proud to look like her sister.

"Olivia said she'd like to watch cartoons while we work out. Is that okay?" Lorelai whispers from across the room, the words tinged with nervousness.

I raise an eyebrow at the questions.

"Of course," I say, turning my attention back to Livi. "What's mine is yours."

"What does that mean?"

"It means you make yourself comfortable here. You eat when you're hungry. You watch television whenever you want."

"Noah."

"Sorry. You watch television whenever your sister says you can." I wink at Olivia, and she tries to do it back to me. Only being successful at blinking both lids rapidly.

"Am I doing it?"

"You're so close," I exclaim. "Keep practicing."

"I'll change and meet you in the gym," Lorelai says as she leaves the room.

I turn on the television and get Olivia settled on the channel she wants. As soon as the picture of brightly colored toons appeared, I all but disappeared to the girl. She's engrossed.

"You holler at us if you need anything, okay," I tell her, running a hand over her head to get her attention.

"Uh-huh."

Smiling, I go change and ready myself for a much-needed session with Lorelai. Drunken sex-fests are not great for my hip. I should try to remember that the next time I'm so in my cups. Or, you know, just not get so wasted to begin with. It does nobody any good, and all my worst decisions are made that way.

I'm getting good at ignoring the lingering self-loathing I feel. Lorelai will hate me if, when, she finds out how I spent the days she was away. It would be better to be upfront, but damn, I've wrecked her enough already. We're finally acting like adults, but it's tenuous, a fragile friendship. I don't want to destroy it again so soon.

It's not fair to her. I know it's not. But it's my decision for the time being, regardless.

Since Lorelai came back into my life, I've acted much like I did after my injury. Losing my career in such a way sent me on a deep, dark spiral into harmful self-indulgence. I've never admitted it to myself, but I didn't just mourn my physical strength or my loss of career dreams. I used that time to mourn my relationship with Lorelai, too.

I didn't do that in college. I was so angry, I pushed aside the other emotions and channeled that into working harder. That way, I never had to question why she left. I could just spend my days believing she was a bitch for leaving me like she did.

Not the healthiest way to deal with it, but I was young and stupid.

I remember laying in the hospital, waiting for the images to come back of my body. Waiting for the news that would change everything. My family was there with me, Mom, Dad, and Connor. But it was her I wanted. Her hand holding mine while I was told it would be a horrible decision to ever suit up for a professional game again.

That's when I mourned the loss of our relationship. And I've never forgiven her for adding that pain to the mountain of it I already faced.

I beat Lorelai to the gym and am running through the stretches she likes for me to start with when she arrives.

"I need a favor," she says as she enters, pulling the door halfway closed behind her.

"What's up?"

"I sent my resume into a few places while Livi was getting her haircut. One place just emailed me. They'd like to interview me the day after tomorrow."

"Where is it?" I ask, my stomach tying itself in knots in anticipation of her answer.

"Mobile. Can I borrow your car? Just for the day?"

"Alabama?" I ask with some disgust.

"Yes, Noah." She sighs. "You snob. It checks the boxes. Farther from Utah, not too far to make the move hard, not Louisiana, and a state with no NFL team."

Fuck, I did tell her that.

"What about Olivia?"

"That was going to be my second question," she says and bites at her lip. "Can you watch her? If it goes well, I'll look at a couple of apartments before driving back."

"Let me think about it while we work."

"Um, okay," she says dejectedly. I'm not going to tell her no. Not exactly. Stalling is what I'm doing. Mobile doesn't settle well in my gut and I'm not sure what to do about that.

She moves behind me and runs her hands down my hips and thighs. Simple assessment, like she always does.

"Why are you so tense?"

"I'm not," I rebut.

"You are." She sighs again when I don't answer. "Never mind, I can guess."

She can't, really. Sure, she can guess what I was up to while she was gone. But not who.

Maybe she never needs to know.

I blink that thought away. It's childish and below me. I own what I do, what I say. With everyone but her, it seems.

"I'll drive you to Mobile and keep Olivia entertained while you interview."

"Really?"

"On one condition."

"I should have known," she mutters.

"You let me take you and Livi shopping for new clothes this afternoon."

"No," she says instantly and steps back. I turn toward her to see I've riled up her temper.

"Why?"

"You dress me like a sex worker, but I don't want you, or any man, dressing Olivia. Ever."

Her eyes are narrowed and shining. She's pissed, and I don't blame her. She's right, after all.

"That's why I want to take you shopping. I owe you a practical wardrobe. I will buy Olivia clothes, but I won't give my input. That's between you and her."

"I can handle all of that myself."

So defiant.

"I know you can, Lorelai," I say, stepping to her, liking how I tower over her even while she's all puffed up with anger. "Though, I would like to know how you ended up stranded in my city. Both of those things aside, I provide for the people in my care. That's you and your sister, currently. Just agree to it."

"No."

"Yes."

"No."

Oh, how I've missed this. The version of Lorelai I loved never gave me an inch during a disagreement. Often, I pushed her buttons for the soul purpose of having this banter with her. Of course, that usually led to naked, sexy times.

She wasn't experienced at first, though I knew she wasn't a virgin. That never stopped her from being an enthusiastic learner. She wasn't shy, and she was curious as hell. Anything I suggested, she'd agree to try. Some were firsts for us both, and I remember so much of our time. When I let myself.

"Why are you broke, Lore?"

"I'm not."

"You were." I laugh lightly at her play. "Tell me why."

Her fists move to her slender hips while she deliberates what to do.

"You agreed to talk," I remind her.

"Did I?"

I lean down, placing my mouth to the shell of her ear. "I didn't force you," I say slowly. "You agreed."

She visibly shivers.

"Let me in. Let me help."

A few shaky breathes later, she speaks.

16
LORELAI

"My mother always called me on my birthday. Every year, without fail. It was the only time she'd sneak away to call. Last year, she called on a different day. My father was sick, dying. She wanted to use the opportunity to get out."

"She couldn't leave whenever she wanted?"

I shake my head.

"No. It's heavily guarded. She assumed there would be chaos when he passed, she wanted to use that as cover. Drew…" I hesitate. Conversations with Noah about Drew have always led to horrible experiences.

If he doesn't keep his promise of no more insults, I'll pack my sister up and leave tonight. I won't let her see me set so low. Not when I'm all she has.

Noah's jaw tightens, and I take a retreating step back.

"None of that," he says, placing his hands on my forearms and pulling me back.

"I don't want to argue."

"We won't. We're just talking. Keep going."

He relaxes and tries to calm his voice. He's trying, so I will too.

"Drew donated enough money to Giving Hope to secure my mother and Olivia a place to hide. They offered them a few months' stay while I figured out our next move. I sold my condo to pay off the guard. It should have been fine. I had savings and a small shit-hole apartment that my boss was letting me rent for cheap. Except, at the last minute, the guard wanted more money."

"You used your savings?"

"Every penny."

"Drew didn't offer any more help?"

I hate reliving this. I'd never felt so alone than I had when it all happened.

"That was the day the story broke about me and Drew. I... I know what it looked like. That he flew me around for clandestine hookups. It wasn't like that. I was in Los Angeles to meet with an FBI agent who's investigating my family's ranch. From there, I flew to Utah to make sure they got out."

"That was the morning after June found you both?"

I nod. To the world, it looked like Drew giving his mistress a sweet sendoff. Reality was he was wishing me luck in saving my sister and at finally having a chance at a relationship with my mother.

"He stayed with you that night after June found you two together."

"No, not really. I had my own room. When he came back from chasing June, I helped him make phone calls to try to get an earlier flight back. His coach fought him on it. By the time he convinced him, there weren't any flights left. The more options that failed, the more unsettled he got. Until eventually he shut down. He stopped talking, wouldn't respond to anything I said. Then he locked himself in the bathroom and screamed like he was dying. I didn't know what to do. I curled up in a chair, and fell asleep waiting for him to come out," I say, swallowing down the emotion clogging my throat. I'd never felt anyone's anguish like that before. I can't imagine I'll ever forget it. "I was worried. I'd never seen anyone so distraught. Hours later when I woke up, he was still in there. Talking to himself like she was locked in there with him. It was the saddest thing I'd ever heard. I was ashamed that I was there to bear witness to it."

"You shouldn't have. That wasn't for you."

"I know, Noah," I say, my heated voice now matching his. "But he was the only friend I had, and I couldn't just leave him like that."

"Friends who fuck."

Dropping my head, I try with everything I have to tamp down the feeling of defeat. Despite his promises, he'll never let this die. What I say now won't matter to him, it doesn't change anything.

"I never stayed the night with him. Not once. We'd fuck, I'd leave. He refused to kiss me, he never performed oral. He wouldn't even use my name, except when it was about my punishment. Which he gave me in return for following all his rules. He was strict with keeping it as impersonal as possible. Nothing he got from me was *about* me. Every time he came, it was to June. I know because he usually said her name. He used my body and I let him so that I didn't have to keep going to strangers for what I needed. I let him because I was using him too." My voice has grown quieter as I've gone on.

Noah's heart is racing. My eyes haven't left his chest. I don't want to see the disdain on his face, not when I already feel it so acutely.

"I'm not asking you to understand, Noah, but maybe you could at least quit throwing it back in my face as if I miss those times with him. I don't. I don't miss how cold it was, or how alone I felt. I don't miss wondering what it would be like to have someone so obsessed with me that it's my face they see no matter who they're with. And the guilt. Oh, hell, the guilt we both felt every time. I don't miss that, either. The only thing I miss is the feeling that someone finally had my back. Even that turned out to be fake. After June found out, he barely responded to me at all. I get it, I do. So much happened in those few short days, but I could have used my friend to talk to."

He doesn't respond. I wait several long moments, but nothing comes.

With so many things to fight for in my life right now, this isn't a battle I want anymore. I'll talk when he wants to talk, but I'm over expecting anything good between us to come of it.

I can't win Noah over. I don't fit in any part of his life, anyway, so why keep trying?

"Lie down," I say, changing the subject. "You're too tight to work out. Let me see if I can loosen it up."

He does. Silently, I massage his right side. I want to press him for what he did to work himself out of shape like this, but I know it's not something I want to hear. Besides, it seems as if I've landed myself in a very one-sided relationship with Noah.

A relieved sigh releases from him as my thumb presses down around his glute and tensor, working out one particularly gnarly knot.

"What happened with your job and apartment?" He finally speaks.

"My boss, Will, was always flirty. In turn, I was always standoffish. I rushed back to Seattle to get back to work. I needed to start saving again since Giving Hope was a temporary solution. But after I was splashed on every tabloid with the local star quarterback, Will became more persistent. The flirting turned into forward advances, then into bribes of reducing my rent even more in exchange for favors. I thought I was handling it okay and he'd get the hint that it was never going to go his way. Until one night I came home to him in my apartment, waiting for me."

"Excuse me?" he says with icy rage.

"You can be *my* whore now, Lorelai. That's what he said when I opened the door. I ran out and called the police. An officer escorted me back in long enough for me to pack a few things. That was the best they'd do because I didn't own the property."

Noah jumps off the massage table and starts pacing the small space, every muscle on his body straining with effort. Veins pop out along his neck and arms.

His anger does beautiful things to his body.

It's so fucked up that I'm turned on by that.

"Fuck. Fuck, fuck, fuck."

"Noah, stop. It's over, I never have to see him again."

As if he'd forgotten I was even in the room, his head snaps to mine when I speak. He rushes me, backs me up until my ass rests against the windowsill, and the coolness of the glass settles over the back of my head.

His hands come up to my face, holding me in place, nose to nose with him. His wolfish eyes positively glowing now.

"Did he hurt you? Did he *fucking* touch you?"

"No. He scared me is all."

"That's *all*?" he asks, clearly thinking that Will's intrusion is worthy of capital punishment.

"You know what I mean. It could have been so much worse."

I could have been raped, beaten, left for dead like June McKenna had been by her stalker in college. Walking away with nothing but fear was luck. I'm not taking it for granted, or taking it lightly. I'm just thankful it wasn't worse.

"Did you press charges?"

"I tried. The cop didn't take it very seriously. He seemed almost amused, honestly. I got a cheap hotel room and tried to find work. I waitressed part time because I wasn't getting any callbacks."

"Why? You worked with top level athletes in San Francisco." His anger hasn't faded. At least it isn't directed at me this time.

"Because I'm Lorelai Simmons and I was looking for work in a city that loves Drew and June McKenna."

Noah takes an almost gasping breath, and I watch as all the gears shift. So many of the missing puzzle pieces finally landing in place for him. He's now forced to consider my side of the story and realizing it's nothing like he imagined.

"You ran out of money and thought the tabloids that were giving you so much free attention could buy you off instead."

I've done a lot of stupid shit in my life. That move is damn near the top of the list.

"I'd hoped they'd be okay with some standard soundbites. I didn't want to give them anything real."

He nods. "And coming here?"

"Idiocy and desperation aren't great bedfellows." I shrug.

"You always were impetuous."

"Impetuous violence," I muse.

"What?"

"Nothing, just something my mother used to say about me. That I followed my heart with impetuous violence."

He places a hand over said heart, and we both feel it stutter.

"This heart," he whispers. It's not a question, and I don't understand the statement. "Let me take you both shopping."

I blink at the subject change.

"No," I say, but he cuts off my refusal by fusing his mouth to mine. It's short, almost chaste. It is life wrapped up in an inevitable heartbreak. I want to pull it closer and shove it away all at once.

"You can't kiss me to get your way, Noah," I say, swimming through the blur of watery eyes. He can't offer such a precious gift to me when I know it's only going to crumble to nothing when I leave.

"I kissed you because I wanted to."

"You can't do that either."

"Your objection has been noted. Now let's go shopping," he states as if we already made the decision.

"I'm not going to win this, am I?"

"Not a chance," he says with a smile.

"Not Nieman's," I say. I don't ever need to go back there. "I choose the stores."

"I pay."

"You buy clothes. I buy shoes and underthings."

"You buy underthings."

"Whatever." I give up with an eyeroll.

"We may have to pry Olivia away from the television. She was engrossed."

"They're still very new for her. I need to try to keep it balanced or I'm afraid she'll be perched in front of a television for sixteen hours straight," I say.

"No televisions where you grew up?"

"That would be outside influence and information. Strictly prohibited."

Noah stares at me for a few beats. His smile fades into a sadder version, and I fear the pity will follow. But then he pulls me into him and wraps his arms around me tightly while he holds me. My cheek rests against his hard pec. The feel of his skin, the smell of him, it's heady. I could lick it up, lick *him* up.

I could stay here in his arms forever, if life were different.

"Thank you," he says to the top of my head.

"For what?"

One hand slowly works up my back and fists gently into my hair, pulling my face up to his.

"For trusting me with your truth."

"You'll want more of it, won't you?"

He nods without breaking eye contact. Though he doesn't say the words, I imagine I hear him say he'll want it all.

17
NOAH

I've seen the memes. I know women have an uncontrolled obsession with Target. Standing here in the middle of this madhouse, I can't fathom why.

The lighting is garish. The people are loud. I'm certain parents have dropped off their younglings to run wild all day without their supervision. Nothing else could explain how there are so many more of them than adults.

And everything in here is hideous.

Lorelai disagrees, of course. Olivia has been wide-eyed and glued to her sister's leg the entire time. I'm guessing she's much more like me and would prefer a dimmer, quieter place to shop. She's a bright child.

My promise has been kept; I haven't given my input. I haven't needed to. Lorelai knows as well as I do that I would veto every item in this store. *Clearly.*

Instead, I follow them from department to department, pushing an ugly red, plastic cart around like I'm nothing more than an impeccably dressed errand boy. We started in the women's department, where Lorelai refused to pick 'more than she needs', as I rolled my eyes profusely. Albeit quietly.

Then it was underwear. I'll give credit where it's due; all the panties here would give me no guilt ripping to shreds off her body.

"Noah?"

"Yes, little one?"

"Do you have a case of the grumps?"

"A what?"

"A case of the grumps. Right, Lie-lie, that's what you said?"

"Yep," she agrees.

We're headed across the aisle to the girls' section next. Though I would prefer to be at nearly any other store, I am oddly excited to watch Olivia shop.

"Does it look like I have a case of the grumps?" I ask, then make a ridiculous face, bugging my eyes and sticking my tongue out at her.

"No." She giggles.

"Then I must not."

Lorelai side-eyes me curiously, so I stick my tongue out at her, too. Olivia giggles more.

"Okay, Livi. Start picking out things you like, and I'll help you find the right size."

"It doesn't have to be dresses, right? You said."

"Right. If you see a dress you think is pretty, you can get it. But it doesn't have to be dresses. You can get pants and shorts, if you want," Lorelai answers, patiently.

"And I won't get in trouble?"

"Do you remember what I said about that?"

"You said we might have to talk, but I'll never be in trouble."

"That's right. So, let's pick some clothes that you want to wear, not that someone else says you should wear. Okay?"

Olivia nods and starts a tentative search through the racks. At first, she only looks. Several long minutes pass before I start noticing her double takes. A dead giveaway that she's interested in something but apprehensive to speak up.

She keeps eyeing a pair of yellow leggings with tiny rainbows printed all over. I elbow her sister gently and nod my head toward the item. Careful to not give any opinion but make sure Lorelai is aware of what's happening.

"Got it," she says to me. "What about these pants, Livi? They look fun."

Olivia gives a nod and a half smile, trying to hide her enthusiasm.

An hour later, I'm packing the bags into the trunk of my car. Olivia took quite some time to start speaking up, but she was getting the hang of it by the time we made it to shoes. Lorelai has her work cut out for her. It's hard not to wonder if she's up for the task.

She has a twisted past, as well, after all. While that will serve Olivia in many ways, it's also a lot for Lorelai to navigate even without the added pressure of a toddler in her care. Alone. In Mobile, Alabama. Or wherever they end up.

The prospect of them moving away than a couple of hours does bring on a case of the grumps, and I find I'm not very conversational on our drive to get dinner.

It's been a long, emotional day. There is a lot to ponder over. Starting with Lorelai's ex-boss, Will. I'm going to fucking bury that man.

No, I won't actually kill him. But I'll make him wish he was dead. Money goes a long way in the world. Connections go even further. Lorelai specializes in sports injuries. I'm sure Will's business relies on athletes. I know athletes, agents, coaches, recruiters, team doctors. If I must call in every last favor I have, I will see that asshole out of business.

It still won't be enough punishment for him, but it's a start.

Swallowing down the rest of what she told me today won't be easy, either. Lorelai's been misunderstood by everyone. Most of all by me. Regardless of the choices she made, she didn't deserve to have her entire life upended because of it. She shouldn't be unemployable and destitute, with zero support in her life. All while attempting to save people from an abusive, fanatical cult.

Drew ended his season playing the best game of his career and the fans loved him for it. He's gained forgiveness from everyone in his life, including the wife he betrayed. While everyone simultaneously shuns Lorelai. That's some deep-rooted misogynistic bullshit right there. I'm ashamed that I partook.

I have my own reasons for being angry with her, sure. There are still issues we need to work through, things I need to understand. Like why she pulled that shit that ended our relationship. Yet, it's getting harder and harder to see why anyone else should hate her. Except June, of course.

"Are we really going to eat bugs?"

"Mudbugs aren't really bugs, Livi," Lorelai answers. I can hear she's trying not to laugh.

We purchased a car seat for her while at that horrible hellscape and it's put her in kicking distance of the back of my seat. I'm not bothered by it. If her legs are swinging, she's happy and I can't get past the need to make this pocket-sized human smile.

Now we're headed to see Babs. I'll drop the girls off first before heading down the street to pick up a replacement phone. Something I should have done at the earliest opportunity. Instead, I rushed to judgement and made horrible decisions.

Lorelai spins my world into full-out bedlam by merely existing alone.

The restaurant is busy when I finally get back, a new phone in hand. The tables, all being communal style, are full. Lorelai and Olivia are surrounded by a group of elderly locals telling them animated stories of urban legends. Lorelai wears a huge grin; Olivia wears a smile of butter that matches her fingers.

With no room for me to sit next to them, I easily lift Livi up and settle her back down on my knee. This suit will likely need to head straight to the dry cleaners, but I'm too hungry to care.

"Just Noah, I ate so many muddy bugs," Olivia says around an ear of corn.

"I can tell, this belly feels so full," I say, patting her tummy lightly.

Lorelai's smile fades as she watches our interaction. A few more clues into her childhood fall into place and more pieces of my heart break away. As hard as it will be to hear it, I need her to tell me. I need to listen to her.

Reaching a hand over to hers, I grasp it firmly until she looks at me.

"It's me, Lore. You're both safe."

"Here, suck the head!" Olivia shoves a crawfish in my face, barely holding on to it in between her slippery fingers. Her other palm reaches for my cheek to steady her reach.

I suck the spicy juice as Lorelai bursts into giggles.

It doesn't matter that it's at my expense; her laughter is the most beautiful thing I've ever seen.

"Here's another," Olivia offers, smearing more stickiness on my other cheek now.

Lorelai continues uncontrollably, and within seconds, the rest of the table has been infected. Babs comes out with a fresh pot for us, dumping in front of me and Olivia.

"The *piti* is good for you, Mr. Noah. So is the *chouchou*," she says with a big smile.

If only that were true.

Hours later, Olivia is asleep, dead to the world in new pink pajamas that fit her. We had hit the toy department too, and she chose an overstuffed alligator that's now tightly tucked under her arm.

Lorelai is on my laptop. Applying for more jobs or researching the best neighborhoods in Mobile, or something of that sort.

I'm showering off all the butter and grease, layer by layer, recounting every single thing that's happened today. It's a mountain of information to take in, to dissect, to decide what to do about any of it.

I put a call into a friend in Seattle to look into this Will character. I also emailed the director of Giving Hope to set up some regular support.

Neither of those does anything, directly, for the two people currently living with me. While it soothes a small amount of knotting in my gut, it doesn't erase it. Not nearly.

The thought of them moving away in the coming days sends me close to panic. I'm unable to reconcile all the feelings I'm having about it. My brain tells me it's the best for them, for all of us. They need to learn to rely on each other, to live on their own, and with their own rules. Only, I wish Lorelai had more good days behind her before rushing away.

If she's not in a stable place, how can she build a stable home? But who am I to tell her what to do?

She was right when she called me her tormenter. Tonight was the first time since she's been here that she had a genuine moment of happiness.

And I want to give her more of that while she's here. And more.

Shutting the shower off, I quickly dry off and pull on a pair of gym shorts. My office light is off when I pass by. I find Lorelai on the sofa where she's made a bed for herself. Her eyes flutter under her closed lids and a soft smile plays at her lips, as if she's enjoying a happy dream.

I should let her be, let her keep hold of whatever is giving her that lazy, content look.

I can't. I want her close for as long as I have her.

I want more than a truce. I want to be her friend. I want to give her some of the things life has so thoroughly denied her. It's all temporary, of course. Maybe this time when she leaves me, it can be with respect instead of betrayal.

Embracing my boorish side, I peel the blanket off her and lift her into my arms. Her arms instinctively wrap around my neck as she snuggles closer.

"You're back from practice early," she says groggily.

When she was mine, she'd often hide out in my dorm room. It was larger and a single, meaning I didn't have a roommate, because of who I was. It was a quiet place for her to study. She worked so hard to learn everything she could. Was always striving to be the best. Sometimes she'd fall asleep while she waited. Those days were my favorite. She didn't rest enough. I felt better when she caught a nap.

I think she's back there in her dream and, no lie, my dick is rock-hard knowing she's dreaming of me.

"I don't have practice anymore, Lorelai. Remember?" I ask, setting her down on my bed.

"What?" She starts to wake back up.

"You were dreaming of me."

"I was not," she denies, heat flaring on her cheeks.

"Liar," I say through a smile. "I have a gift for you."

"What?" she repeats.

"When was the last time you were kissed?"

"You kissed me today." Her eyes darken, and she scoots back on the bed, trying to pull her legs up to her chest. I move to still them.

"That's not what I'm asking, and you know it."

"I don't…"

"No more lies."

Her eyes glisten and yet another piece of my ego falls away into the abyss. How did I not see how broken she was? How sad, and hurt, and alone…

Humans aren't meant to live without companionship, affection, or care. How long has she been without all of them?

"Years," she says it softly, but I hear the agony as if she's roared it through soul-breaking pain.

"I'm going to change that now. Because I want to. Because we can be better versions of ourselves than we were yesterday. Because I'm sorry that I didn't *see* you."

I see the effect of my words; she's breaking down in a million small convulsions. No tears, but she's damn near going to hyperventilate.

"Lorelai," I snap to get her attention. "Breathe with me."

Then I steal her chance. I catch every stutter from her mouth into my own, forcing her to match my rhythm. Keeping it slow and gentle, I wrap an arm around her and lower her down as I climb up over her. I feel her tremble. Worried she's not feeling the same as me, I back off and open my eyes.

Her stare is wide and watery. Two small tears fall out when she blinks up at me.

"Is this okay?"

"You make me dizzy. You hated me just yesterday."

"I never hated you."

"You don't treat people the way you treated me if you like them, Noah," she says.

"I acted out of hurt, not hate."

Her mouth opens as if she's going to speak, but she doesn't. I wait her out, but nothing comes.

"Say it, Lorelai."

"I'm sorry I hurt you. That was the worst way for me to handle our situation."

Now, I'm the one taking a moment. It's difficult to not react with her. Anyone else could have a difficult conversation with me without elevating my emotions. She shreds my nerves like no other.

However, truce has been called. And if I want her to tell me her truths, I need to learn to properly control myself around her.

"I don't know what our situation was. Will you tell me?"

"It's hard to know where to start," she says, turning her head to the side.

"Do you want me to ask questions?"

"No," she says, but nods her head. I try not to laugh; it's obviously not a humorous situation.

"Were you with Drew while you were with me?"

"Never," she exclaims, snapping her back to me. She holds my face, then. "Have you thought that all this time?"

My heart tells me to lie to her. Tell her that I haven't always wondered that, because that would remove the pain in her voice. It wouldn't be helpful to either of us, though. It definitely wouldn't be true to me.

"I couldn't be sure."

"Oh, Noah," she says softly, closing her eyes again. "I would have never. I loved you. More than anything."

"Then why, Lorelai? You taunted me into hurting you and then you left me."

One night, Lorelai asked me if I'd spank her. I laughed her off at first, until I realized she was asking in earnest. The suggestion baffled me. Hurting her in any way was so far beyond anything I could imagine.

When I told her I needed time to think about it, admittedly, I thought it was a fleeting fancy. Something she'd get over and forget about.

A week later, she brought it back up.

And again, and again. She became almost agitated about it. Then she went out one night with friends instead of coming to see me. She posted pictures of her night out on her social media. Every picture had Drew in it.

Jealousy made me agree to try what she wanted. Until recently, the night I spanked her lived in my mind as the worst night of my life. When I refused to do it again, she left me. Since she's been back, I've added more nights to my horrible list.

We've both made bad decisions.

I need to know what led to hers.

18
LORELAI

"Everything about my life had been dictated or ruled by others," I say. There's no way to make Noah understand the way my head processes situations. Especially because I can't understand them myself. I'll try though. I have to try. "When my mother sent me away, I didn't understand what a gift it was. I wanted to go back because I didn't know anything else. Until I did. When I learned that I could have dreams of my own, and obtain them, I wanted everything."

Noah still lies atop me. His face only inches from mine, his taste still on my lips. I want to escape to the other side of the room, carve some distance between us while I tell him about the worst day of my life. I also want to climb inside him and never leave his warmth.

"Except to be what held someone else from obtaining their dreams. I never wanted to be that."

"You weren't, Lorelai."

"I was. Remember the truth of it all, Noah. Not just the parts you've been telling yourself for so long. Remember that you started sleeping in a little later when I was there in your bed. Remember that you were late to practice three times in the last month we were together. Because you didn't want to leave me."

"That's college, it didn't mean anything."

"No more lies, Noah."

He huffs because he knows. He knows that he didn't do any of that before, or after, me.

"I refused to be the reason you didn't fulfill your dreams. You would have done the same for me."

"Not with the malice you threw my way," he barks, and I flinch.

"No, of course not," I hesitate before continuing. "You saw through so much of my bullshit. So many of my defenses. I knew that if I didn't make you hate me, you'd never let me leave. You were already so uncomfortable from spanking me. I decided to use that to bait Drew. It was my best chance at being unforgivable."

His jaw clenches under my palms, causing the bristle of his two-day growth to tickle my fingertips. My focus is there, not at the emotions playing all over his features while he reconciles them all.

I won't get to feel him at all soon.

"What did you tell him? He came at me as if I was a serial abuser."

"I didn't tell him that." It's hard to get the words out; so much guilt blocks the words. "I told him you liked it more than I did. That I thought you might be a sadist, and that was too reminiscent of my father. My intention was to make it a me problem, but Drew reacted more than I anticipated. I think more so from his own childhood. God, I fucked up so badly, Noah. I could have ruined your entire career, which was the exact opposite of what I wanted."

"You didn't though. You wrecked my heart, not my career."

"But I could have. You should hate me for that. Drew could have easily gone public and made things hard for you."

"It's up to me to decide to hate you or not, Lorelai. Let me make up my own mind as I learn what really happened."

"Okay," I say softly.

"You'd fucked him before?"

It always comes back to that.

"Once." I nod. "He was rougher than you were with me. Not in a bad way, just different. I thought maybe he'd be okay with what I needed and you hated."

"I didn't understand what was being asked of me, Lorelai. I still don't."

His frustration is obvious. I can't blame him; he's right to be upset that I never explained.

"I have a hard time going very long without punishment. It was a regular part of my childhood, deserved or not. When I moved in with Aunt Alice, I struggled. She'd try so hard to convince me that I wasn't doing anything to deserve scolding, but it never worked. She'd ground me or take away a privilege on occasion just to try to pacify my rabid need."

Poor Alice. The amount of shit she had to deal with was so unfair to her. I appreciate her efforts, but I've always wondered if it helped lead to her untimely heart attack. Not just due to her worrying about me, but also my mother and all the other innocents my father held captive.

I didn't have her for very long. The impression she made on me is priceless, regardless. I hope to be what she was to me, and more, to Olivia.

Safety. Understanding. Non-judgmental. She was all those things to me, and they were all things I never knew existed until her.

"College was hard. I didn't like the constant presence of so many people. I hated communal living; it was too reminiscent of the ranch and didn't feel secure. It weighed on me all the time. Some days, I'd be so panicked I wouldn't sleep at all. When you let me start using your room, it was the greatest gift you could have given me, at the time."

Noah soothes my hair back from my face. I wiggle underneath him, and he widens his legs to allow me more room. Only it presses his groin into mine and all my nerve endings spark at once.

They're screaming for me to roll Noah over and fuck him blindly. Stupid, stupid body.

"That quiet time wasn't enough to ease the anxiety?"

"No. My father used a rod."

"Fuck, Lorelai. That's why you handed me a crop?"

"I'm sorry I didn't try to explain," I say, nodding.

"You let me hurt you." He spits the words, but it's a pain directed at himself, not at me.

"You didn't hurt me; I told you that. The more lackadaisical you became about football, the more horrible I felt about myself. I knew it was because of me and I hated myself for it. I needed what you gave me that night. But that was the problem. I needed it and you hated it."

He rests his forehead on mine. I wait as patiently as I can for him to collect the words he wants to say.

"I would have learned. I *did* learn."

"I know. Hopefully, you learned because you wanted to. Because you like it. Not because I needed it."

He closes his eyes, and again, we lie in the silence that surrounds us. There is noise wafting up from the street. Tourists still enjoying the night. It feels so far away, another world altogether. As if he and I are cocooned in a bubble of our own making, impenetrable by outside influence.

We've never been that, though. We were good together, but we weren't a force. Our love didn't have the chance to grow into something so strong.

I'll never regret that I left Noah. I'm ashamed of the way I did it, but I know leaving was the right thing. At the time.

I will always wish that it could have been different. That it still could be. If wishes always came true, there wouldn't be anything left to strive for. I know I'll never have Noah the way I want. Despite that, from here on, I'll always try to be a woman who could deserve him.

"You didn't have to break my heart," he whispers against my lips. The words feel like a million needles sinking into my heart. One by one.

Loving this man is a slow death.

"I did. You needed to focus. I needed to give you that. For both of us. It wasn't just your heart that broke that day." My voice hitches. "I hope you can believe that. It was the worst day of my life, and I'd had many of those by that point."

"I believe you," he says and peppers kisses across my brow. "It's not easy for me to admit it, but I know you're right in some ways. I would have scorched the earth to keep you from ever being harmed or sad."

"Fire and brimstone?" I ask, trying for some levity.

"Fuck that biblical shit. It has no place with us."

Us.

That's not a word in my vocabular pertaining to Noah. His lips move against mine, deepening his ministrations. It's a matching cadence to the gentle rocking his hips have picked up. A hand finds its way under my sleep shirt, causing my skin to flutter under it as he runs it up my side to rest just under my breasts.

They're not overly large. Dance and gymnastic saw to that, I suppose. I've never achieved ample cleavage, even with great bras. Noah never minded my subtle curves. I can't help wondering if that's another taste of his that's changed. The women he's been with since I arrived have been beautiful, hourglass shaped.

It's difficult to remember that it doesn't matter, that we're not an us, when his warm words skate down my body.

"Is that why you didn't like Pope? Because of all his preaching?"

"Why am I in your bed, Noah?" I change the subject. He's gotten a lot out of me today. I didn't even make him work for any of it.

That's where I am a whore. I'm a complete fiend for kindness. I'll lap the scraps of it up off the floor.

That's not okay. I can't do that anymore. Olivia deserves a strong caretaker, a strong role model. There's already so much stacked against us.

Noah pulls his head up, gaining a better view of me.

"Are you changing the subject on me?"

I nod.

"Has it been too hard? Too much today? I have a lot of questions, but there's time."

That makes me blink. There isn't time. I'm out of here as soon as I can be. If it's not soon, I'll fall for Noah so hard my skull will split. And it would be just as well, because I don't know how to survive having him and losing him all over again.

"You haven't earned any more. I've told you what I owe you, why I broke it off with you to begin with. You got more from me today because you played nice. Anything more about me doesn't come with one day of you not on my ass for every mistake I've made in my life."

He climbs up to his knees now, one on either side of abdomen. It gives me a nice view of his bare chest and heat rushes to places it ought not.

Noah is so hard to ignore. Especially, when he peers down at me, like if he looks long enough, he'll figure me all out.

"How do you see me going about earning it?"

"What exactly is *it*, Noah? What are you after, and why?"

He huffs again in exasperation. Obviously, he's not used to obstacles in the way of what he wants. Roadblocks are my specialty.

"I want to know you, Lorelai. The real you."

"Why?"

"There doesn't have to be a reason. Why shouldn't I want to know you?" He moves his hands to his hips but doesn't get off me.

"Because I'm leaving soon. Because I broke your heart in a horrific way. Because your family hates me. Or, how about because I nearly ruined the marriage of two of your best friends? How many reasons do you need?"

"Not a single one of those is a reason that we can't be friends now."

"Are you feeling okay? Do you have a fever?"

"Of course not." He laughs. "I can keep different parts of my life separate from the others. I'm a fully functional adult."

He may not mean it the way I take it, but suddenly I feel like Noah's dirty little secret. Coming off the back of being Drew McKenna's, it's an even bigger blow.

"Get off me."

"Lorelai…"

"Get the fuck off me, Noah." I seethe through gritted teeth.

"Hey, okay," he soothes and moves to stand. "What just happened?"

I try to calm my racing heartbeat from the burst of adrenaline that accompanies my temper. Not the easiest thing for a hothead like me. I hold my hand up for him to give me a minute, not wanting to lose myself and fly off the handle.

I'm fucking better than this. I have to be better than this.

Olivia's tear-stained face from when I picked her up in Utah flashes behind my eyelids. She barely knows me. I had only been able to spend a handful of hours with them after they escaped, before I had to fly back to Seattle to try to build a life for us all.

She's put so much faith and trust in me. I think it's because she intuitively recognizes something in me that matches her. I can't be sure, but I know I can't blow it.

"I'm done. That's what happened. I'm not allowing you to make the rules for me anymore, because I can't trust that they'll come from a place that has Olivia's best interest in mind."

"What did I say that makes you think I don't have her best interests in mind? Or yours, for that matter?"

Standing from the bed, I take a few steps toward the door before I look back over my shoulder.

"We're not secrets to be hidden away from the people in your life that you really care about. I'm never letting Olivia feel like the adults in her life are ashamed of her. The only people I will let get close to either of us will be people who want us as much as we want them."

I leave him with that. But not before he delivers one final hit.

"You are wrong about something, Lorelai. The NFL wasn't my only dream. You were one, too."

Just like that, my heart turns to cold stone and sinks into the dark depths of my toxic fucking soul.

19
LORELAI

I fell asleep on the sofa last night. But I'm waking up in Noah's bed.
 The sneaky bastard.

He's not only plastered to me, but he also has one leg tossed over mine, effectively keeping me in place. It's how we used to sleep. My nose buried in his chest, his chin resting on my head. It's the only time I've ever felt safe.

It breaks my heart, but I give myself a moment to take him in anyway. Inhaling deeply, I try to place what he smells like. It's clean but manly, like he worked out all day and walked home in fresh rain.

I want to bottle it up. Which is a stupid thought since it's probably his soap. Irish Spring's patented panty-dropping scent or some shit.

Speaking of panties…

That's all I have on, besides my sports bra that I didn't take off before I passed out. My oversized sleep shirt seems to have walked off my body in the middle of the night.

"Oof," Noah exhales when I give him a jab in his side. "The fuck?"

"You are an overbearing prick, Anders. Do you know that?"

"I do." Sleep drags the words out slow and low.

"Why am I in your bed, and where are my pajamas?"

"Oxytocin."

"What?"

"It's a hormone. When activated by skin-to-skin contact, it reduces stress."

"I know what it is." I sigh. "Why did you think I needed a boost?"

"You were sleeping restlessly."

"How do you know that?"

His arms tighten around me, his leg hitching higher. But he doesn't answer.

"Were you watching me sleep?"

Still no answer.

"Are you plotting to kill me?"

Laughter bursts out of him, and his chest ripples with the action. I blame lack of caffeine for my foggy judgment when I stick my tongue out, using it to flick his nipple.

It's right fucking there. What else am I supposed to do in my non-caffeinated delirium?

"Do that again and you're getting railed so deep into this mattress it will take you hours to dig yourself out."

Promise?

Damn, I need out of this bed.

"You ever heard of consent?" I push gently to get him to ease up. He doesn't, of course.

"Yes. And I'd never do anything to you without it. Me wanting to comfort you doesn't make me a villain."

"Let me up. I need coffee. And clothes, you fucking pervert," I say, pressing at his chest again.

"Not just yet. I like sleepy morning talks," he says while scooting down to my level. When we're nose to nose, just like last night, he continues, "You were agitated when you went to bed last night. I didn't like it because I know I was the reason. I told you that you and Olivia are both safe with me and then I said something carelessly that made you think you don't mean anything to me. I apologize for how it came out. I didn't mean that I'd keep you from them. I meant that I'd keep their judgment from you. This is a new situation for both of you and I don't want to add to that stress, or let my family and friends add to it. Okay?"

It's my turn to sit silently, not knowing what to make of Noah and all this gentleness.

"You don't trust me, and I deserve that. You should, at least, know me well enough to know that I would never knowingly let a child suffer. I will help you and Olivia. I do have what's best for the both of you at heart," he says and presses a light kiss to my nose. "Let's try to be friendly, Lorelai."

"Friends don't strip unconscious friends down to their skivvies while they sleep, Noah."

"First of all, who says skivvies? Second, I think we can make up our own rules for this friendship. My vote for rule one is that we have as much skin-to-skin time as possible. You're a mom now; you should really control your stress levels."

"I'm a sister. And you're vetoed."

"Do you have that power?"

His voice deepens a few octaves and takes on a dark sultriness that I feel in my core.

"I'm certainly not giving it to you. I don't even know you."

I try to wriggle my way out of his hold again.

"Hold on," he says as one hand palms the back of my head, forcing me to look at him. "You know me."

"No, I don't. I don't understand you at all. You should hate me and instead you're cuddling me. You should have left me on the street, instead you move me in and pay me way too much for way too little. All I know of you is what I've been able to glean from scouring the internet. Every day I'd wonder if I would see you dating, or engaged, or married. When the pictures of you and June—It doesn't matter. Let me up."

"It matters, Lorelai. When you saw the pictures, what happened?"

"You don't need me to say it, Noah," I painfully whisper. "You know me enough to know what I thought."

"I didn't know you until the past couple of days."

"And I still don't know you at all."

"You do. You know the most important things."

"Why don't you hate me for what I did to you?"

"I just don't." He shrugs. "I don't agree with how you approached the situation. But I'm trying to understand that you didn't have the same life experiences to pull from as I did. Let's not overthink it. It's in the past and we're different people now. We move forward, not back."

All I can do is blink up at him in awe.

The conversation ends when Olivia's voice calls from down the hall.

"Lie-lie?"

"Damnit, where's my shirt?"

Noah jumps up, grabs a t-shirt from his dresser door and slips it over my head as soon as I sit up. It smells the same as him. I want to bathe in this scent. Because I'm a glutton for punishment.

Ugh.

"Good morning, Livi," I say, exiting his room.

"Morning."

"How did you sleep?"

"Good. Nobody is in there to wake me up," she says, pointing to the guest room.

"Nope," I reply, trying to keep the sorrow out of my voice.

"Can I have cereal?"

"Yes, ma'am."

I settle her at the table with a big bowl of cereal, then grab myself a cup of coffee. My hand shakes around the mug.

"What was that about?" Noah asks, steadying my hand with his.

"Something I saved her from." All the daughters slept in shared bedrooms at the main house on the ranch. As the girls got older and wiser to what was happening, it wasn't uncommon to wake up to someone crying hysterically or having a nightmare. It was the worst when someone was about to be married off.

Again, that wasn't something I understood at the time. But with age comes knowledge. I know now that the girls were kept separate to keep a watchful eye on us. Not for our protection, but for control. We were spoon-fed only the information my father deemed necessary. We were kept naïve.

Until the day we weren't. The day a girl would be told her fate.

The wails of terrified young girls will haunt me forever.

"What?"

I turn from staring out the window to staring at him.

"I'm going to take her out to lunch today. I'd like to let her see some of the city."

Noah sighs at my change of subject.

"My treat. We can walk down to the river."

"Whatever you say, Daddy."

"Sarcasm suits you. But watch it," he says quietly. Then he swats my ass. Quick and sharp, and he covers the sound with a fake little cough, so Olivia doesn't hear.

It's a reminder that I need to steel myself against his charming and flirty side. Noah is detrimental to my heart which is already far too weak and fragile.

Olivia comes alive when we get to the waterfront. A band is playing live music. She's an instant fan and wastes no time jumping into the small crowd of other children dancing wildly to it.

Noah keeps an eagle eye on her even though he smiles and laughs at her awkward movements. I love that she loves this and simultaneously worry about how well she'll do living with only me. She's a friendly girl who loves chatting and company. What if I'm not enough for her? I mean, I'll have to find childcare, but when we're home, I'll be busy with other responsibilities like cooking and cleaning and whatnot. She's lived her whole four years with a multitude of kids to play with daily; I can't give her that level of companionship.

"What if I fuck this up?"

Noah's hand finds mine, his thumb rubbing soothing circles on top of it. It's so familiar, as if it hasn't been years.

"The fact that you're worried makes me think you're going to be just fine," he says. "It's the parents who think they'll be great at it all that I'd be concerned with."

"So, you're saying have zero confidence in myself and second-guess everything? Perfect."

He laughs, then drops my hand, only to reposition his arm around my shoulders. Pulling me in, he rests his chin on the top of my head.

"You've got this, Lorelai. It's clear as day you love her and would walk over hot glass shards on bare feet for her."

"I hope you're right."

"Look at me," he commands. I tip my head up to look at him, and once my face is open to his and the warm glow of sunshine, his mouth dips down to taste mine. It's only a second of two, but it's maybe the sweetest thing he's done for me since I got here. "You've got this."

"Thank you."

"You're welcome," he answers at the same time a throat clears.

In synchronicity, we look up at the noise.

Drew and June. He's tense and glaring at us both, while June clings to his arm with watery eyes.

And just like that, I'm all but forgotten by Noah. He stands abruptly and steps to them, pulling them away a short distance. Far enough that I can't hear the quiet words exchanged over the sound of the music.

I train my attention on Livi, instead. They aren't my business, no matter how much I want to know what's being said. About me.

Livi's hand in hand with another girl of similar age, spinning each other around in circles. Hair flying in their faces, they giggle.

"It isn't like that," I hear Noah say when the song ends.

"Sure looks like it," Drew returns.

I peek from the corner of my eye to see Noah wrapping an arm around June now. My throat plummets down somewhere around my ankles. My new 'friendship' with Noah is already causing the problems I warned it would. Besides his words making me feel exactly like I knew they would, I don't want to be a complication for Noah.

"Just Noah, did you see my new friend?" Olivia hollers as she runs toward him at full speed.

"Livi," I try to avert her, but she ignores me and crashes into his leg.

"I'm sorry, I must have missed it, Miss Olivia," he says as I stand to retrieve my sister.

"You weren't watching me." She pouts.

She's too attached to him already. This won't end well when we leave, and I'll be the one left to pick up the pieces of her tiny broken heart.

"Livi, do you want to go for a walk? I bet we can find some ice cream along the way?"

She gives Noah a sad look but takes my hand.

"You have her?" Drew asks. I can't tell if it's awe or an accusation. As if I'm unfit.

Which only raises my hackles.

"Who is she?" June asks softly, nuzzling further into Noah's hold.

Nobody says anything and my gaze bounces between them all as it dawns on me. She has no idea that Drew was a part of getting my mother and sister out.

Replaying the few conversations I've had with her, I don't think she knows anything about me.

"You didn't tell her?" I ask Drew incredulously.

I messaged Drew when my mother and Olivia got out and he'd congratulated me. After that, he quickly turned sour to most communication with me. He didn't cut me off completely, at first. Occasionally, he'd send a pained reply of his own. But those messages never responded directly to anything I said or asked. I had the feeling he wasn't really reading what I sent him.

It didn't take long before he stopped responding altogether. But I assumed he'd told June about my part in all this. Not to defend me, of course, but as a hint of an explanation as to what we were to one another. Which wasn't much of anything now that I see it more clearly.

I thought we were friends.

Like so many times before, I was wrong.

Nothing he could say makes me fucking her husband any better. But at least maybe she'd be able to see that I wasn't maliciously going after her man or actively trying to break them up. Again, not better, but maybe less threatening?

"He said it wasn't his story to tell." June is the one to finally speak.

I want to feel grateful for his small kindness. Because my childhood trauma, that I still carry with me every day, isn't his to tell. But if ever a circumstance existed that he should say something to someone, it's ours. And that someone should have been June.

I tilt my head up to the sky and get control of myself, of my emotions that don't know what to do in this moment. I'm all over the place and nowhere at all.

"I'm taking my sister for a walk," I say to Noah who hasn't moved from comforting June. The look he wears is one I'm not equipped to decipher right now. The pain of once again feeling like I'm alone in the world, after having someone by my side for such a short period of time, stings more than I imagined.

"You should tell her," I say to Drew.

Then I leave the threesome, my sister in tow, peeking over her shoulder at Noah.

20

NOAH

"Her sister?"

I don't look away from the retreating blonde heads. When I saw Drew and June standing there, I immediately noticed June's discomfort at me being snuggled up with the ex-mistress of her husband.

Trying to diffuse the situation quickly and quietly didn't work.

They're both on to me and my latent feelings regarding Lorelai. Neither of them is comfortable with them. Which only reminds me of all the reasons Lorelai said we can't be friends. I don't want to accept that. The people I have in my life should be the people I choose to have there.

So why did I feel so guilty when they saw me comforting Lorelai? And why do I feel so guilty that I let Lorelai and Olivia walk away just now?

"Yes. She was just made legal guardian to Olivia."

"Where's her mom?" Drew asks.

"She went back to the ranch."

"Ah, fuck."

"What's the ranch? What is happening?" June's voice pitches an octave higher.

"Hey, Junie, calm down. Let's go sit and we can explain," Drew soothes.

We walk a couple of blocks to a small, quiet, coffee shop and pick a table in a secluded corner. Drew's hardly inconspicuous as a giant of a man and a superstar quarterback, but luckily nobody seems to be giving us anything but cursory glances. As soon as our orders are set in front of us, he starts explaining things.

I'll admit; it's admirable that he had the balls to keep quiet about Lorelai's past with June. It's a testament to how confident he was in winning back his wife. It's also a testament to how forgiving of people June is. Most wouldn't have let that stand.

Me, for example. Obviously, by how ruthlessly I treated Lorelai until just a couple of days ago. I wanted to grill her on every detail of every minute of the life she lived without me in it.

"Lorelai grew up on a polygamist compound. Her mother snuck her off when she was twelve because her father was already making plans to marry her off," Drew says.

My coffee cup clanks to the table because in my dismay, I can't seem to control my own hands.

She didn't tell me that part.

"Oh my god," June gasps, a hand raising to cover her mouth. "That's awful."

"Her father became terminally ill last year. Her mother contacted her, saying she wanted to leave and bring Olivia with her, when he died. I donated to a charity that helps people from situations like that, in trade for a place for them to stay."

June's eyes well up with tears, but it's not because she's upset with Drew for helping. She's far too kind to ever deny anyone help. Including the family of someone she dislikes as much as Lorelai.

"They got out the day after you caught Drew and Lorelai together. They stayed with the charity until her mother decided to go back a couple of days ago. She signed custody over to Lorelai," I fill in. "Lorelai's been trying to find a way to support them herself these last few months, but things haven't gone well."

"In what ways?" June asks.

"She sold her condo in Seattle to pay off the guard at the compound, but at the last minute, he wanted more. It took all her savings to pay him off. Then her boss sexually harassed her and broke into her apartment.

On top of that, no one in Seattle wanted to hire the mistress of the hometown star quarterback."

Drew sighs, because he hates when anyone refers to Lorelai as his mistress or girlfriend. I want to kick his ass for making this shit about him right now.

"Shut the fuck up, McKenna," I growl, still reeling about a twelve-year-old Lorelai facing marriage to someone likely triple her age. Or more.

"I didn't know any of that," he says, holding his hands up in surrender.

"What's she going to do?" June asks in a quiet voice. She's probably trying to reconcile all her feelings. Feeling empathetic for someone you despise is a confusing situation, to say the least.

"She's interviewing in Mobile tomorrow. If it goes well, they'll move there. Try to pick up the pieces."

June and Drew both sit, silently studying me while I finish my cappuccino.

"Was she... was she physically abused?"

"Yes," I answer.

"Sexually?" she asks.

I don't know. *I don't fucking know.* Because I either didn't care to ask or didn't dare to ask. Neither is okay.

"I asked her that once and she said no," Drew answers.

In this instance, I hate Drew McKenna. Why does he have information about Lorelai that I don't? She was never his. She was mine and I should have all these answers.

I know, deep in the depths of my tainted soul, it's because I didn't care enough. There was always something of higher importance in my life. I came before Lorelai, even when I thought I loved her.

I didn't know what love meant. I still don't. It's why I never fought for her. It's why I treated her like nothing but a toy that I could torture at my pleasure.

"I need some damn air," I say, standing. "Make him tell you the rest, June. Make him tell you what happened that night at the hotel, and why she was there."

I wander the city for an hour or so. Lost to my imagination, my anger.

My jealousy. It takes that much time to get ahold of myself. To get to a place where I can have a conversation with Lorelai and not be mad that she never felt like she could confide in me.

Lorelai and Olivia are in the bathroom when I get home. It's bath time, and I eavesdrop on their conversation through the door that's only half closed.

"Will Noah come with us?"

"No, Livi. When we move, it's just going to be me and you."

"But we'll visit lots."

"I don't know, bug. We might be a little far away for that."

"How far?" Olivia asks, panic clear in her voice. My heart drops to my stomach.

"Kind of far. I know it's hard to understand, but we'll make new friends. Better friends," Lorelai says, brutally wounding me.

Better? What the fuck does that mean? Nobody can be a better friend than *me*.

I stop listening and go change, not leaving my bedroom again until I hear the blonde duo turn on the television.

"Hi, ladies. How was your walk?" I try to force cheerfulness through my sour mood.

"Fine," Lorelai says.

"Yeah." Olivia sighs.

"Miss Olivia, that didn't sound very genuine."

"What's genuine?"

"True," I answer.

"Our walk was fine," she says with a pout. "We went to some stores, and I met another new friend. But then Lie-lie said you're not moving with us." Her little arms cross over her chest.

"Well, I live here. I like living in New Orleans. I don't think I could move away. But if you're not awfully far away, I could come visit."

She nods her head, but I'm not sure she believes me.

Lorelai hasn't said anything or even looked at me.

"Lore, do you have time to work out?"

She shoots me an incredulous look. Clearly, she's pissed at me. I'm a little pissed at her, too.

This ought to be fun.

"Fine." She rises from the couch. She's already dressed for a workout, so I follow her to the home gym, leaving Olivia to zone out to cartoons.

"Stretch," Lorelai barks when we're in the gym.

"What's wrong?"

"Nothing."

"Liar."

"I decided to take a bus to Mobile tomorrow. I don't know anyone else to ask, so can you please watch Olivia?" she asks, and I feel like it cost her something to ask me that. As if she'd rather eat worms than ask me any favor at all.

"I'll drive you both, we already discussed that."

"That was before."

"Before what?"

Lorelai's whole demeanor changes in the blink of an eye. Her eyes flash, nostrils flare as her shoulders rise and reel back a few more inches.

"Before I found out you fucked the only person who was even remotely a friend to me in this city. And I can only guess that you did that out of pure spite for me," she hisses in a voice barely over a whispered breath. Even she doesn't want to hear the words again.

And fuck me, she's right.

"He's upset, by the way. He expected a call after you spent the better part of two days in his bed."

She turns from me, and I see her shoulders shake with rage and sadness.

"Lorelai, I'm sorry."

"Why? You don't owe me anything but money."

I could live a hundred years and never be able to forget how dejected she sounds right now. This woman has been beaten down time and time again, and I've spent the past few weeks determined to expose every bruise.

"Hey." I step up behind her, then place a hand on her shoulder. She flinches away from my touch as if I struck her.

"Do not touch me, Noah. Don't pretend you care."

"I do care."

"I don't believe that. And I don't want to talk about this. Or anything, anymore. I may have done bad things in my life, but I'm not a bad person. I'm not vicious or vindictive. You can't say the same thing, can you?"

I can't. All I can do is stare at her with the heavy weight of knowing she's right.

"I'll bring Olivia with me tomorrow if you won't watch her."

"Of course I'll watch her. But let me drive you."

"No."

"Fuck, you're stubborn."

She shrugs.

"I want my money tomorrow, too." She heads for the door. "Work yourself out from now on."

21
LORELAI

The bus ads an extra hour to my trip to Mobile. At least I don't have to deal with Noah, though, and that's worth it.

My heart is so wrapped up in him that my brain forgot itself for a hot minute. All it took to reel itself back in was Alim excitedly whispering to me the story of how he bagged the most eligible bachelor in the city. And how they had fucked like bunnies for the two days they were holed up in his apartment.

I regret taking Olivia by the shop to meet him. Like so many times before, I was wounded and wanted to cling to a small slice of kindness. Thinking Alim could be the balm to my wounded pride, I headed straight there from leaving Noah and his newfound besties.

What a horrible mistake.

Noah told me in college that he wasn't 'entirely straight'. I didn't care; I never felt threatened by anyone else invading our relationship. Maybe because I always expected I'd be the downfall of it. Or maybe because he doted on me in so many ways. Perhaps both.

So, it isn't a surprise that he slept with a man. It shouldn't be a surprise that he was malicious, either. He's been that since the night I flew into New Orleans. I had just let my guard down, is all.

His quick maneuver to console June yesterday when she saw him comforting me should have been enough to build it back up. Yet somehow, I still thought there was a chance he was on my side.

Noah makes me stupid. Or, more stupid. I can't afford that. Not anymore.

Luckily, the bus stops just a few doors down from the office I'm headed to. Anxiety is working through me. I tamp it down by reminding myself that I am a damn good physical therapist, with an excellent resume. Regardless of my bad luck, or consequences of my own dumbass decisions, I know what I'm doing in this field.

A tall woman, who I'd guess to be in her early fifties greets me when I walk in.

"Lorelai," she calls.

"Yes, hi. Are you Janelle?" I hold out my hand to shake hers.

"The one and only. It's nice to meet you. Come on back to the office," she says, gesturing to a hallway off to the side of the lobby. I follow after a quick glance around.

It's not a large facility, but it's well equipped and nothing looks more than a couple of years old. A few clients are scattered about, each with their own therapist or trainer.

Janelle holds a door open for me, and I step in, taking a seat in front of a large glass desk. Everything is modern and bright with sun shining in from a window behind her chair.

"Did you find us all right? You were coming from New Orleans, correct?"

"Yes, and yes. It was a breeze."

"Good to hear," she says, pulling my resume into her hands. "This is exceptional. You must have worked with some heavy hitters."

Literally. I worked with not only a famous designated hitter in Major League Baseball after he tore his rotator cuff, but I've also worked with a couple professional boxers.

My resume doesn't refer names, but the firms I've worked with have a very established reputation in the sports industry.

"I have. My experience covers multiple sports and athletes with a myriad of injuries."

"All fully recovered, I presume?" She gives me a smirk. Of course, not all recover fully. There's only so much we can do. We aren't miracle workers, despite how badly some people wish us to be.

"To the best of their abilities." I smile.

"I'll be honest; this interview isn't one I needed to have."

My chest tightens, readying myself for yet another blow.

"You're so overqualified for this job, I'd be stupid not to hire you. This was just formality. The job is yours, if you want it."

Oh, thank fuck.

"Really?"

"Truly," she says with a big grin. "How soon do you think you can start? I've been contacted by a client who grew up in these parts. He's moving back and wants to come in three times a week. He's something of a celebrity, and honestly, I don't think I can trust anyone I have on staff to be discreet. We've never had anyone of his caliber in here before. I'm hoping you can take him on."

"When does he want to start?"

"Two weeks."

"Since we're being honest. I just gained custody of my four-year-old sister. I'll need to line up daycare and find a place to live. As soon as I confirm those two things up, I'm all yours." Hopefully, my new single-mom status isn't a deal breaker for her. Janelle has an easy, laid-back demeanor, and something tells me she isn't going to balk at this.

"It just so happens my youngest daughter has a daycare. I'm sure she'd love to watch your sister. It's small, never more than a handful of kids at once, if that sounds okay?"

It sounds too good to be true. But I'm not telling her that.

"It sounds like I just need to line up a place to live. I don't need to head back to New Orleans right away. I'll take the afternoon to look for something. I'd appreciate any advice you have though, since I don't know the city at all."

"Honey, I will give you all the ins and outs if it gets you here as quickly as possible. Whatever you need, you ask. I've been a single mom since my daughters were nine and six. Anything you go through, I've been there, and I'm happy to dish advice."

"Thank you. I appreciate it more than you know."

Janelle's face grows serious, motherly even.

"I think I know more than I should. And I'll have you know that I do not care about your past personal life. You had a clean slate with me when you walked through that front door and only you can mar it. I've been through my fair share of drama and I'm not judging you based on anything but what you show me. Understand?"

"Thank you," I say with all sincerity.

"You're welcome, Lorelai. Now let's get you acquainted with your new workplace and city."

Six hours later, I'm walking into Noah's building.

Janelle called her daughter, Kiki, to confirm that she had a space for Olivia. Then, as promised, she filled me in on the best neighborhoods to look in. We hashed out pay, which was easy because I'd accept just about anything. Also, because she's paying me quite fairly. It won't be a lavish lifestyle, but it will be comfortable enough. It certainly isn't what I made on the west coast, but Olivia and I are not fussy girls to begin with. We'll do just fine.

I'd searched online for rentals and come across a couple small houses being rented by a property management company. They were available to show me one, and I instantly fell in love with it.

When I say small, I really mean tiny. It's perfect for us, regardless. Two bedrooms, one bath that, thankfully, has a tub, a cute kitchen, and even a vegetable garden out back. It's ancient but clean and fits my budget, if on the top end of it.

It will be nice for Olivia to have a yard after growing up with so much land to run around on.

Best of all, it's empty and we can move in right away.

Which means I can get away from Noah. And Drew and June. But mostly Noah. I'm equally happy and sad about it. You don't realize how much you've missed someone until they're right there in your life again. Now I have to experience the pain of losing him all over again. Not that I really had him this time.

Janelle's words play through my head. A clean slate. I feel like we'll get that in Mobile. It's not a celebrity hot spot; I won't be hounded by press wanting to know which star athlete's bed I'm in. I can focus on Olivia and myself, and the life we deserve.

When I enter his condo, I hear the television. The screen is alive with colorful animals dancing and singing. The back of Noah's head is visible as he sits on the sofa, but it's tipped to the side. Asleep.

Stepping closer, I find Olivia stretched out next to him. Also asleep, with one arm reaching over her head so her hand can firmly wrap around Noah's index finger.

I'm struck with the thought that I'll never be able to give her this. I can be a mom to her, but she'll never have a dad. With luck, she'll forget all about our real father. He'll never be replaced with anyone who deserves the title.

I know, with my heart of hearts, I'll never love anyone but the man in front of me right now. The last few years have taught me that. If I was going to get over him, I'd have done it.

I'll be forever his. He'll never be mine. I spent the entire bus ride back here making my peace with that. It's okay, because I'll have Livi. Most importantly, she'll have me.

As I gently pick her up, I see Noah jerk awake at the small tug on his hand. I ignore him and settle her into bed.

When I come back out, he's still there. On the sofa, my temporary bed.

"How did it go?"

"Great. I start as soon as I can find a car to get us there."

Noah's face pales and a dazed expression overtakes his features.

"Maybe you shouldn't rush into anything?"

"Maybe you should mind your own business. Do you have my money?"

His eyes dart behind me. Turning, I see a check sitting on the kitchen counter. When I reach it, anger sweeps through me.

"This is too much. Write a new one for the correct amount."

"Lorelai, listen," he begins but stops when I rip the check to pieces.

"Write a new one."

"Let me help you."

"I don't want anything more than I've earned, Noah. Write a new check. Or we'll leave with what I have."

Noah heaves out a long breath, trying to rein in his temper. He's not great at being questioned or battled.

"You're only saying this because you're mad at me, I get it."

"Do not do that. You don't know me any more than I know you. Stop pretending you do. And don't fucking psychoanalyze me. You aren't a therapist, let alone mine."

I see the moment his temper breaks. Readying myself, I make a small retreat toward the kitchen.

"You're right, I don't know you. In fact, it was Drew who told me the reason your mother got you off that hellscape of a ranch you grew up on was because you were being married off. We were in a relationship for almost a year, but he's the one you confided in."

This asshole.

"I'm sorry. When would have been a good time to tell you? When you were working so hard to achieve your lifelong dream? Or maybe the other night when you were fucking your playmate against my door? I could have opened it up and said, *'Hey Noah, do you want to hear about the time I was almost a child bride? It was the week after I'd had my very first period. They made me stand on a pedestal for hours while eighteen different men came to inspect me. I had to smile for them. Twirl for them. Open my mouth wide for them,'* " I'm sobbing now. The damn breaks loose with the recounting of the worst moment in my entire life. I've never told anyone. Drew knew that's why I got out, but he didn't get the details. Those are mine. It's not my shame to bear but bear it I do. "Why do you suppose they'd care how wide a child could open her mouth, Noah? Is that what you want to know about me? If your cock fits as well as they thought theirs would?"

"Fucking hell," he curses and tries to wrap me up in his arms. I fight, but he's so much bigger than me I have no way to win. "Shh, I'm sorry. I'm so fucking sorry."

"I was sixteen when it clicked for me. I didn't understand before that," I say as I struggle to get away from him. It's useless as he wraps his arms around me, picks me up with ease and sits us both down on the sofa. "Alice thought I was having a mental breakdown. I didn't speak for days and cut up every dress I owned. One old man had stuck his fingers in my mouth; I thought he was checking how good my teeth were. I was so naïve."

Noah cradles me in his lap, my back to his front. A hand cups my cheek, and he nuzzles the top of my head. Nothing more is said for a few minutes, until I feel the tears drop on my scalp.

"Don't cry for me, Noah."

"Someone should. Why not me?"

"Because nothing has changed. I'm the same person I was last week, or last year. You wouldn't have cried for me, then." I wipe at my tears. I hate them. My father would have loved them.

"I'm not the same person I was last week, Lore. Let me care about you."

"It's pity, Noah. That's all. Last week you hated me, this week you pity me."

"Don't tell me how I feel."

"You've shown me how you feel. You've proven time and time again that you're always going to think the worst about me first. Drew didn't get those details I just told you, by the way."

We sit in silence after that. Long quiet moments filled with him pressing kisses to the crown of my head as my tears begin to dry.

"If I asked you specifics about your time on the compound, would you tell me?"

Would I? Should I?

We keep coming back to the same spot. I don't belong in his life here. There's no point to me giving and giving, all while he takes and takes. I still know nothing about this version of him.

"If I asked you did you sleep with June, would you tell me?"

He tenses under me. That's answer enough.

"Where did you think I went when I was in Utah picking up Olivia?"

Again, he stays mute.

"You need to let me go now, Noah."

22
NOAH

Three days later, I'm strapping Livi's car seat into Lorelai's truck. I pushed for a different vehicle, but she wanted one that she'd be able to haul furniture in. She did purchase a twin-sized bed and all the embellishments for Olivia. It's loaded in the back.

I don't know what she plans to sleep on as she says she'll 'make do'.

Other than their clothes, she won't take anything else from me. I tried. These past few days have been brutal between us. Neither very willing to budge.

She wears her exhaustion like a veil. One that I crowned her beautiful head with.

Nothing about this feels right. Though I pushed her to this, I don't want them to leave. I suggested following her to her new place, at least helping her set up her sister's bed. She won't allow it. She won't give me an inch.

Because I've already taken enough. Even that wouldn't stop me from taking more. Taking it all.

In another life, I would.

The door to my building opens behind me, the sound of Olivia's crying filling my ears. She's afraid and sad. I'm just fucking angry.

"Noah," she whimpers.

Turning to her, I kneel so she can jump into my arms.

"Hey, baby girl."

"Lie-lie says it's time to go."

"I know, Livi," I say, hugging her tight. "You and your sister are going to have a big adventure in a new city. There are so many new friends there for you to meet. And I need you and Lorelai to take care of one another. Can you do that for me?"

"Uh-huh," she sniffles. "But who's going to take care of you?"

Damnit, I love this kid.

I've spent the past few days with her at my side. Lorelai's been busy making arrangements and not speaking to me, so all my free time was given to Olivia. I don't regret it, but it makes this moment more difficult.

"I'll take care of myself. You remember you can call me anytime you want. Any time," I emphasize. I made her memorize my phone number. We even practiced it many times with Lorelai's phone. She's a smart girl, it didn't take long, and I like knowing that if anything happens, she knows what to do. We discussed 9-1-1, too, and various emergencies.

"I remember," she says through more tears. Lifting her up, I settle her into her booster seat and buckle her in. She snuggles her face into her stuffed alligator, and I turn away so she won't see my own emotions.

But then there is Lorelai. Shoulders back, chin held high, with a look of pure fucking, agonizing sorrow. She's within arm's reach, so I snag her by the elbow and pull her to me.

There's a moment of hesitation, a quick flash of questioning something in that complicated head of hers. Before I can ask her about it, her arms wrap around my neck and her mouth seals with mine.

Her kiss is heaven wrapped in hell. Hope clouded by disappointment. It is the sweetest tasting bitter goodbye I could imagine.

I inhale it. Burn her into every cell of my body. If this is the last time I have her in my arms, I'll fucking remember it forever.

She stops the kiss slowly but doesn't immediately retreat. With her eyes still shut tightly, I rest my forehead to hers and wait her out. Her lips tremble, telling me she's trying to compose herself enough to speak.

"I've loved you since I understood what the word meant," she says shakily. My heart pounds harder with each syllable. "I'll always regret that we couldn't... *can't* be what each other needs."

"Lore," I say, but she presses her mouth back to mine to shut me up. A gentle kiss so full of longing.

"Don't say anything, this is hard enough," she says, finally opening those steely eyes. "Goodbye, Noah."

Her voice breaks over my name at the same time she pulls away from me.

I watch, unmoving. As she checks on her sister, then shuts the passenger door. As she walks to the driver's side and gets in without a glance back. As they drive away.

Toward a new life, a new beginning. One they both need and equally deserve.

To me, it feels like an ending. And not a happy one.

I didn't even say goodbye.

A month later, I'm spending the first night in my new house.

Alone.

Me: This is my new address, please store it.

I text her regularly. I can't seem to quit, even though she hardly responds. She's good at answering if I compose the text around Olivia. So, that's what I try to do.

Waiting an hour with no response, I message again. It's nearly nine o'clock at night, so they should be home.

Me: Please confirm receipt.

Lorelai: Receipt confirmed.

Me: Did you store it?

Lorelai: Yes.

Nothing much has changed. Only distance.

Agonizing fucking distance.

Olivia calls every other night like clockwork. Every other night, I eagerly wait for the phone to ring.

She has a new best friend. *Charlie.* He's six and they met at daycare. Olivia constantly regales me with tales of Charlie. I'm happy for her; she's seeming to be adjusting well.

I'm not. As proven by the idea that I'm jealous of a six-year-old snot-nosed kid that gets to spend five days a week with my girl. Or by the fact that my body feels like shit. I don't want to work out anymore. I still meet Drew when he's in town, but I'm not doing a lot outside of that.

I've even gone back to eating eggs.

"You're depressed," June says to me the following morning.

"Hardly." I scoff.

She's here to meet my designer. June loves this kind of thing. I couldn't care less about it right now.

"You have horrible self-awareness, my friend."

"I'm just tired. It was a big move, to a big house. I need some time to adjust."

She doesn't believe me. I see it in how she scans my face, carefully scrutinizing me.

The doorbell rings, and I open it to Harlow, my designer. We've never met in person, but she was highly recommended.

She's a stunner under red waves of curls. Her high cheekbones are dotted with a splash of freckles and punctuated with fully rosy lips.

I notice. I'm a man, of course I notice. Normally, my dick would think we should escort her to the nearest room with a lockable door and fuck her until she can't walk straight.

Today, it doesn't seem to care.

"Harlow, I'm Noah. Welcome," I say, gesturing her through the front door.

"Nice to meet you, Noah," she gives me a flirty smile, and suddenly I want to escort her out of my house altogether.

"This is my friend, June."

"Hi, Harlow. Nice to meet you." June reaches a hand for her to shake, and Harlow's smile drops a millimeter. It makes me increasingly more comfortable, having June here as a buffer to whatever flirtatious intentions Harlow may have. Which is weird; I've never been uncomfortable around pretty women before.

What the fuck is wrong with me?

We start with the main living areas downstairs. I fill Harlow in on all my tastes and budget while she makes notes and takes measurements. All the while June nudges me with her elbow because I continually stare off at nothing, tuning out the women and their questions.

Then we move upstairs to the bedrooms. Starting with the office, then the room I've designated as my home gym, followed by the guest rooms.

"What are we thinking for this one?" Harlow asks from the doorway of the final guest bedroom. It has a small sitting room on one side and a large walk-in closet on the other.

I stare into the empty space for a minute, my imagination running wild.

"A canopy bed set in between the two windows on that wall." I point to where I want it. "Something girly, but not overly childish. She doesn't like pink. Turquoise is her favorite. She's good at drawing and puzzles. Make the sitting room a place that accommodates that with a desk, easel, one of those puzzle tables. Outfit the closet with low hanging bars, so she can reach everything she needs to. It needs to be bright and airy. Maybe full of flowers, she likes flowers. Daisies, I think. She said those are what she likes best. Make it something special and fun."

"Noah," June whispers, placing a hand on my shoulder.

"She'll visit. She'll want her own room when she visits."

Harlow does the same in this room as she has in each of the others—snaps a few pictures on her phone, measures, jots notes.

"Is the main bedroom next," she asks when her scrutiny of Olivia's room is complete.

"No. You won't be needed in the main bedroom."

"Oh," she says, startled. "I just assumed."

"That room's fine. I think we've covered everything I need from you."

"Of course." She's obviously taken aback by my mood.

I don't really give a fuck, honestly.

"How long before you think you can get started, Harlow?" June gestures for the woman to follow her back down the hall.

I stay put. Imagining I hear a squeaky voice hollering 'Just Noah' as little footsteps pitter-patter toward me.

Then I imagine the blonde woman that would be following her.

June's right. I'm depressed.

Loneliness sunk in as soon as they pulled away. It's amazing how a child changes your entire life in such a short period of time. I barely knew her before they moved, but I'd burn this city down if that's what it took to keep her snorting in laughter.

Leaning against the wall, I slide my back against it and sink down to sit on the floor.

Eventually, June finds me here.

"Harlow is gone. She said she'll be able to start next week."

"Good."

"Can I sit with you?"

"Stupid question, my sweet June," I answer, holding a hand to help her down.

She takes it and settles in next to me, close enough that our shoulders bump.

"Is this my fault?"

"What do you mean?" I turn to look at her, and she wears the same sad expression I fear I've worn for weeks.

"I'm not stupid, Noah. I know you're sad they're gone. But are they gone because of me?"

"Ah, June. No," I say, tilting my head back against the wall. "In a way, yes, you play a part. But they're gone because of me."

"Elaborate."

"She said she doesn't fit in my life. I can't very well argue that. My mom hates her, you and Drew hate her. I spite fucked the only friend she was making in the city." I sigh. "She's right; she doesn't fit."

"Noah! You did what?"

"The night she flew to Utah, I didn't know where she'd gone. It was the first night Drew left. I tracked her phone to the airport, but before we had the chance to communicate, I broke my phone. I went to the last place I knew she'd been. Met her friend. Spent two days in his bed."

A sharp slap lands on my bicep.

"What do you mean you tracked her phone?"

I grimace.

"What the hell is wrong with you?"

"I didn't trust her," I try to explain. "I was protecting you just as much as I was protecting myself."

"For the record, Anders"—her eyes narrow on my face—"in the

future, if you think protecting me requires violating another woman's private life, don't protect me."

"You make it sound bad."

"Because it is."

"Agree to disagree?"

"Hell no."

"Nothing I can do about it now."

"Oh my god, you're still tracking her!"

"Well, no. But I can," I say, flinching at how rigid she's become.

"If I didn't love you, I'd break up with you right now. That's some next level stalkerish shit."

Ouch.

If anyone knows about stalkers, it's June who had one that attacked her and left her just outside death's door.

She's not wrong, of course. I am, for not seeing it as a violation. It was a precaution, for the safety and well-being of all involved. Stubborn as I am, I still see it as that. I can't help that I like knowing she's still alive and moving. Or that I can find her at the touch of my finger.

Fuck.

"I don't know who you are anymore," she says.

"Elaborate," I parrot.

"That night I came to your condo…" She sighs a little, before continuing. "I thought you'd sleep with me because you disliked Drew and Lorelai so much that you'd want that revenge. You didn't take it, Noah. You knew what it would mean for all of us if you did. What's changed?"

"I wanted her to hurt. Like I hurt." I let my eyes fall close, blocking out the sunshine from the window. I don't deserve to be in the sun right now. I deserve the shadows.

"Did she? *Is* she?"

"I don't know if it's hurt she feels. Or if she's numb and determined. I told you; I think I broke her."

"That's hurt," she says with emphasis. "What are you going to do about it?"

There's a trace of nervousness, bordering fear in her voice, and my stomach riots. No matter what I do, a woman I care about hurts. No matter what I do, I hurt. There is no easy answer.

I can't fix this. And that, more than anything, pisses me off.

"What can I do, June? They left. Lorelai fled from me as fast as she could and took that little nugget of joy with her. Even if I could convince them to come back, and nothing says I could, because I was that horrible to her, what then? Do I subject them to regular scorn from people I love? Do I bring her over to your house when you invite me to dinner?" Standing, I pace the room in agitation. "I've spent the past month trying to find a solution and coming up empty. I want them in my life. I want to protect them from all the things nobody else ever protected them from. But I want to do the same for you. I think the only way I can do both is if I let her live her life away from here. I can try to build trust with her, but it won't be easy. Perhaps, eventually, she'll let me in enough to feel like I'm helping."

I don't look at June as I wait for her to say something. Anything. After a few moments, I hear her stand and the soft click of heels as she walks out of the room.

"I'm not willing to be the villain in your love story, Noah. If my only choices are you miserable without them, or you happy with them… Which do you think I'd choose?"

23
LORELAI

It's been six weeks since I started working with Miles Jameson. A decade ago, everyone knew his name. He was a young, hot Hollywood star on the rise. If you believed the tabloids, the sudden fame got the better of him. Excess drove him off a cliff. Almost, literally.

In his case, the tabloids were right.

He was involved in a horrible auto accident that left his fiancée in a coma for months, and his own body a mangled mess.

Miles, much like me, is trying to pick up what pieces are left and glue them into a new picture of what his life could look like. A talented producer wants to give him the chance at a comeback. Miles is fighting hard for it.

Three days a week, two-hour sessions. I've been tough on him and he's yet to complain once.

"You think you can handle a few more of those, Jameson?"

I have him doing Swans on the Wunda chair. His grimace says he isn't loving it.

"I can handle anything you throw at me, darlin'."

I smile. It's what he calls me when he doesn't like me very much. Something I caught on to quickly. It sounds like typical Southern charm, but it's got an insulting undertone to it. Once the workout is over, he'll be back to calling me Lore.

It's cute, really. I like Miles. He likes me in return. The work we're doing is much more than physical therapy. He's paying me to train him, and much like I did with Noah, I help him with a nutrition plan.

He's been sober for thirteen months and eight days. Now, he's ready to be healthy, too. It feels good to be helping people again. Noah was different. The price I paid in helping him heal his body was too high. I couldn't ever just feel good about the work we did.

I only wish Olivia was adjusting so well.

She's doing okay, all things considered. She's resilient and just as stubborn as me, which helps her when she's fighting through something.

There's just so much that's new to her, she's easily overwhelmed. There have been a few meltdowns. I hate to say, they're mostly because of the boundaries I set with other people. Mainly Noah. She wants to call him daily, sometimes it's several times a day. Trying to ween her off him is difficult. It's not that I want to cut them off from each other, I don't. I don't want to take anything from Olivia that does her good. But I worry where too much attachment to him will lead.

We've set similar rules regarding her friend Charlie. Living the way we both did, she doesn't understand the separation of homes, and families, and why they don't share mothers.

There have been some impossible conversations. I know more are in our future. Those moments are few and far between, though. For the most part, we're both thriving here in Mobile.

Our free time consists of learning the city and searching for fun items to fill our rental house with. She wanted to paint the walls in her bedroom, but the landlord wouldn't allow it. Instead, we thrifted a nightstand and a child size table and painted those.

She's fallen in love with a diner called Bob's downtown, insisting we go every Friday night because she likes the ice they use, and grits are her new favorite food.

Her adventurous spirit makes me adventurous. Each time she decides she wants to try something new, I pause to think of what new thing I could be doing, or learning. Ultimately, I'd like to help more people like her and me. I just don't know what that looks like yet.

The days pass quickly now, and I'm content with our current situation. Until I crawl into bed every night and all the distractions fade away. That's when I wallow, when I mourn. When I try to convince my stupid heart that it can move on.

She's a loyal shit, though. Forever pining for a man that doesn't love us, or even deserve us.

I've spent many years believing I didn't deserve him, especially this last one. I'm learning that's not the case. Learning to love myself is hard, but I'm getting there. Knowing that my mistakes don't mean I can't demand respect has come easier.

I am more than the sum of my few bad decisions.

That's a Miles Jameson mantra. He tries very hard to live by it and reminds me, regularly, that I need to do the same. He, too, spent years disliking himself. We understand each other in that way, and I think it helps when you don't feel so alone in the world. I haven't confided in him about my childhood, but he was already aware of my scandalous affair, thanks to the gossip sites.

He made it clear early on that wasn't an issue for him, and more so, that he understood being misunderstood by the public at large.

Janelle's been a great boss, too. She's a fierce, no-nonsense woman, that supports her employees in every way she can. Most of us are women, so she makes sure we're safe and that no clients get away with anything we don't want. I've even seen her side-eyeing Miles on a few occasions. He's flirty. Janelle makes sure it doesn't cross any lines.

Miles doesn't seem the type though. He gives off heavy southern gentleman vibes. It's a good thing that's not my kink, because Miles Jameson is fine as hell.

He towers over me at several inches above six-foot. He's built like an Olympic swimmer but has the face of a man who's been through battles. There's a constant five o'clock shadow, dark like the messy hair atop his head that often falls over one eye. A small scar, about an inch long, mars his temple at the hairline.

I bet women lick it when they're fucking him.

"Lore?"

"Sorry." I blink the thought away. Sadly, his sexiness only raises a small tingle in my broken nether regions.

Fucking traitorous vagina.

"Where'd you go just now?" There's only worry in his tone. Luckily, he's not so attuned to my brainwaves.

"Nowhere I need to be."

"You all right?"

"Yeah, yeah. I'm good. Let's move over to the TRX."

"Darlin'," he groans. "I think you're trying to kill me."

"Not a chance, Jameson. I want to see this movie you keep telling me about. It won't get made if I kill you."

Miles starts filming the beginning of June. Which leaves us two more months. It's plenty of time since he's in decent shape already. No matter how many times I remind him of that, he can't shake the nerves. I suppose that's understandable.

He left Hollywood on ghastly terms; it takes a lot of guts to step back into that world.

This new role of his apparently requires 'a whole heap of nudity'. Miles is concerned any ounce of fat is going to stir the body critics. Instead, he wants all the audience members thirsty for his next role.

I haven't seen him nude, obviously, but from what I have seen, he has nothing to worry about.

We finish up his after TRX and stretching. Miles is my last client for the day, and as it is Friday, I have a date with my mini-me. As has become habit, Miles pulls me in for a goodbye hug, pressing a kiss to the top of my head.

"I'll see you Monday, Lore."

"Bye, Miles. Take it easy," I call as I try to be sly in watching his incredible ass walk out the door.

"That isn't strictly professional behavior now, is it?" The deep voice is right behind me, making me jump damn near out of my skin.

Spinning around, I place a hand over my racing heart.

"You scared me," I say, startled that I didn't notice him enter the building

"I see that," he says through a smile that looks anything but happy. His eyes are trained behind me, at the door.

"How are you here?"

"I have a car. I drove it."

"*Why* are you here, Noah," I ask, rolling my eyes at him.

"Mr. Anders would like to make some appointments with you," Janelle interrupts him from across the room. "Only if you're available, of course."

Her meaning is clear. She won't force me to work with Noah. I appreciate her even more for it.

"What's wrong?" I ask him.

"It doesn't feel right," he says it so softly, with so much feeling. My pussy clenches with desire for him to mean his life without me. Like I said, my vagina is a hooptie; she needs a full overhaul. "Even when I walk, it doesn't feel right."

Right.

His hip.

My dumb pussy needs earplugs.

"Walk. Let me see."

He does, and again, his hip is sitting too high.

"Noah. What did you do?"

"I think it was the move. I took on too much." He steps closer to me. Too close. "Will you work with me again?"

"Why me?"

"You are the best. Why not you?"

I slow blink. Praise will get him everywhere with me. It's like kryptonite for me.

"You can come in once a week. That's it. The rest of the work you can do at your own home gym. I assume the new house has one." If I'm forcing boundaries on Olivia, I better force them on Noah, too.

He nods.

"What day works best for you?"

"Friday evenings," he says in a growly voice.

"My Friday evening appointment is filled for the next two months," I say, glaring at him. He's being completely obvious.

"Can you shuffle it? I have work, this is the best time for me to leave the city."

"No. You aren't my priority. I've committed to him." I stumble over the words when Noah's jaw cracks and his mouth tightens. "I… I'm not moving it for you. Pick a different day."

"I'll come in after him." His lips barely move as he says it, holding himself together. I don't understand why he's being so unreasonable. Or why he's so worked up.

"I have a standing date on Friday night. That doesn't work either."

His fists clench at his and his head whips to the side as he averts his gaze from mine.

"Why do you push me, Lorelai," he says, taking a dangerous step closer to me. He stares down at me for a few beats, and my heartbeat pounds. Suddenly, he steps back and rushes for the door, as if his irritation is too much for him to handle just now.

What the fuck?

"Honey, I don't know what the hell just happened between the two of you. But I'm pretty sure I'm delivering twins in nine-months' time. The sexual whatever that was is enough to have half the damn block pregnant," she says, waving a finger after Noah.

"It's not like that," I say, dazed.

"Oh, I know you didn't just say that," she cackles. Her laughter can be heard for the next several minutes as I gather my stuff to leave.

I head outside to wait for Kiki. She walks Olivia here on Friday nights when she comes to meet her mom. They have their own standing date on Friday nights. I think theirs includes alcohol, though. Not sticky fingers, ketchup-stained faces, and bath time.

I wouldn't trade it, though.

"Just Noah!" Olivia sees him before I do, letting go of Kiki's hand as she runs to him. With all the faith in the world, she leaps as high and far as she can. Knowing Noah will catch her.

They cling to each other as if they've been lost for ages and only now found their way home. I try not to be sensitive about it, but how? Wiping away a tear, I hope the guilt that I'm why they don't have regular visits vanishes with it.

"I've missed you, Miss Olivia."

"That sounds silly." She laughs.

"You sound silly," he says, then blows a raspberry into her neck, sending her into a fit of giggles.

Janelle locks the door behind me.

"I take it back; I think it's triplets. And I don't even have viable eggs."

"Oh my god," I say, humored but exasperated.

"Have a good weekend, Lorelai." She walks away with a wave, grabbing KiKi's elbow as she goes.

"Sure, I'd love to," Noah tells Livi.

"Yay! Lie-lie, did you hear?"

"What?"

"Noah's going to go to Bob's with us!"

Noah's looking at me differently now. A lightness has taken over him. Gone is whatever demon possessed him a few moments ago.

"Is he now?"

"Yes. It's a *date*," he says.

24

NOAH

"Should I drive?"

"No, it's only a few blocks. We like the walk," Lorelai answers. I can't tell if she's mad, happy, or confused that I showed up like this. Choosing to believe she's delighted by my impeccable presence, I grab her hand with the one not currently wrapped around her little sister.

"Lead the way, ladies."

"It's that way," Olivia points.

"You know the way?"

"Uh-huh, it's easy. We go this way. Then that way," she says, pointing to our right. "Then we'll see the sign that spells bee oh bee. That means Bob's."

A proud grin brightens her face.

"Miss Olivia, have you been away so long that you know how to read now?"

She nods, as if it's a given.

Lorelai laughs lightly. I squeeze her hand and pull her a little closer. Confusion warps her pretty face. She appears a little dazed, even. But not mad. Or maybe that's just my imagination.

Olivia's palm lands on my cheek, pulling my face back to hers.

"You have got to try the grits, Noah. They're so very delicious. If you promise not to get a tummy ache, you can ask them to put an egg on top."

"Oh my, that does sound so very delicious."

"I know." She sighs.

Now Lorelai and I both laugh.

Bob's is exactly where Livi said it would be. While I wouldn't pick this place in a hundred years, I don't complain. It's clearly become a special place for these two.

I do order grits with an egg on top, and I promise the smallest sister that my tummy will be fine. The big sister gives me a side-eye, but I reach over and grab her hand under the table.

Which makes her return to her confused and quiet state. I don't know what I'm doing any more than her, but it feels good, and I haven't felt good for a long while.

A server, different from the younger woman who took our order, stops by the table. This one is in her sixties, silver hair piled in a tight twist on the back of her head. I'd be surprised if this isn't the only job she ever worked, just by the familiar comfortability she gives off.

"Well, if it isn't the Simmons sisters back again," she exclaims. Olivia's smile falters, but she waves at the woman. "And who is this handsome gentleman?"

"That's Noah. He was Lie-lie's friend, and I was scared of him 'cause he looked grumpy. But that's just sometimes, so now we're friends, too."

"Hello, Noah." She laughs. "Y'all need anything, you know how to holler."

She moves to another table and begins an animated conversation with those patrons as well. I understand why they like the place.

"Livi, remember what I said?"

"You said soon. I remember," she answers with a slight pout.

"What's wrong?"

"We don't have the same last name. I'm working with an attorney to get it changed."

"You want to have the same last name as Lorelai?"

"Yeah, else how will everybody know we're family? Charlie has the same last name as his brother."

"Ah, I see. I'm sure it will get sorted, you just have to have patience."

"That's the same thing you said," she says, looking at Lorelai.

"It must be the truth, then," Lorelai says, trying to reassure Olivia.

They chatter about it for a little while longer until Olivia's drink arrives. It's a lemonade with the 'good ice' and it sucks up all her attention.

"Are you covered with the attorney? I have an excellent one if you need."

"I think he can handle it. It's supposed to be straight forward, with what my mother already signed. It's just that these things take time and toddlers don't really understand that."

"Sure," I say. "But if it looks like you need a bigger team, please let me know, Lorelai. I can help. I want to help."

Her mouth opens, and I know the intention is to ask me something. *For* something. She doesn't, however. Instead, she closes her mouth and nods.

Un-fucking-acceptable.

But right now, in the middle of Bob's, isn't the time to push it.

Olivia's sour attitude doesn't make a second appearance.

After we eat dinner, we start the short walk back to my car. But a panic unlike I've ever felt hits me like a ton of bricks. It's reminiscent of waiting for the doctors to deliver me the news I knew would end my career. Only worse.

It's so visceral, it threatens to bring my dinner back up. I'm not ready.

"Where's your truck?"

"At home," Lorelai answers.

"It's close enough to walk?"

"It's just right there, silly." Olivia points in the opposite direction of Bob's.

"I'll walk you," I say.

"You don't need to do that, Noah. We can manage."

I can't.

I fucking can't.

"I'll walk you."

Her eyes bounce between mine, trying to read me, just as I am her. She nods, only slightly, but it's enough for oxygen to once again start flowing through me.

I'm losing my ever-loving mind.

We walk to a small cottage on a quaint block where the city stops being all business and starts getting quiet. It's white with a powder-blue door that could use a fresh coat of paint. The roof will need to be replaced in the next few years, but the windows are on the newer side and the shutters look sturdy and functional.

Both houses bordering hers have small bicycles lying haphazardly in the front yard. It's a family block; I'm sure Olivia likes that.

"Come see my room!" Olivia's tiny hand pulls at mine, but I look to Lorelai for permission to enter.

A soft smile appears, and I take it as a go-ahead.

Olivia shows me every inch of the house. We finish in her room with her telling me about all the furniture they "found and furbished" to make it hers. There's a small television in the corner and she turns it to a cartoon. Pulling me down to sit on the floor, she curls up in my lap to watch.

In five minutes, her pint-sized snores alert me to her state. I tuck her into bed and go find Lorelai in the kitchen where she's nursing a cup of tea.

"Some bald-headed cartoon character put her to sleep."

"That does it every time."

I decide not to waste time. If our past is any indicator, this amicable night can turn volatile at any time.

"What were you going to ask me earlier?'

"Nothing," she says, looking down into her tea.

"Don't do that," I say, stepping closer and using a single finger to raise her chin back up. "Ask me."

"I don't know if it's a good idea."

"You'll know once you ask."

She sets her mug down on the counter next to where we stand and wraps her arms around herself.

"What is it?" I soften my tone as best as I can.

"I still need to appoint someone as Olivia's guardian if anything happens to me."

I blink. I didn't know what to expect, but it wasn't this.

"Me," I say without hesitation.

"Is that a smart choice?"

"It's the smartest choice. It's the only choice."

Lorelai looks back down.

"I don't want you to accept that potential responsibility because it's the only choice I have. That's not fair to anyone."

"Lorelai, it's the *only* choice," I repeat firmly this time.

"Besides," she continues, as if I haven't spoken at all. "You always wanted a family. Someday you'll meet someone and have babies, then how would Livi fit into all that? I'm just not sure it's the wisest thing to do."

If I wasn't so attuned to this woman, I could have missed the waver in her words. It cost her something to say this.

It cost me to hear it.

"Lorelai, listen to me. I am the only choice. Because if you don't name me, I'm going to lose my shit altogether. On you. Right now, and every day after until you do what I'm telling you to do. Olivia will always be welcome with me. Always. I'll be damned if some stranger gets to raise our girl."

Her head snaps up.

"You mean that?"

"Damn it, yes. Completely."

"Thank you," she says on an exhale. "I've been fretting over it. You're who she's taken to best, of course. But since you and I don't get along so well, I didn't know… Anyway, it's temporary until she takes to someone that I think offers her the stability she'll need."

I cut off the words with my mouth. Pushing my tongue in to taste her while I lift her by the hips and settle her onto the counter. At a better level now, I can deepen it, take more control. Her surprise bleeds into a matching desire.

We sync with each other fully. My hands go to her hair. She mirrors the move, pulling me closer. As close as I can get with her thighs straddling my waist.

Dragging one hand down, I trace her jaw, her neck, then her breast. I take my time and don't stop until I'm at the waistband of her leggings and her hands are at my belt.

Just as I am about to dip below, she stops and pulls away.

"What are we doing?"

"Getting along."

She laughs without humor.

"Nothing has changed, Noah."

Everything has changed. My reason for being has shifted off the only axis it has ever existed.

"What do you need from me?"

She thinks for a moment. I silently wait, hoping she answers with something that will bring her closer, not push us further apart.

"Something true. Something meaningful. Even if it's painful."

For everything she's given me of herself, I haven't given her any of me. That's what she's asking. She wants my secrets. My mistakes. I pushed for hers; it's only fair. Except, her confessions made me care about her again. I'm afraid mine will make her hate me more. One thing is certain, we can't keep circling this with no outcome. We move forward or we give up.

"You were right about your friend. I didn't know where you were. Drew had left that morning for a two-night trip, and instead of giving you the benefit of the doubt, I got drunk and fucked him to spite you."

Her lids shutter and her breath hitches.

"Look at me," I command and wait until she does. "It's weighed on me since I sobered up and realized how awful it was. To you, to him, even to Drew. I'm sorry."

"You always were good at hitting your mark," she says, knowing that was what was drilled in by coaches my whole life. "It's horrible enough that you thought I was with Drew. Only made worse by the fact that it was the most important time in both mine and Livi's lives and all you thought about was scoring more revenge."

"I didn't know. You can't think I would have reacted the same way had I known why you were at the airport."

"How did you know I was at the airport if you didn't get my messages?"

Ah, shit.

"That's probably not something you want to know," I hedge, because what the fuck else should I do? She's already pissed; this information will blow her top.

"I assure you it is." There it is, that temper I used to love. Now... not so much.

"There's an app on your phone."

"That lets you track me?" The question doesn't come out hysterical, but it's borderline.

I let my head fall; it's answer enough.

"What the hell is wrong with you?"

"Nothing now," I lie. So much is wrong. "But when you first arrived in New Orleans, I didn't know what to believe or if I could trust you at all. I thought it was best."

"You're more awful than I thought."

"I'm not."

"You are."

"Give me your phone. I'll remove it."

"It's still there?"

"Not once you give me your phone."

Lorelai reaches into the back pocket of her shorts and pulls it out. I take it from her and immediately navigate to the app, letting her watch me as I uninstall it.

"Done. You can stop glaring at me like I'm a psychopath now."

"Hardly," she snipes.

And despite how serious the situation is, I smile. Because I like our banter. I miss it. Even when she's pissed at me, I like her attention. Jesus, I'm like a bratty kid with her.

"I'll apologize again. I'm sorry that I jumped to conclusions. That I sought to hurt you instead of hearing you. I regret so much of the way I've treated you."

"And what about the stalker app? Are you sorry about that?"

I grimace.

"Less so. I hate that because of the app, I did horrible things. Though I'm not sorry I like knowing where you and Olivia are and that you're safe."

I give her a minute to study me, hoping she sees my sincerity, and that my intentions, at least now, aren't nefarious.

"You aren't forgiven," she finally says, but she's somewhat calmer.

"What do you need from me?" I ask again. I'll keep asking until I get her to trust me, which seems to be getting further out of reach.

"More."

I want to steal the word from the air and shove it back in her mouth.

"Are you going to set me up as Olivia's guardian?" Tit for tat. That's how we seem to work best.

"Yes," she states as if there was never a doubt. "Against my better judgment, but I don't want to take things away from her. She adores you, and despite the shit you do to me, I know you'd take care of her."

"Good fucking girl."

Lorelai's attitude changes right then from caged up and tense to something like a messy, glazed cinnamon roll. Her eyes darken, nipples pebble, shoulders drop, and she leans closer to me without even realizing it.

"Lorelai, is it possible your kink isn't punishment but praise?" I let the words fall softly, quietly over her upturned face.

"Can't it be both?"

Fair point.

"How have you been dealing with all that?"

"I've been trying to ignore it. Staying busy helps."

"When was the last time you came?"

She looks down instead of answering me.

"Answer me, Lorelai."

"Three nights ago."

"How?" And so help me, if it wasn't by herself, somebody will end up dead.

"With my fingers."

Thank fuck.

"What were you thinking about?"

Her lips tighten.

"Lorelai," I warn.

"I don't owe you this, Noah."

"No, you don't owe me anything. We're just having a friendly conversation. It could easily turn less so if you don't answer me."

"Threatening me?"

"Promising you, sweetheart."

I see it, the way she likes the endearment. How it softens her even as she tries to hide it.

"Who were you fantasizing of?"

"You know," she says in a pained whisper.

No, but I suspect. I hope. Fair or not, I want her as tortured over me as I am over her.

"Was it my fingers in your cunt? Or my cock?"

Her hips push forward enough off the edge of the counter to rub against my groin. She tries to pull away, but I wrap my hand around her waist and pull her back.

"My cock, then," I say with dark humor. "Confirm it."

"Y… yes," she says on a heavy sigh.

"Well done," I praise her. "It doesn't have to be a fantasy, you know?"

"It does," she says, her fists coming up to my chest, keeping some separation.

"No, baby, it doesn't. Take what you need from me."

"I can't, Noah. I can't take it; you have to give it. But you don't. Not to me."

She lets the words pour out. Each one like a knife stabbing me in my guilty heart. Because she's right. She's been right on so many things that I've been determined to believe are wrong.

Lorelai isn't asking me to give my body to her, she's asking me to give her my soul. I know this leads down a hard road, but once again, I ask.

"What do you need from me?"

A loud rolling thunder roars outside and rain pelts the windows. It's as ominous as her next words.

"The truth. About everything. About you and June and Drew."

This truth will hurt her. I know it. She knows it. I want to deny it, but I can't.

"I didn't fuck either of them, if that's what you're asking," I say. It's stupid, because of course that's what she's asking. "I came close with June once before her and Drew got back together. Then after, we played. The three of us."

She pushes me back so she can stand, but her legs give under her and only my arm still wrapped around her keeps her from falling to the hardwood beneath her bare feet.

"Why?" she whispers. I don't know how to answer because I'm not sure of the question.

"Why?" This time, it's louder. Filled with so much agony, and her fists beat at my chest as she repeats it.

"Lorelai, stop."

She pushes hard and wrenches away from me. Turning, she heads to the back door, just off the kitchen.

"Lorelai."

She doesn't stop, doesn't listen. Opening the door, she steps out.

"Fuck."

I follow, and by the time I get to the door, she's standing in the middle of the small back yard. Thankfully, it's surrounded by a high privacy fence that no neighbors can see into. Because Lorelai has stripped off her t-shirt already, and her shorts and underwear quickly follow.

"What the fuck are you thinking?" I rush to her through the rain. She pushes me away from her.

"Why?" she yells.

"Why what?" I yell back over the thunder still rolling above us.

She's naked now, soaking wet in the downpour showering us both.

"Why am I the only villain? Why am I the only one not forgiven? Why am I the one hated and alone?"

"Come inside, we'll talk."

"Fuck you, Noah," she says, and the defeat I hear makes me want to vomit. "I've spent so many years hoping to be forgiven by you. But I don't need it anymore. I'm forgiving myself. I'm letting all my guilt wash away."

"Lore." I try to reach for her, but she swats me away.

"I'm worthy of happiness, Noah. I'm worthy of kindness, and fucking love. I won't let you, or anyone else, reduce me down to my one worst mistake."

"Will you please come inside?"

"No. I'm right where I need to be. Free from my father's abuse. Free from June's hate. Free from Drew's judgment. Free from your spite," she says through the water falling from both her eyes and the sky. "Here, I'm free to be me. Woman, sister, mother. Flaws and all. I'm done letting others dictate my life and my feelings. I'm not your punching bag. I'm not Drew's scapegoat. I'm just me, learning from my mistakes and growing into the person I was always supposed to be."

She throws her arms out and twirls in the small puddle forming at her feet. Lorelai, naked and wet, free for maybe the first time in her life, is the most exquisite thing I've ever laid eyes on.

Her pale skin glows in the moonlight. I wipe away the rain from my face to see her more clearly. To see her for the first time. How she wants to be seen.

Strong and independent. Now without scars, not without troubles. A real human who feels pain just like the rest of us.

"You can call me every horrible name you want. You can fuck every friend I have. None of it matters anymore, Noah. Your opinion of me doesn't matter, and I'm done letting you wound me. You think you get to come here and tell me all you regret, and I'll just forgive you? You wouldn't do the same for me. I know whether I'm a good person or not, and you don't get to decide that for me. And you sure as hell don't get to punish me for the shit you make up in your head!"

The world should all burn in hell for how we've treated Lorelai and her like. With double standards and deep-rooted misogyny. I'm guilty; so many of us are. Calling women whores who are just trying to survive the only way they know how. Blaming them and their beauty, their desirability, for all the mistakes of men.

She wasn't in the right when she entered an affair with Drew, but she was less wrong than him. She didn't owe anyone her honesty and loyalty. Women claim that they shouldn't betray their own kind, but women are also the cattiest bunch and the first to turn on each other for the least offense. Forgiving him and not her, seeing his hard work to grow and change, yet not recognizing that she's capable of the same— that was bullshit. And I played into it.

Lorelai is the one spinning but it's my world being turned upside down.

I'm about to strip out of my own clothes and join her in letting the rain wash away our sins, when another burst of thunder roars, punctuated by a bolt of lightning brightening up the night sky.

Fucking hell.

Rushing to her, I haul her naked body over my shoulder and head back to the house. A hard bite is delivered into my back.

"Put me down or I do it again," she yells.

"Don't you fucking dare." I enforce each word with a swat to her backside. She quivers, then stills.

Her responsiveness makes me hard. As does her obstinance. I always enjoyed it when she played, when she challenged me. Not many women ever have, none like her.

Lorelai made me laugh. No matter how stressed I was over football or school, she always found a way to ease it and show me a good time. It was part of what made me always want to be around her. Always want her around. I missed that the most when she left—the laughter.

But I recognize the truth of the situation. The reasons she thought she needed to leave me. I had lost some of my focus, and that's why I didn't fight for her as I should have. She's also wrong. Lorelai thinks she needed me more than I needed her. That's not at all true. I did need her. I *wanted* her.

I never had fun with a woman after her. Until June. Guilt softens my erection. I don't know how to be true to both women. Each of whom I need in separate ways. Each of whom need me in separate ways.

"That was a stupid thing to do," I tell her when I deposit her at the edge of her bed.

"It didn't feel stupid. It felt amazing."

"It was reckless. You don't get to be reckless anymore."

Her bottom lip trembles, making my cock twitch. Lorelai is the most fuckable thing I've ever laid eyes on. But tonight, vulnerable, naked, and wet, it's all I can think about.

"What do you need from me, Lorelai?"

She laughs but it doesn't sound right. There's no lightness to it.

"I need you to leave, Noah. You can come in once a week. Tuesday, Wednesday, or Thursday at five. Pick one. I'll even let you take Olivia out after your session. She misses you, and I won't steal that away from either of you," she says before pausing to lick her lips. They can't be dry with rain drops still running down her face. "But that's all you get from me."

I kneel in front of her and place my hands on her thighs.

"Can we please talk about this? I don't want you to hate me, Lore."

"I haven't wanted you to hate me for years. We don't always get what we want."

"I never hated you, Lorelai. I was hurt and confused, but it was never hatred I felt," I say, fingers pressing into her flesh as if I can push the words into her skin and make her believe them.

"Your actions speak very differently, Noah."

I let my head fall into her lap and inhale the scent of her skin mixed with the fresh rain.

Since they've moved to Alabama, I've had more than enough time to consider the truth of my relationship with Lorelai. I can see that in college, I was a balm to her wounds. I recognize now the fragility she showed at the start and how it faded over time. As if when I was near, she was being healed; the wounds from her childhood slowly being stitched back together and the skin growing whole.

Now I'm the knife further opening each cut.

"That's over, Lorelai. It will be different from now on."

"I know. Not because you say so, but because I do. Go home now. You can text me which appointment you want."

I'm both unbelievably proud of her strength and utterly pissed off that she's using it to push me away. I deserve it. We both know it. But this, whatever this is between us—be it friendship or something more—isn't over. *No. I'm just getting started!*

"I'll take Wednesday. Then I'll spend time with Livi before heading back," I say, looking up from her lap. I don't say the rest. She knows, better than most, how underhanded and overbearing I can be. I'll do whatever it takes to get what I want.

What I want more than anything right now are Lorelai and Olivia in my life.

25
LORELAI

"The key is owning up to your choices, Lore. Then learning from them. I did that, and I think that's why I'm getting this second chance."

Miles is working through his post-workout stretches. Like every session, he talks through them. The conversation is never about the physical work he's putting in, though. Always it's about the mental tasks he checks off his daily to-do list.

"I feel that, Jameson. I don't make excuses for the awful things I've done. I did them. Some I regret fully; some I regret partially. Either way, I've learned. I am learning. I'll keep learning until I'm happy with who I am. If ever. If not," I say with a shrug, "then I guess I just keep working at it."

"But you don't hate yourself anymore, right? That's important too."

"I don't have time for hate in my life, Miles. Hate has never been a powerful word in my vocabulary of feelings. The only person I've ever truly hated is dead. I'm burying that emotion with him."

"Good for you. Wish that was a lesson I'd learned earlier in life."

"There's time, Miles." I help him with his current stretch, trailing my hand down his thigh as I increase the pressure. "Our stories aren't finished until we're in the grave."

"You're a good egg, Lorelai. Don't let anyone tell you different."

Not long ago, his sentiment would have made me emotional. Or super needy for more. Not now, though.

I'm proud of myself. And of the progress I've made. I was selfish. I was the villain in someone else's life. Now… now I am the good egg Miles believes me to be. I'm never going back to anything less.

"Same to you, Jameson."

He looks less confident than I feel. While I don't know much more about his past addictions and what led to them. No more than what media reported, anyway. I know who Miles Jameson is now. Kind, caring, self-reflective. Worthy of my friendship. As I am his. You can't spend six hours a week with someone without getting to know them.

Miles and I have a special kind of friendship. It's so free of judgment and outside pressure. Three times a week, we get a workout in pure honesty. It's incredibly therapeutic.

I've told him more about my past these last two weeks. Like most people, he doesn't get the grittier details, but he knows I grew up in a religious, pedophilic cult. I've told him the things I'm least proud about in my life. Those things being what I did to June McKenna. I'm not hiding that part of my life away; I'm facing it head-on.

In return, he told me he's least proud of the injuries that were caused to Bellamy, his ex-fiancée. He said it's the only thing he wishes he could completely re-write in his life. They haven't spoken since shortly after she awoke from her four-month long coma.

It choked him up when he told me that, so I know how much it still hurts him. How much he missed her was clearly written all over his face. He doesn't expect to ever be forgiven by Bellamy. I get it; I don't ever expect June to forgive me. It would be an impossible ask.

Miles is right, though. We don't have to continue to hate ourselves. It would get us nowhere. In my case, it wouldn't be good for Olivia, either.

"Tight ass incoming," Miles says in a hushed whisper. "If you want to hold this stretch a few beats longer so I can see his face get all screwed up, I won't mind." He sends me a cheeky wink as I run my hand down his other leg.

Noah makes a point to be early for his Wednesday workouts. He happened to pick the only day that Miles has an earlier workout with me, as if he knew that. He probably did, seeing as he'd been stalking me through my own phone.

Noah's early arrival isn't lost on Miles who's turned it into a game. He's much flirtier when Noah is in audience. Miles says he likes to see Mr. Perfect come undone. They're both ridiculous, but I like to see Miles entertained, so I play along. Noah's jaw clenching is just an added bonus.

"That's awfully tight, Jameson," I call, somehow keeping a straight face as humor dances in his eyes.

"Darlin', you don't know the meaning of the word. I could teach you, though."

"Ah, are you asking me out on a date, Miles?"

"Call it whatever you'd like, beautiful."

"All right, you charmer, you're done for the day," I say, reaching down to give him a hand up.

Miles goes to retrieve his belongings, and I begin cleaning the equipment we've used.

Noah steps closer when he sees I'm nearly done, at the same time Miles returns to give me his goodbye hug. It's normally a very casual, friendly gesture. This time, Miles wraps his arms around my waist, lifting me off my feet until I'm eye level with him.

"Thank you for today, Lore. You're the best gal a guy could have in his life." Then he kisses the bridge of my nose, tenderly and lasting, before placing me back on my feet. "When you're ready for that date, you let me know. I promise the best time of your life."

"I'll keep that in mind. Have a good weekend, Jameson."

Miles doesn't date. This is a conversation we've had already. He says he's a perpetual friend with benefits type of guy. In his heart, I think he's still committed to the promises he made to Bellamy. It's romantic if you're into tragic types of epic romances. Which I guess, I kind of am.

On more than one occasion, he's hinted at having that arrangement with me.

On more than one occasion, I've thought about accepting.

What can I say? He's hot as hell, and we're grown, healthy adults.

"Are all your clients that unprofessional?"

"You call it unprofessional; I call it panty-dropping," I say, patting Noah's chest. "You know how to get started."

He huffs but gets to the stretches I always have him perform first.

Like the past two weeks, I don't attempt to engage Noah in conversation outside of the work we're doing. He peppers me with questions about Olivia and my life, but I'm adept at avoidance when it comes to speaking about myself.

He's getting little out of me. Which is fine since he's gotten enough already. About twenty minutes into our relatively silent workout, he changes the game on me.

"You already know that when we started seeing each other in college, I'd never been in much of a relationship before. I rarely did repeats with women because I didn't want attachments," he says. I'm uncertain about why he's bringing any of this up. But he doesn't give me a chance to ask. "You were different from the start. You were unexpected and you humored me. Nobody ever made me laugh before. I never had fun with a woman outside of the bed.

"My whole life, I'd been able to anticipate other people's reactions. Never with you though. You were a curveball. I loved it. I'm not sure I ever told you that," he muses. "That I loved you. I did. I should have been clear about that."

My hands falter where they're guiding his body into a pose. I shake them out and take a step away from him. He never did tell me. I believed he loved me, but it was hard to trust. At one point, I believed my father loved me, too.

"When you left, I was angry, and I turned that into my drive for the NFL. That last season, my senior year, I played the best I'd ever had. I blamed you for it when I should have thanked you. You're right, I had lost some of my focus. You noticed and while I'd like to believe we could have worked it out, I don't know if I'd have had the same results. You have always been the greatest distraction to me," he says as he stands up.

Turning around, he bends slightly to look at me directly.

"That's not your fault, you know? It's nothing you did; it's just who you are and what you meant to me. You understand?"

I return a shaky, dazed nod.

"Good, sweetheart. Now come put your hands back on me."

We finish his workout in relative silence. Noah, very relaxed, while I'm drowning in a fog and trying hard not to cling to the admittance that he loved me. It doesn't matter now, all things considered. It's nice to know that I wasn't deluding myself, but it doesn't change anything.

Except that it's the closest thing to "I love you" I've ever heard. I don't mean only from a man. My parents never said it either. Nor Aunt Alice. I do know she felt it, but she was as damaged as me. It probably wasn't a feeling she trusted either.

I'll make it a point to tell Olivia as often as I can. She'll never have to wonder. She'll *know*.

"Do you want to go with us tonight? We're headed to a place called Dumbwaiter. Olivia is very excited to try shrimp on her grits."

He asks me every week. Each time I decline. This time is meant for them. I know Olivia adores it. She calls it her *Just Noah and Livi night*.

"She told me," I say, but I shake my head. "You two have a good dinner. I'll see you back at my house."

This is the routine. He asks, I decline, he goes to pick up Olivia and after they've had a meal at some random restaurant much more refined than Bob's, he drops her back at my house. He never stays long; he hasn't tried to push my boundaries.

It's his turn to nod, before offering a small wave and heading out the door.

Once home, I eat a quick salad for my own dinner, then start on the project I've been trying to perfect for nearly a month.

Goddamned homemade bread.

My mother made it every day. Many of the mothers did, but our mother added rosemary, so we always knew it was hers. Olivia misses it. If I'm honest with myself, I miss it too. But for the love of all things, I can't get it right. I refuse to give up, though. I won't be beaten by a loaf of bread.

Eight recipes tried. All failed. I make each one several times, to be sure. It's time to admit that it isn't the recipes, it's me. Regardless of how closely I follow each step, I'm doing something wrong.

This current loaf is added evidence. I knew it when I pulled it out of the oven, heavy in my hands. It's dense, not light and fluffy.

"Fuck," I say as I drop it into the bin. Another wasted attempt.

"Lie-Lie, language!"

Noah laughs lightly as he follows my sister in the front door.

"That was a bad one. That costs fifty cents," Olivia says, her tiny fists landing on her hips. She scolds my language often, so we made a deal. The really bad words mean I must put money in a jar that she calls the Special Day jar. When it has enough money in it, we'll pick somewhere special to spend the day, like the beach or the zoo.

We'd do that regardless, but this way makes her feel like we've earned it somehow. I'm not sure how I feel about that exactly—her need to earn good things in her life, but we'll work through all that together, in time.

So many things about her personality remind me of mine. Behaviors I never saw as problematic until I didn't like that she did them.

I say Miles and my friendship has been therapeutic, but not nearly as much as having Olivia in my life. She teaches me new things every day. I'm a better person because she's in my life. My mother gave me the best gift she ever could have the day she stole Olivia out of that compound and gave her to me.

"Sorry, Livi," I say and go to my purse for my tithe.

She walks over to the trash and peeks in.

"Another one?"

"Yeah, I'll get it right one of these days. I promise."

"I know you will," she says with a toothy smile, always so full of confidence in me. She prances off to her room, leaving me alone with Noah, who now is taking his own look into the trash.

"What's that about?"

"My mother always made rosemary bread. We miss it, but I can't quite figure it out."

He continues to stare at the brick of a loaf of bread for a few beats before he shuts the lid and looks up.

"You and Miles are becoming friendly."

I've been having longer and longer stretches of times between temper flareups since moving to Mobile. But if anyone knows how to raise my hackles, it's Noah fucking Anders.

"Yes. You going to try to fuck him, too? I'm not sure that's his preference, but for you, he may make an exception."

Noah is on me in an instant, backing me up against the wall, his entire body pressing into mine. One hand finds my nape, giving it a gentle tug. The other finds an ass cheek and grips it firmly, pulling my groin into his.

"I told you we were done with that, sweetheart. We're playing nice now, learning to be friends," he whispers the words onto my own lips. "Jameson isn't the one I want to fuck."

Noah's mouth steals away any comeback I had in mind, giving me a short, but searing, kiss. It scrambles my brain, and I stand awestruck when he pulls back far enough to lick the bridge of my nose. The same spot Miles kissed earlier.

"I'll see you next week, Lorelai."

Sunday morning, I'm washing up the breakfast dishes when our doorbell rings. We've never gotten unexpected visitors before. Olivia is as startled as I am and hides behind me as I open the door to one of the last people I'd ever expect.

Grace Anders stands in her picture-perfect embodiment of stoic beauty. Tall, slender, impeccably dressed in pressed khaki pants and a silk blouse that matches the rosiness of her cheeks.

"Um, hi," I greet in confusion. "Oh god. Is Noah okay?" Panic settles in my chest. I can't think of any reason she'd be here, unless something bad has happened. But then again, I don't know why she'd tell me if it had.

"He's fine, dear," she says with a smile so much like her son's. "Can I come in? I'd like to speak to you about something."

She called me dear. Right? I didn't just imagine that.

"Who is she?" Livi tugs on my t-shirt to get my attention.

"This is Noah's mother," I answer, stepping back to let Grace in. If she's here to say something awful, I'd hope she'd consider doing it away from my toddler's ears. But she called me dear. You don't call someone that if you're about to say something horrible. Or maybe they do in the south.

Fuck, I don't know.

"Hello, Olivia," Grace says and squats to Livi's level. "Noah has told me so much about you."

"He did?" She sounds amazed.

"Yes, he speaks about you quite often. He tells me of all your Just Noah and Livi nights." Olivia beams at that.

"Do you want to see my bedroom?" Olivia asks. It's her favorite place and she's always eager to show off her very own bedroom.

"Of course! Maybe I can have a quick chat with your sister first. Would that be okay?"

"Sure," Olivia sings and twirls off down the short hallway to her room.

We both watch her go, not speaking until we hear her television turn on and the sound of a cartoon carrying down the hall.

"What's this about?" Though I try to sound casual, there's something like threat in my tone. I don't care if Grace is Noah's mother. If she's come here to insult me in front of Olivia, I'll stand my ground.

"I deserve that, I'm sure," Grace says, contrite. "You broke my baby's heart, and I took it personally. It's not an excuse, mind you, just an explanation. I can see you understand being protective of your children."

"Yes…"

"Noah and I had a long talk about you the other day. He told me why you left him, and he told me some, not much, but enough of your past."

"And?"

"And…" Grace laughs. I assume she's a little amused that I haven't yet let my guard down with her. "I want to help, Lorelai. That's all. Being a mother is hard work, and you weren't even offered the nine-month preparation period. It's my understanding that your own mother isn't able to offer you support or guidance. While I've made my fair share of mistakes, I like to think I raised two good men. Let me help. Please?"

"How exactly?"

"Well, I thought we'd start by the three of us making rosemary bread together. I hear it's been troublesome, and I happen to be quite a decent baker."

Several hours later, Olivia is passed out on the couch, a half-eaten piece of bread resting on her full belly. I'm sure emotion plays over me, and I rush to school my features before Grace sees.

But like a true boy-mom, she notices everything.

Her arm comes to rest across my back.

"You're doing a fine job, Lorelai. She's a great girl, and despite everything, seems very well adjusted."

"Thank you," I say, the words breaking apart as I try to piece them together.

"You're welcome. Can we agree on a clean slate? You're both very important to my son and I would like to get to know you without the preconceived notions. If you'll let me."

"I'd like that. But I don't know what the future holds for me and Noah. We're civil, at best, these days."

Grace gives me a squeeze of understanding.

"I know. But that doesn't mean you and I can't work on our own friendship. If you need anything, I hope you'll reach out."

26
NOAH

"She thought something happened to you, Noah. You should have warned her."

"Mom, I told you. She would have declined. How did it go otherwise?"

My mother pried plenty of information out of me a few nights back. I'd been telling her how much fun I had taking Olivia out to a nicer restaurant. Olivia was excited by everything that was so new for her, and her enthusiasm was contagious. Several times throughout our meal, the neighboring tables giggled at her comments. And by the end of the meal, she had the entire wait staff wrapped around her finger.

Mom, like any good mother, was worried about my attachment, and Olivia's to me. That led to a more serious conversation about Lorelai's unique predicament.

Which in turn led to why Lorelai broke up with me back in the day.

My mother is stubborn, like me. But she isn't hateful. She disliked Lorelai because she's overly protective of my brother and me. At heart, she's all about being non-judgmental and giving chances. Except she felt she needed my approval for that with Lorelai. She was fairly upset with herself when she learned all that Lorelai has been through. Once past that, she was all about what she could do to help a new mother.

I let her take that on. Because Lorelai could use the support whether she believes that or not. Also, because I want my mom to know them the way I do.

For my part, I've been in touch with Giving Hope again, letting them know that if any other girls get out of that cursed ranch, I'm to be contacted for any expenses needed for their care. There isn't much I can do, outside of financial support, but I've made them aware that my pockets are deep where they're concerned. If Lorelai has more relatives escaping, I want to ensure they're cared for.

I've also been keeping tabs on Will. Whose client list is quickly dwindling. It still isn't what he deserves, but I'll find a way to make him pay. Even if it takes a trip to Seattle myself. Which becomes more and more tempting the more I think about it.

"Splendid. Olivia is a spitfire," my mom says, and even through the phone, I can hear her smile.

"She's the fucking greatest, Mom."

"She really is, Noah. I can see why you adore her."

I hear it, her worry. I was hoping it would vanish after she got to know them some.

"It's going to be okay. Stop worrying," I try to placate.

"For me, certainly. I can be friends with those two completely independently of you and the other people you have in your life. The question is, can you?"

"Yes."

I don't know how yet; the picture isn't complete in my head. But I'm nothing if not determined, and that determination is fixed on figuring this out. Finding a way to have all the people I care about in my life, where they belong. And all of them being happy, healthy, and safe.

It's an inherent need, at this point. It's instinct, constantly speaking to me because we're not there yet. At the place where everyone is under my protection and in my care. I've always been controlling to an extent. But this deep, soul-burning, crushing desire is a whole new level. It's fucking consuming.

My mother is silent for a moment. Contemplating me.

"I only spent an afternoon with her. But it was enough for me to see her true character, to see why you'd love her."

"Livi would be impossible not to love."

"You know I wasn't speaking of Olivia, Noah."

It's Wednesday, and once again, I'm early to my appointment with Lorelai. I know what's happening; I've always known. Jameson is amused by me. I couldn't give a fuck.

He can play whatever games he'd like, and of course, Lorelai can join in. She gets a sense of payback from it. And, probably, I deserve that, so I let her have it. The games they play soften her up. Soft Lorelai is as much a favorite of mine as riled Lorelai is. It's the indifference I don't like, the in-between feelings that make her not care if I'm here or not.

I'm not jealous of Miles Jameson. But if Lorelai is happier thinking I am, I'll give her that. I'll give her everything she needs, even if she doesn't realize it.

So, I'll continue to arrive early, letting them play their games. I can be the brunt of their jokes. It does give me the opportunity to see where, exactly, he puts his mark on her. Only for me to replace it with my own later.

If she's going to carry a man's scent, it sure as fuck is going to be mine.

Like the past three weeks, Lorelai's hands linger on him while he finishes his last stretches. His eyes trail her body. Can't blame him there; she's gorgeous with her tight ass, subtle curves, and the glow of her pale skin that's beginning to show a kiss of sun.

He stands, whispers something in her ear that makes her blush, and I give the appropriate response. Tensing my muscles, clenching my fists.

"How are you today, Mr. Anders?" Janelle, Lorelai's boss, steps up next to me.

"Quite well, thank you," I respond easily.

"I'm on to you, by the way. Those two don't see it, but I do."

I turn my head to her, giving her a wink.

"Would you be good for her?" she asks me. "She deserves that. A partner in life. Someone she can always rely on. If you can't give her that, you need to let her go."

My smile falters. I could say yes, but the truth is I've already failed at that. Miserably.

"Thank you for looking after her, Janelle. And Olivia. I know she appreciates it, but I do, as well."

"She hasn't needed much from me, but if that time comes, I'll always have her back. You can count on that," she says, patting my arm before she wanders off.

I look back at Lorelai in time to see Jameson's hand lingering low at the small of her back while he hugs her goodbye. She's in yoga pants and a sports bra, leaving bare skin for his fingers to fondle.

I don't like it.

Not one bit.

But I'm not jealous.

Jameson saunters by me and out the door, looking smug. Looking like he's going to be in my woman's bed tonight. I know better. Lorelai's not that easy. And that's another slap in the face, because not that long ago, I treated her as if she was.

Lifting my chin to Miles, I stride toward Lorelai.

"Have you had a good week?"

She peers at me over her shoulder as she wipes down equipment.

"You sent your mother."

"You'll learn soon enough that my mother only does what she wants."

"You told her about the bread. You gave her my address."

"Yes. And yes. But it was her idea. I only supplied the necessary information. Did I do wrong?"

She huffs a little as she turns to face me.

"No," she says on a sigh. "You should have asked me, but I appreciate Grace's help. I made another loaf by myself, and it turned out just as good."

"I'm glad."

"You still should have asked."

"Noted." I'd do it again, but I don't have to tell her that.

Her eyes narrow.

"You'd do it again, wouldn't you?"

I laugh. Loudly and genuinely, but I don't answer. There's no need.

She says she doesn't know me, but that's not entirely true. She knows the right stuff, the core of who I've always been.

Lorelai points to the mats, and I start running through my pre-workout stretches. As usual, she doesn't speak much more than what's necessary. Waiting until about halfway through the session, I begin to talk.

"For a year after we broke up, I didn't have sex with anyone. Nobody held my interest for long enough. After the draft and moving back to Louisiana, I decided it was time. Not for sex, necessarily, but to learn. I never wanted to be in a position of hurting someone like I had hurt you."

"Noah, we've discussed this. You didn't."

"I didn't understand that then, Lore. With the windfall signing bonus and salary I was making, I joined Lupus et Agnus and found myself a tutor. Her name was Fabienne. She was a switch, which was perfect because she could teach me to dominate while being submissive to me. Quickly, I realized I liked it. Dominating. Not extremely, but enough to know that I was in control. And for my partner to know it, too."

"Don't turn your foot out," Lorelai instructs, guiding me where she wants me. I can feel her fingers shudder. I'm not telling her these things to upset her or excite her. Only to fill her in on the parts of my life she missed.

"I also found that I liked Fabienne. We were together for almost two years," I say, and Lorelai removes her hand from me as if I burned her. "In our own way, that is. It was an open relationship of sorts. We each fucked plenty of other people with one another's permission. Or, often, we'd share them."

"I didn't know you'd been in a relationship. There were never reports." Her voice stutters as much as her hand. I should feel bad about that, but I hang on the fact that she kept tabs on me instead.

"You wouldn't have. Fabienne is profusely private. That worked well for me because I didn't want the media attention of the new star quarterback dating a woman old enough to be his mother. It wasn't real dating anyhow. Eventually it fizzled out as I always knew it would. But by then, I was comfortable with the club, with the fringe lifestyle."

The relationship I had with Fabienne was never meant to be long-term. We both understood that going in. It was convenient and fun. Until it wasn't anymore, and we both moved on. She's since found another man, younger than I am, and she's been with him for years now.

"It was the only other relationship that was more than friendship I had."

I turn my foot out again, purposefully.

"You don't consider what was between you and June as something more?" Lorelai's hand, as I expected, reaches to adjust my foot.

"No. It wasn't like that. She was hurt, confused, trying to learn about herself as much as she was figuring out Drew. But she never stopped loving him. I could see that the first night I took her out to dinner," I say and study her expression. It doesn't change, though. She's focused on my form. "If I had seen any indication that she truly wanted me to fuck her brains out, I would have."

Still, she doesn't flinch.

"Did you think I had something more with her?"

"I suspected." She shrugs. "June's pretty great, who'd blame you? But I know what you mean, she's loved him through a lot. I couldn't imagine watching the man you love sleep his way through half the co-eds at a large university and still come out loving him the same on the other side. But she did."

"That, and worse."

Her head snaps up.

"I know, Noah. I was there."

"I'm not blaming you, Lorelai."

"Aren't you? Haven't you been?"

"I did, yes. I believed you were manipulative, conniving. Maybe even evil enough to try to steal someone else's husband," I tell her and reach for her hand so she can't back away. "I know better now. You both made a bad choice, but you're both working very hard on being better people. I respect that, and there's nothing more that can be asked of either of you. None of us are without faults. I'm more concerned with what we do when we know better."

She nods but won't look at me as I squeeze her hand.

"I do have one question, though."

"What?"

"Would you have stopped if you hadn't been caught?"

"I can't say with any certainty what would have happened. Every time, we both said it needed to be the last. It was definitely weighing on us heavily. Neither of us wanted to keep doing it. That sounds stupid though, like an excuse."

"You've never made excuses for it. Not really."

"I can't," she says, shrugging again. "We didn't want to be hurting June. Drew more so than me, of course. But I hated it, too. That, and the knowledge that I'd be primary caregiver to my mother and my sister... well, I knew the end was near. I only wish we'd come to that conclusion sooner. Or, better yet, never started up at all."

Her words are spoken so softly, but I know every one of them is true.

"I believe you, for what that's worth."

"It's not worth a lot, to be honest."

It would be, had I not fucked Alim. Had I given her the same opportunity at friendship I gave Drew.

Nodding, I squeeze her hand once more, letting her know I understand.

When the hour is up, I ask, like always, if she'll join her sister and me. She, of course, refuses, and I head straight to Kiki's to pick up my best little friend.

"Are you going to tell me where we're going yet?" Olivia asks as I buckle her into her car seat.

"I told you, it's a surprise."

"I don't think I like those."

"Have you ever had one before?" I laugh.

"No."

"Well, let's go see if you like them or not."

It turns out she does, and we enjoy another dinner. When we walk back into Lorelai's house, she squeals and runs to her sister.

"We ate in the sky, Lie-lie!"

"I'm sorry, what?" Lorelai laughs while picking her up.

"It was in a so very tall building, and I could see the whole city!"

"That sounds amazing. What did you have to eat?"

"Shrimpy grits," she says through a wide smile.

"Again?"

"With an egg!"

"Oh boy, I bet you loved that."

Olivia nods and wiggles her way out of Lorelai's arms, running off to her room. This is her routine now on Wednesdays. When we get back, she goes to get ready for bed. When it's time for me to leave, she'll be half asleep watching her silly cartoon.

It gives me time with her sister, so I like this routine.

Lorelai has changed since coming home, now donning a pair of her workout shorts and one of her faded t-shirts.

"Your sister had a great idea tonight," I say softly as I crowd her space. She backs up a step, but it only puts her where I want her. Her back to the wall, harder for her to scurry away.

"What?"

"She thinks we should start having Just Noah and Lie-lie nights. So that you can eat in the sky, too. She thinks you're being left out."

"Four year olds don't really understand that sort of thing."

"I think she understands just fine. Besides, I agree with her."

I make another small move froward, forcing her chin to rise to keep eye contact with me.

"Go to dinner with me, Lorelai."

"I don't think that's a good idea."

"I don't agree. Let's do it so we can know who's right."

Her lips twitch as she fights the smile, and it feels like the biggest victory of my life. Being drafted into the NFL, coming back and winning games from impossible odds—none of my achievements compare to cracking Lorelai Simmons' shell.

She doesn't say anything, so I press a little closer. Wrap my hand around her waist and slide to the back. Lean down infinitesimally more.

"Say yes."

"I don't see how I can. What about Olivia?"

"I'll take care of all the arrangements. All you need to do is say yes."

"Noah," she says. Anticipating another refusal, I dip down and press a kiss on her lips. Light, almost friendly. Almost.

"It's one dinner. Have some fun with me, like we used to."

"We're not who we used to be," she replies. I'm not sure it's intentional, but she rises to her toes to say it across my lips.

"No, we aren't, sweetheart. We're better than we used to be." With my hands still wrapped around her, I spin her so her front is to the wall, and I can press into her back. Slowly, I slide down her body into a crouch. Lifting up her shirt with one hand, and dragging down her shorts, just enough, with the other. I lap at the skin that Jameson touched. Pulling my tongue across her skin as it erupts in small spasms beneath.

She's needy, but I know it's too soon. She's not ready to accept me that way. Into her bed, into her body.

Righting her clothes, I palm her stomach and stand tall and close behind her.

"One night, Lorelai," I say into her hair. "One night of us as we are now. We can leave the past where it belongs and just have a good time. Say yes, baby."

27
LORELAI

I said yes. Maybe that's stupid. Or wrong. I'll end up hurt in the end, most likely. Yet I can't seem to regret saying that one small word. So instead, I focus on not getting my hopes up, not being overly invested. It's two tentative friends going out for a meal. Nothing more.

Full forgiveness for the way he treated me hasn't come. But something he said hit home to me. It's what we do when we know better. He can't turn back time any more than I can. We can't undo our wrongs. All we have is time to improve and learn. If he's offering me that chance, I can't very well deny him the same.

A quick commitment wasn't something I could do, however. Wanting the time for the idea to settle, I told him I'd go the following Saturday. It's now Wednesday again, and I am down to just a few more days.

"Calm down, darlin'."

"Sorry," I say, startled back to reality.

"When was the last time you went on a date?"

"Oof, do we have to do this?"

"That long, huh." Miles laughs. "Want to go on a practice date with me first?"

"I can't handle one man in my life, even when he's barely in it. What would possibly give you the idea that I could juggle two?"

"Don't underestimate yourself, Lore. You can handle anything Tight-ass throws your way."

I hope he's right.

"Speaking of, shouldn't he be here by now? Lurking like he does," Miles says. Noah isn't early today, but just as Miles says it, he walks in the door, cellphone to his ear.

"I'll make it work." I hear him say before he ends the call, tossing his duffle bag and phone in the same corner he always does.

"I'll see you Friday," Miles says, giving me a warm hug. He places a lingering kiss to the side of my neck as he does. It's the most intimate he's ever been. From my position, I'm looking directly at Noah as it happens.

His eyes focus like lasers to the spot and a calculating expression takes over him.

I cock my head.

"Take it easy, Jameson. You worked hard today, don't overdo it."

Miles leaves, and Noah strides over to watch me go through the motions of cleaning all the equipment.

"Do you want to lick me now or later?"

"Excuse me?" Noah laughs. "I'm certain that's not appropriate office talk, sweetheart."

Turning to him, I tilt my head, exposing my neck.

"It's right there."

"I fucking know exactly where it is," he rasps out. His voice turning deep and growly. "I'll take care of it in private. Finish cleaning up and work me out."

Damn.

My body grows heavy, the cleaning wipe in my hand floating to the floor as I lose function… everywhere.

"Stop looking at me like that, Lorelai. Unless you want to skip this workout and head straight to your place for a different one. Just know that I'm picking up Olivia in an hour and that isn't nearly enough time for me sate you the way you need."

How the hell was that supposed to make me less horny?

"I… I just need a minute. Start stretching."

"You'll need more than a minute, baby. But you go get yourself together, I'll be here when you get back," he says smugly.

"Bastard," I whisper as I leave. His laughter roars behind me.

"You splashing cold water on your face or other parts?" Janelle joins his cackling as I pass her. I grin at her amusement but give her the bird, only making her laughter louder.

After my cooldown, we get to work. We may slowly be stabilizing our footing, but I'm still leery of it all, and am quiet while I run him through the work I want him to do today.

It doesn't take long for him to fill the silence.

"I heard it before I felt it. Maybe that's common with injuries like mine, I don't know. But it's what I remember the most. Not the pain but the sound. Of bone breaking and my life changing."

I help him shift his form, allowing my hand to run along the hip he speaks of.

"I'm lucky, really. I made it farther than most. I'm not bitter about that anymore. I used to be though. You wouldn't have recognized the man I became after getting out of the hospital."

He takes a long inhale followed by a longer exhale.

"That's not true, I guess. You'd recognize him better than anyone, because I let myself fall into that hole when you showed back up in my life," he says, making eye contact. I quickly look away though. "I was mad because you weren't there."

"Where?"

"At the hospital when the doctors gave me the news. Fuck, on the field with me as I laid there waiting to be carried off. I wanted *you*."

I can't not look at him now. This confession shocks me to my core.

"Even after all that time? And what I'd done?"

"Even then, Lorelai."

"Not Fabienne?"

"She didn't even cross my mind. You did."

"I don't know what to say," I tell him, doing my best to contain the overwhelming emotion. The pure fucking heartbreak of it all. "I wanted to be there, too. I'm so sorry, Noah."

"Look at me, sweetheart," he says, pulling me into his chest. "It's not your fault."

"How can you say that?"

"Because it's true. We both fucked up. You should have been honest with me, but I should have seen something bigger was happening. I should have fought for you."

"You can't say stuff like that to me," I say, burying my face in his chest. He's been sweating a little, and like the weirdo I am, I find it comforting.

Never did I dream of Noah fighting for me. The thought makes me dizzy. Had he, I probably would have broken completely and followed him anywhere. Instead, he did what I expected. What everyone in my life had done before and has done since. He let me go.

"I think the truth is exactly what I need to be saying to you. And you to me. Deal?"

"You can lie to me if it keeps me from crying," I say, knowing he'll know it's a lie.

"I wasn't trying to make you cry. You keep saying you don't know me, and I'm fixing that. Eyes on me, Lorelai," he says. He must see the question on my face, the one that screams that nothing has changed. He reads me like I'm his favorite book. "Neither of us knows what the future holds. Let's take this one day at a time, okay?"

"That terrifies me, Noah, but I'll try. For real though, stop making me cry. I haven't cried this much since…"

"Don't. You don't need to go back there anymore. I'll do my best to not make you cry anymore," he says, his head falling to rest on mine. Forehead to forehead. "Go home now. I'll see you back there after I feed our girl."

They get back later than usual, and Noah is carrying Olivia in his arms, fast asleep. I nod toward her room and follow him back. She's dead weight as I strip her down and pull her favorite nightgown over her.

"You wore her out," I tell him when I meet him back in the small living room. He sits on the sofa I bought—one of the few things we bought new.

"We ran into one of those disgusting traveling carnivals. She was too nervous to go on any rides, but she liked the games. And the cotton candy."

"You spoil her," I say, trying for a stern tone and failing.

"She deserves a little spoiling," he says, his hand reaching out for my wrist so he can pull me down into his lap. "So do you."

"I've done nothing to deserve spoiling."

Noah pulls my legs up and twists me around as if my height and weight are nothing. When he has me sideways and comfortable, he pushes my hair back and runs his lips across the spot Miles kissed.

"Bullshit, Lorelai. You gave up everything you had to save a girl you didn't even know from a life of rape and abuse."

"I did what anyone would do in my position," I say.

"Again, bullshit. Now shut up and let me finish my task."

He starts at my collarbone, and slowly, so damned slowly, traces up the column of my neck, not stopping until he reaches my earlobe.

"I don't like his skin on your skin." He catches my lobe in his teeth and gives a gentle tug, making me gasp. "I don't like wondering every week if it's going to be the one where he wins you over with that fake southern charm and you end up in his bed."

"It's not like that, he doesn't do relationships."

"You don't have to be in a relationship to fuck." His mouth travels back down my neck, pressing kisses all along the way.

"He did offer up a friends with benefits arrangement."

Before I know what's happening, Noah has me lying flat on my back, his body pressed fully atop mine. Hands in hands, he reaches our arms above our heads and stares down at me.

"Did you consider saying yes?"

"Yes," I say after swallowing hard. Noah overwhelms me entirely. Our hearts beat hard against each other as his cock makes itself known against my leg. It's intoxicating.

His eyes close while he composes himself, his fingers gripping mine more tightly.

"But you didn't," he says slowly, as if to convince himself.

"I said I'd keep it in mind."

"And have you," he growls at me, at the same time he grinds his groin into me. I lose the ability of a verbal response. I give a slight nod, instead. "Why do you push me, Lorelai?"

"Because the most beautiful thing I've ever seen in my life is you when your typically smooth edges show sharp points and you can't decide whether to throttle me, fuck me, or do both simultaneously."

Noah blinks down at me as if I've stunned him.

"I'm going to go home now because if I stay any longer, I'm going to need to be doing it with my dick inside you."

An audible moan escapes, and I stretch my body underneath him.

"Stop that, Lorelai. When I finally fuck you again, it's going to take time and I won't be getting out of bed until you're comatose and I've spent myself over every inch of you."

"Holy shit."

"We don't have that kind of time tonight, baby. Besides, you get a date first. So, I'll see you Saturday," he says. Then he bites the spot on my neck that Miles kissed, while also tickling his fingers into my sides.

I erupt in a squirm of laughter, but he doesn't relent for a few minutes. Not until he, too, is laughing, and I need a second to catch my breath.

"I've missed that laughter," he tells me while getting up. I pull myself up and follow him to the door. Just before he walks out, I reach for his hand, making him stop.

"Have a good week," I say. I like this. The new peacefulness between us. "And thank you."

"For what?"

"For making Olivia a priority in your life."

An apprehensive look flashes on his features for a quick flash, then he reaches to cup my cheek.

"Not just Olivia. I'll see you in a few days. Stay safe." He rubs his thumb across my lips, then leaves.

Suddenly, that peacefulness I enjoyed just a minute ago feels different.

28

NOAH

"Quit asking me, Anders. It's planned for Wednesday. Her actual birthday," Drew says.

June's birthday is Wednesday. Drew's planned a big party. Of course, I want to be there.

Only.

Wednesday. Olivia. Lorelai.

I'll have to cancel my day in Mobile, and I'm disgruntled about it. Extremely.

Not just because I don't like adjusting my plans or letting down people that rely on me. But because of the complicated situation. If I were dating anyone else, I'd invite her along. Hell, June would expect me to. And while this thing between me and Lorelai is new, that's what I see it as.

My heart says we're dating. Or will be after tomorrow night, when I take her on one.

I'm finding myself in the exact position Lorelai told me I would be. Avoiding hurting someone is getting more and more complicated.

"Stop brooding."

"Stop talking." Drew and I are working out today. He thinks he needs to put in extra time to get game ready as training camp approaches. I think he's vain as fuck. One look at him tells me he's in the best shape of his life.

Yeah, I look. Fucking sue me. The man is better looking than he has any right to be. That's my bitterness talking, of course.

"Dude, I get it. You don't want to shuffle your night with Olivia. I'm sorry that you feel like you need to do that. But I've already told you Bryce and all his girls will be there. You can bring her."

"Stop talking, McKenna."

"He's got one about her same age, I'm sure they'd have a great time."

"Shut the fuck up, Drew. Before I lose my shit entirely," I say. He drops his weights and crosses his arms over his chest. He's about to start arguing with me. But if he does, he'll be returning home to his wife with a broken fucking jaw. "Do not say a fucking word. A big part of my predicament is because of you, do you understand that?"

"Noah," he begins.

"If you had fucked your wife properly, if you had started up with anyone but Lorelai." I hold up fingers. "A million other options and you chose the one that makes it impossible for me to claim what's fucking mine without complications."

"Noah."

"I can't just take what I want without hurting my best friend."

"Noah."

"No, Drew. Do not fucking speak, unless it's to tell me how the fuck I fix this."

"You fucking done?"

I swallow hard, mentally shaking myself back into the here and now. I've backed Drew against the wall. I sigh and back up a few steps.

"I'm nowhere near done, you arrogant prick. How the hell am I supposed to invite Olivia and not Lorelai?"

It's Drew's turn to sigh now. He scratches at his scalp, pulling his hair askew. "I'm sorry, man. I didn't think that through."

"Your special trait," I snipe.

"Fuck you, Noah," he snaps back, his cheeks red with anger. "I don't need you to remind me of my fuckups. You aren't my father. You also know how hard I'm working at being a better person."

"So is she."

"I get that. Again, I'm sorry. I'd fix it if I could. You know I would."

I do know. Despite what Drew did to his wife, the man really does have a good heart. He's almost as caring as June is. Much more than I am, for sure. His fuckup doesn't change that, and he is different than he was when June and I first became friends.

His growth doesn't do anything to alleviate my situation, however.

I didn't sleep much last night as my conversation with Drew weighs on my dreams. I don't have a solution, but I'm determined. Today, I'm putting it aside. Maybe that's not fair, but it's what I'm doing. It's Saturday and I'm focusing on nothing except having a good time with Lorelai.

Nerves race through me. It's an unfamiliar feeling. Yet not entirely. A little reminiscent of the day of the NFL draft, and the morning of my first professional game. Not the same though. This is more anticipation sprinkled with nervousness. Not the other way around.

I've meticulously taken care of everything with the single purpose of giving Lorelai a great night. And hopefully morning.

Lorelai opens her door to us, and both my mother and I freeze. Stunned.

"Oh, Lorelai," my mother says, a hand raising to her heart. "You're beautiful, dear."

"Thank you, Grace."

My mother rushes into the house to the excited voice of Livi.

"What's happening?" Lorelai whispers.

I can't answer right away; I'm too busy taking her in. My mom was right, she's beautiful. Lorelai always dresses casually comfortable. Even in college, she'd wear dresses on occasion but was never overly done up. Now, mostly, she's in various forms of workout gear. The only times I've seen her in something different were when I forced it on her. Those outfits weren't this.

The dress she wears is a short number, made of a blue printed fabric. Threads of green and silver shimmer in it, which help to call more attention to her eyes. The sleeves are long, the neck high, with small ruffle detail at the hem. It fits to her form as if it was tailored specifically for her. It's subtle in how sexy it is. It's classy, even. It's unlike anything I've ever seen her wear, and knowing she wore it for me makes me more anxious to rip it off her.

"Is this okay," she asks, as she attempts to smooth wrinkles in her dress that don't exist. "You're always so put together; I didn't want to look like a shlub next to you. But I didn't know where we were going either. Am I underdressed?"

"Do you remember the night you forced me to introduce myself to you?"

"Is that how it happened?" she asks, eyes narrowing on me, but her lips upturn slightly.

"You know it is." I laugh. "You walked in wearing cut-off denim shorts, a vintage looking NASA t-shirt, and converse hi-tops that looked like you'd worn them every day for a decade."

"Your point?"

"My point is that it didn't matter. It's never mattered what you've worn. Your confidence always shone through and you were always the most gorgeous woman in the room. Wherever that attitude went, try and find it again. Because it still doesn't matter. But, for the record, you are perfect. You're not underdressed, but I hope to change that by the end of the night."

Her mouth opens in surprise. Reaching under her chin with a single finger, I push it back closed.

"My mother is here to stay with Olivia. She has more baking planned. Cookies, I think. Are you ready to go?"

"I'm not sure. Do I need anything?"

"Just you."

"Then I guess so. Let me say bye to Livi."

Following her in, we find Olivia sitting on the kitchen counter eagerly watching as my mother measures ingredients into a bowl.

"Noah tells me you're an exceptional egg cracker, Olivia. Can you put two in?"

"Oh yes," she answers in the same awe-struck voice she uses so often. It's my favorite of all her different voices. It means she's experiencing a first of some sort and I like it when I'm there to witness it. I'm not sure what this first is. Maybe it's one-on-one time with a motherly woman who has no expectations of her; I don't know. But I'm happy to see it and I want to experience more of them.

I want to experience all of them.

"Livi, I'm leaving with Noah now. I want you to have fun with Grace, okay?"

"I will. Oh! I have to tell Noah something!"

Olivia scoots to the edge of the counter, and Lorelai lifts her down so she can run to me. I squat down for her.

"Can you buy Lie-lie dessert?" She's whispering directly in my ear, making me laugh as the words tickle.

"I can if you want me to."

"I do! I don't have monies, but I want to do a nice thing for her. Because she does nice things for me."

"I'll buy her the biggest dessert I can find and tell her it's from you. Deal?" I hold my hand out and she shakes it with her little one.

"Deal!"

"What was that about?" Lorelai asks as we walk out to my car.

"She had a favor to ask." I shrug as if it isn't a big deal. It is, though. It's giant.

"You're not going to tell me."

"Not just yet."

Opening the passenger door for her, I hold her hand while she gets in. Then I reach over and pull the seatbelt across her, buckling it up.

"I'm a whole ass grown-up. I can do that myself."

"It's too early in the evening to be talking about your ass, sweetheart," I say, pressing a kiss on her cheek before I shut her door and walk around to mine. I notice the smile she's trying to hide and take it as indication that I have a decent chance of ending this night exactly where I want to be.

Inside Lorelai.

I take her to a small restaurant I found online. Once seated, we order drinks and I ask for a platter of Murder Points oysters for an appetizer. It brings a smile back to Lorelai's lips.

"When did you learn Pilates?" I've been telling her parts of my life she missed, but she's yet to fill in the blanks of her history.

"A few years ago. I wasn't in the position to go back to school full-time. With Pilates, I could go through the instructor training course on Saturdays and Sundays. It took almost a year, but I enjoy it. And I think it benefits a lot of my clients."

"You worked seven days a week for almost a year?"

"Yeah." She shrugs.

"That's some serious dedication, Lore," I tell her. "Did you have any free time?"

"Enough, I guess. I still had plenty of time to binge horror movies and serial killer documentaries in the evenings."

"You have a fucked-up way of finding relaxation."

"Thank you," she says with a big grin.

"Are you certified to teach yoga, too?"

"I am. Similar process, but didn't take as long. I can teach Barre, as well."

She takes a sip of her drink, makes a sound of approval, then takes another.

"You didn't have much of a life outside of work and school, did you?"

"No," she says with a shake of her head. "But it was on my terms and that's what mattered."

"Have you heard anything from your mother?" It's not a quick subject change. I could tell by her expression she was thinking about her childhood and all the choices that were being made for her life without her consent.

"No."

"Do you want to talk about that?"

"Is this a therapy session or a date?"

"Are we on a date, sweetheart?" She blushes, and it's exquisite. "It is a fucking date, to be clear."

We eat the oysters and then our meals. The server comes back to ask if we want dessert. Lorelai is about to decline when I interrupt and ask for a piece of the butternut squash pie to share.

"You might have to eat more than your fair share of that," she says.

"Fine. But when Olivia asks, you can tell her I bought you a big, delicious dessert."

"What?"

"She wanted to do something nice for you, because you do so many nice things for her."

"What?" This time it comes out stilted, full of emotion.

"I think it means she loves you, Lorelai."

"You can't say that stuff to me, Noah."

"I can." I laugh. "Go ahead, cry. It's sweet as fuck, it makes me teary-eyed, too."

"You don't look like it."

"It's my secret power."

"How many do you have?"

"Wouldn't you like to know?"

Her eyes go wide, clearly telling me she would.

"Where are we going now?" Lorelai asks after we conclude our meal and we're back in the car.

"It's a surprise."

It's not far, we're pulling into the parking lot within minutes.

"A movie?"

"Not quite."

"Noah."

"It's a surprise," I emphasize.

We walk up to the will call booth. I give my name and the woman pushes the tickets through the slot. Lorelai grabs them before me.

"Noah," she breathes, looking at them.

"I'm sure you've been before. But—" I stop when she cuts me off.

"I haven't."

"Really?" I ask. She shakes her head. "You always wanted to, though."

"You remember that?"

"I remember everything," I tell her before grabbing her hand and leading her into the theater to watch a late showing of *The Rocky Horror Picture Show*.

For the next nearly two hours, I watch her sing along with others in the audience, all while I hold her hand that squeezes mine each time she's excited about something. A few times, she rises to dance. I rise with her and step behind her so I can feel her move against me and so she doesn't give anyone behind a show. Her dress rises dangerously high when her arms are above her head and she's bouncing around with such enthusiasm. She's too engrossed to even notice.

By the time it's over, I'm hard, and she's relaxed with a huge smile brightening her face. Lorelai throws her arms around my neck and beams up at me.

"You had a good time?"

"The best, Noah," she tells me, then kisses me slowly but chastely.

"I'm glad," I say, smiling against her lips. "You ready to go?"

"Mmhmm."

"Come on, then."

I lead her, hand in hand, back to the car. When I buckle her up again, she grins at me while I do it, but doesn't comment on my overbearing nature. It's presumptuous of me to start driving back across the city to the hotel I have for the night. I've been called worse.

"Noah?"

"Yes?" I answer without taking my eyes off the busy street.

"How can I thank you for such a perfect Just Noah and Lorelai night?"

"You don't need to thank me, Lore."

"But if I want to?"

Movement catches my eye and I quickly glance over to see her slide the seat back. She's kicked her shoes off and one bare foot comes to rest on the dashboard.

"What are you doing?"

"Getting comfortable," she says on a sigh. "While I think of the ways I can express how much I appreciate tonight."

"Lorelai."

"If things were different between us, I'd take you home. I'd change into something strappy and revealing. Something that gives you easy access," she stops talking and moans.

Another glance shows me her dress pulled up enough for her fingers to enter her cunt. My fingers clench on the steering wheel.

We're not nearly close enough to the hotel.

"Lorelai," I warn again.

"I guess that's just a fantasy though. Because you learn your lessons and won't fuck me again."

Fucking hell.

"So, I'll have to pretend. That it's your fingers dipping into me right now. I'll imagine it's your cock fucking me in every way imaginable."

Four minutes, I calculate. That's how long it will take to get us to the hotel. Safely, anyway.

"Oh god," she calls out, breathy and needy.

"You fucking brat," I mumble, changing lanes in the hopes it gets me there even seconds faster.

"Mmm, I am. So bratty. I should be spanked, made to behave." Her foot braces against the dash, her hips thrusting up. "I need someone to teach me a lesson."

"You're not wrong," I growl, making the turn onto the street the hotel sits on.

"I know I'm so naughty."

I catch her bringing her fingers to her mouth, sucking them in, all while her eyes stay glued to mine.

"You'll pay for that, Lorelai."

"I hope so," she moans the words.

The next two minutes are torture. Lorelai continues to torment me with sounds of her own pleasure. I'm a damned powder keg by the time the hotel comes into sight.

"Pull your dress down. Now. Before a valet gets a look at what you've done to yourself, and I become homicidal."

"Yes, Daddy."

Jesus.

Pulling up, I barely have the car in park before I'm out and throwing the keys to the valet. Rushing to the passenger side, I pull Lorelai out by the hand. I'd haul her over my shoulder if I didn't care about causing a scene.

She already looks thoroughly fucked and I've yet to even touch her.

"Have a good evening, Mr. Anders," the valet calls in a cheeky tone. I want to strangle him for seeing her this way.

"Why do you fucking push me, Lorelai?" I ask once safely alone, ensconced in the elevator.

"Is your mother all right staying with Olivia a bit longer?"

The question makes me blink through my sexual daze.

"My mother is staying the night at your house."

"Presumptuous," she whispers with a small smile.

"Determined," I return, stepping into her.

"To get inside my panties?" she teases.

"To get inside you."

Her smirk vanishes and her eyes dilate and bounce over my face. She's probably looking for the lie. She won't find it, and I feel bad that she even considers I'll deny her tonight.

That's on me.

The elevator door dings upon opening. I lift Lorelai up off her feet, front to front, her hands wrapping around my neck. One tangles into my hair and her lips taste my neck. I grip her ass where my hand keeps her pinned to me.

The walk to the end of the hall is excruciating. But we get there, and I get the door open without dropping my fragile cargo. I place her on her feet just inside the door.

Immediately, her hands pull her dress up and over her head. It leaves her in white lace cups covering her breasts under blue triangle straps. The same blue straps wrap around her hips in crotchless panties.

I loop my fingers in the waistband and pull her to me.

"Presumptuous?"

"Determined," she throws back.

I drop to a crouch, and pulling one of her knees over my shoulder, I finally take the taste I've wanted since she began her torment. I could feast on her taste for the rest of my life and never tire of it. I swirl my tongue a few times and nip at her clit until I feel her begin to shake.

And then I stop.

I stand.

"What do you need from me, Lorelai?"

29
LORELAI

A loaded question if ever I heard one.

I *want* everything from him. I want him at my side always. Making every decision with me, the easy and the difficult. I *want* to build a life together. A home, a family. I *want* a future with Noah Anders. I want to be the mother of his children. I want to be precious to him.

I've never wanted anything more. Not even to escape my father. I'd endure years more of my childhood if I knew Noah was waiting on the other side.

What I *need* is different.

It's something I shouldn't ask for, because I'll rely on it, and I need to rely on myself. I need to learn to live without this.

But it's been months since he gave me what I like, and the manic parts of my brain convince me that if we take it just one more time, we'll be okay for long enough to adjust to a new way. It's a lie. The sane parts of me know it, but they aren't as vocal. Not as loud. They can't win the battle.

A chill runs up my arms and I move with it, my nipples growing impossibly hard.

"I…" I can't seem to get the words out. Unsure of how he'll react, the situation being much like the first time. But we aren't the same people we were. I'm stronger. He's different.

"Say it, Lorelai. Tell me what you want me to do."

"I want you to punish me," I say, finally finding the same confidence I had in the car.

"For what?"

Noah's the only person to ever ask, and I'm taken aback by it.

My father created things to punish me for. It never mattered if I was perfectly good or mischievously naughty. He'd punish me either way for some feigned offense. He'd say I needed the *rod* to learn how to properly behave, to submit to him and a future husband. His hand was never used; instead he'd opt for a stick, a crop, a cane. Canes were the worst, the most lasting.

The random men at clubs couldn't have cared less. They needed to give as much as I needed to get. They punished me for faceless women who had wronged them somehow. Maybe a mother who was too stern, or not stern enough. A wife who refuses to give them their full attention, or who doesn't know they are as kinky as they are. Much like the situation Drew found himself in with June. Drew punished me for his own faults and mistakes. He appeased my needs because I let him appease his while pretending my body was his wife's.

Each situation was as degrading as the next. But I never saw it that way. I still don't. I like it and I won't be ashamed about it. Only how I sometimes went about getting it. I didn't care, I took it all. I took it however I could get it. If given the choice, I'd only go to one man for it. Forever. But that's a dream. Noah hasn't offered that.

"Does it matter?"

"Of course it does."

"It never did to anyone else."

His warm fingers curl around my chin, lifting my face up to his.

"I'm not anyone else, Lorelai. I'll give it to you, if you tell me why."

Noah's thumb rubs circles around the corner of my mouth, pulling my lip slightly each time. I open and suck it in, watching as his eyes grow wolfish. I curl my tongue, cradling him the same way I would if it was his perfect dick in my mouth.

His fingers tighten and his thumb takes control of the movement.

"Attempts at distracting me won't help. I already want to fuck you into next week. But I can want two things at once. Tell me what I'm punishing you for?"

He slides his thumb out slowly, and I suck the entire way, releasing it with a pop.

"For being born with tainted life blood. For being too pretty, too young. For being stubborn and impetuous. For trying too hard and not nearly hard enough. For leaving you. For finding my way back to you. For being an utter fucking failure far too often. Take your pick, Noah."

"You're asking me to punish you for your whole life. Even the parts you have no control over?"

"I'm saying it doesn't matter. Do it for whatever reason you'd like. Do it because I'm a whore," I bait. I don't want a therapy session from Noah. I want his hands on me. I want his body pressed against mine and his mouth busy with other tasks.

He only gives that to me when he's angry.

"What did you call yourself?"

"A whore. It's what I am, isn't it? You reminded me for weeks." I trail my hands up to his tie, pulling it loose, dragging it out of his buttoned-up collar. "Tie me up, show me how you'd treat a common whore. Not that high-priced one you dragged home to torture me with."

"You want me to tie you up, Lorelai?"

"I want you to do whatever you want to do to me, Noah."

"Are you very sure of that?" His voice deepens, darkens, as his suit jacket falls to the floor. It's followed shortly by his crisp shirt. My hands join in, undoing his belt and fly. I drag them down as I kneel at his feet, removing his wing-tip boots. I toss them aside, add his socks to the pile, and help him step out of his pants and boxer-briefs.

When he's fully naked, I peer up at him through my lashes.

"Whatever you want, Noah," I repeat with clarity and confidence.

A flash of doubt passes over him, but it quickly subsides when I raise an eyebrow at him.

"Forearms on the bed, ass in the air," he barks, and I positively melt while I rush to comply.

The first smack lands when I'm barely in position. It's followed quickly by several more.

"What I want, Lorelai, is my stolen years back. I *want* for you to have never been duplicitous," he growls through clenched teeth while he continues to land blows. One after another on the same spot. Damn, it's going to sting for days. "I *want* for you to have been open and honest with me. I want to not be in the position I am now."

Fantasies. We all have them. I can't give him this one, nobody can.

"I'll punish you but not for the reasons you think you need it," he says and switches to my other ass cheek. "This is for thinking so lowly of yourself. For calling yourself a whore when we both know you're not."

I gasp at the power those words hold over me. Realization that I needed Noah to acknowledge that, verbally, hits hard. My arms falter under me, and I struggle to stay put under his punishing blows.

"This is for thinking you're weak."

Smack.

"This is for doubting you can be the mother Olivia needs."

Smack.

"This is for letting me believe the worst for so long."

Smack.

"This is for letting me treat you like shit for weeks."

More smacks follow each lesson.

They stop as suddenly as they started. His touch turns into a gentle kneading.

"How do you feel?" he asks, and I only now realize I'm gasping through heavy breathes.

"Good," I say after a quick self-check.

"How good?" His fingers, two of them, thrust inside me, leaving me gasping for another reason entirely.

"Oh god," I moan. My body instinctively moves to get closer to him, to find the pleasure it's so desperate for.

"Even as wet as you are, your cunt is like a vise on my fingers. Imagine what it would feel like with my dick inside you."

Blood pumps through me so hard and fast, I hear it in my head. I don't want to imagine him inside me, I want to feel it. Though he's naked and hard, I have no idea what his plans are. He said before he'd not fuck me, and he's stubborn enough to follow through. I might die if he does follow through with it from the biggest case of blue vagina ever imagined.

"Don't tease," I whine.

When his fingers leave me, I'm ready to jump up and fight with him. There must be a way to convince him to give this to me. Just once.

He grabs my hips, and in a single, fluid motion, flips me over.

"Look at me, Lorelai. If you think I can walk anywhere, let alone away, with my dick this hard, you're crazy."

Of course, my eyes travel to the area affected. And, holy shit, there's never been a more perfect dick in existence. They should make a mold and produce Noah Ander's dildos in mass. Every woman should experience it, just not the real thing. I want that all to myself.

It's long, standing proudly in front of his chiseled body. There's not an ounce of fat on him. Built as the example of a perfect male specimen with corded muscles and veins protruding along his arms.

Licking my lips, I watch with rapt attention as he strokes his own length.

"Did I say you could touch yourself, Lorelai?"

I didn't realize that I was. But I don't stop immediately. Instead, dipping my fingers farther in before bringing them up to hover in front of my lips. I stretch my tongue out and lick once.

"Do you want to taste," I ask him, holding them out to him.

"Not like that," he replies. Noah bends down and comes back up with his tie in his hand. "Arms above your head, stretch them up to the headboard."

Quickly, I scoot further up. The headboard has slats that I grab on to, making it easier for him to bind me to it. Excitement has my breasts heavy and heaving. I don't know what he has planned, but that's what gets me worked up the most. The anticipation, threaded with a bit of fear and anxiety. Trusting Noah not to hurt me physically is one thing, but knowing he can torture me in so many ways is another.

It doesn't matter. I'll take what he gives.

He loops his neckpiece around my wrists and the slat. Gasping when he pulls it tight, I sound much more wanton than shocked.

I am. I so am.

"There's no running away from me this time, Lorelai," Noah says. It's an ominous warning that has heat rushing to my cunt.

He smiles, and it takes my breath away. It's genuine and easy, something he rarely shares with me. Livi gets it, June gets it. But this one is mine.

"Knees up to your chest, sweetheart. Let me see that pretty, wet pussy."

I do as he asks. Thank fuck for flexibility and a strong core. As soon as my ass starts rising off the bed, his hands slip under it, bringing it further up to him as he crawls closer to me on the bed. As if he can't wait any longer, or he's been starving for days, as soon as I'm where he wants me, his head dives down. His tongue plunges in while his hands support my lower back high off the bed. The position makes it so I only see him as his eyes pierce into mine.

It's intoxicating—how he studies me while he works voodoo with his tongue. It's intimate. Much more intimate than I've been in years. Since him.

I've alluded, but I wonder if he truly understands how sparse sex has been for me. And even when I did have it, it wasn't intimate. It was cold mechanics. A means to an end that only ever fulfilled one thing for me. My partners didn't see me.

For the first time in so long, I feel present to a man.

It's terrifying in its intensity. Fear that I'll become needy and addicted to it, as his smile, wins over. I shut my eyes to it.

Noah isn't pleased by it and lands another hard palm to my already stinging ass cheek.

"You can blink, but you do not get to close your eyes to me," he says roughly. "There will be no question as to who is fucking you."

Oh god. He's really going to fuck me this time. I'm weak with need for him.

I'll be stronger tomorrow, I mentally pinky-swear with myself.

"Put your legs over my shoulders, Lore. I want you to fuck the shit out of my mouth until all I taste is your release." With his hands still supporting me, I comply, and one thumb moves up the seam to swirl inside my pussy for a moment.

Then it's gone and his mouth is back, and I use the leverage of my hands gripping the headboard and my knees thrown over his shoulder to do exactly what he asked.

I writhe against his mouth; that magical tongue of his diving deeper than seems possible. My head is the only thing still touching the bed underneath me, everything else is high in the air supported by him as he helps my lower body rise and thrust.

The orgasm edges, grows closer and closer, just barely out of reach. When Noah's thumb, slick with my own pleasure, presses into my ass, I fucking explode.

He matches the motion of his thumb to his tongue, making my thighs clench so tight around his head that if I was in my right mind, which I most certainly am not, I would worry I was hurting him.

Except he's making sounds of approval in between lapping and sucking. Noah doesn't stop until my muscles unclench and all there is left for me to do is desperately try to slow my racing pulse.

"Fucking hell, Noah."

"That was good, baby," he says softly against my pussy, making me shiver, his thumb still slowly moving in and out of my ass. "I'm taking this tonight. But not before I take that foul mouth of yours."

His touch leaves me, and he crawls up my body. Lifting my head, he props a pillow behind me, getting me to the height he wants.

"Open your mouth, and don't you dare close those eyes."

Noah wastes no time thrusting in as soon as my mouth is wide enough. He's on his knees which rest on either side of my head. He grips the top of the headboard, peering at me as he quickly pushes in and slowly drags back out. His eyes never leave mine, so I see what gives him the most pleasure. Noah likes it when I twist my tongue around the head of his cock; he loves it when my throat relaxes enough for him to fully be seated inside my mouth.

Pulling it out, he gives me a moment to catch my breath. I don't need it though; I need more of him. I shimmy down as far as I can so I can suck his heavy sack into my mouth. So I can lap at him. His knees widen, lowering himself but also giving me more access. I run my tongue back as far as I can get in this position. It's not as far as I'd like, but he gets my intention and his cock twitches with excitement.

Then he moves. His hand clasping around mine as his body lays atop the length of mine. A question crosses his face.

"Anything you want, Noah." It's confirmation enough for him and his eyes dance with more emotion.

Noah Anders is a very dirty man. I'm not sure anything would be off the table for him. While I am not as widely experienced as he is, there isn't a lot I wouldn't try with him. If he wanted my tongue in his ass, I'd do it. He's never had any qualms doing it for me. It only seems fair. Besides, imagining the pleasure he'd get from it turns me into a quivering mess.

His hands pull the lace bra down, exposing my alert nipples. His head dips to suck one in. I push my chest up into him and raise my legs to lock around his waist. His cock nestles along me.

So close.

Noah switches to the other breast, slowly torturing me with small movements of his hips. It's not enough, never enough.

"Noah, please."

"Hmm." He makes questioning sounds around the breast in his mouth.

"Please, I need more."

"More what?"

"You. I need more of you."

His teeth clamp onto a breast, gently biting and pulling.

"Please," I cry.

"Be specific, baby. What do you want?"

"I want you in me, Noah. Please get the fuck inside me."

Noah laughs against my skin, making me squirm.

"It's not funny, Noah. Put your cock in my vagina. Please."

Now he's really laughing, his body convulsing against mine. Not in the way I want it to.

"You're an asshole," I cry.

So fast, he's up on his knees, pulling both my legs up. He tosses them over his shoulders and swats the underside of my ass.

"Watch that mouth or I'll shove something in there to keep you quiet."

"Promise?" I ask on a sigh.

"I didn't say it would be my cock. That has other places to be."

"Any time now."

Noah pushes into me quickly and fully.

The world falls away as we both still. I can feel his rushing pulse through his cock as it races as fast as mine. I can't breathe as his eyes boring into mine glaze over with the same sensation. The same feeling that this is right. That this is everything.

That this is home.

Noah falls over me, his hands framing my face, and his nose nuzzling against mine.

"I just need a minute of sweetness. I just need a minute to…" he says but doesn't finish.

The words he doesn't say could be anything. To remember the past. To savor this moment. To memorize it, because it will be the last time.

My fists form in the ties as that thought crosses my mind. It's the most logical one. My heart wants a suit of armor to guard against it.

Because if anything, this moment makes me remember how incredible we were together. How much I loved him. How much I still do and always will. How much it's never felt like this with anyone and how it never will again.

My mouth opens to beg, or plead, or make promises. I don't know. He steals the chance of words or thoughts away with his kiss. It starts so gentle, so loving that I want to die in this moment because life will never be better than this.

His hips don't begin to move until the kiss grows into something more. Something less sweet and more crude. Noah rises back up to his knees and yanks my body down further onto his cock, causing my hands to pull against the headboard.

The pain is enough to bring me to my senses.

Fuck.

"Shit. Condom."

"What?"

"Do you have a condom?"

"You aren't on birth control," he says like it's a revelation.

"No. I haven't needed it, nor have I had time find a doctor."

"Of course." He sounds so nonchalant about it. "I didn't bring anything. I'm clean, though. You can trust that."

"That's not the only concern."

"I know you're clean," he says.

"Noah."

"I am not concerned, Lorelai," he says slowly, adamantly. "Okay?"

So, so slowly he pulls away an inch or two, then moves back in. I think I should tell him to stop, but I feel like I *need* him to keep going.

"Do you have limits, Lorelai?"

"We're not discussing this further?"

"I don't need to. We can, if you need it."

I try to sit up, forgetting that I'm tied to the bed. Noah places a hand over my heart.

"Calm down, sweetheart."

"I haven't been on anything for weeks and weeks, Noah. I could get pregnant."

As I speak, his hand travels down my sternum, between my breasts, and stops over my belly.

"Would you be upset by that? By another Olivia?"

No. The answer comes to me immediately. I'd carry ten of Noah's babies and I'd take ten more Olivias. But…

"What are you saying, Noah? Be very clear."

"I'm saying, Lorelai, that I've never pictured the mother of my children." He pauses for me to blink a couple of times. "…as anyone but you. If I get you pregnant, I'm just fulfilling another dream."

Oh my god.

"You can't say things like that to me, Noah."

"Stop saying that. Don't ask me things you don't want me to tell you the truth about."

"Noah."

His hand covers my mouth.

"Quiet now. If you want me to stop, tell me to stop. If not, answer my question. Do you have limits?"

In normal situations? Yes. I had a long list with the strangers at the club. Most especially, penetration was off the table. That was only the first rule, the most important.

With Noah?

"No."

"You sure?"

"None," I answer confidently. "Anything you want, Noah."

I don't think I'm ovulating; the chance of pregnancy is slim. And since he's still moving in and out of me little by little, my brain is out of fucking commission anyway. Straight thinking is too much to ask.

But I'm confident I wouldn't regret Noah's baby. Even if it makes our complicated situation stickier.

"I'm going to fuck you now, Lorelai."

30

NOAH

She doesn't understand. She can't possibly know what it does to me. To be inside her. To want to grow our child inside her. To have that possibility right in front of me. I can't not take it. I want it. I want her.

I'm choosing Lorelai in my life. I'm fighting for her.

In the dirtiest way possible. I never saw myself as some creepy breeder. But here we are. When she asked for a condom, my entire being screamed never. I'm not afraid of binding her to me forever with a child. I *crave* doing it.

Being inside her feels more than just familiar. It feels right, it's where I belong. Like two souls adrift for too long finally finding their way back together. We've had a rough voyage, and it's not over yet, but Lorelai is mine.

I slam into her to prove the point in my own head.

She moans with pleasure, stretching her perfect body and pushing her chest up. Her tits framed in the sexy bra straps make my mouth water. I want my mouth all over her, but I want to see her writhing under me more.

I do it again and again, each time gaining the same reaction. Her eyes never leave my face, but there's something more than pleasure. The fear she always carries with her, even when buried deep, is trying to surface. I hate it. Even more because I've done nothing to stop it.

She doesn't trust that this is real. Or that we are lasting. Despite that I just proclaimed her the mother of my future children, she's not convinced I'm committed.

Running the hand that's been resting on her abdomen up to her throat, I massage it for a moment. Slowly increasing the pressure as I continue battering into her.

"You're mine, sweetheart. One way or another, you've always been mine. You always will be," I tell her, hoping to see some of the apprehension fall away. "Legs up wide, baby. Let me closer."

She's so agile and strong, she has no problem complying, and I can push further in, my sack seated against her ass. Using the hand not wrapped around her neck to tangle into the straps of her bra, I pull her toward me with each thrust, forcing an exhale out of her to match our pace.

Even as I lean down, pushing her knees down into her, she manages easily. I keep going until we're forehead to forehead.

"I want that mouth. Kiss me like you mean it."

"I always mean it," she says softly.

"Then kiss me like you'll die if you don't."

She stretches her head up to me meet me. Mouth to mouth, I imagine what she's telling me with her kiss. That she's telling me the same things I'm telling her.

I can't be too close to her; I can't be too deep. My hips roll over and over, but it's not enough. So, I ride her harder and harder, never breaking the kiss. Until she's gasping for breath around the tongue I have shoved far down her throat. And until I can't control anything anymore.

"Come for me, Noah," she says, pulling away only an inch.

Because she's always had power over me, I obey.

"Fuck, only you." No one else makes me feel like she does. Every nerve ending lights up like a motherfucking inferno as I flow into her. Lorelai moans my name like a prayer. Her legs wrap around me, keeping me as tight to her as she, too, falls apart. I don't stop fucking her until she's past it, spent, limp in my arms.

"How are your wrists?"

She wiggles them, checking over herself.

"They're fine."

"Good, sweetheart. Do you have more in you?"

"Oh my god, do you?" She laughs. "You did all the work. All I had to do was lie here and enjoy."

"That's how it works. When I fuck you, the responsibility for us both to get off is mine."

"And if I want to fuck you?"

"Do you want to ride me or peg me, baby?" Lorelai is stunned into silence, and I grin down at her. "I'll let you do either, on occasion. But mostly it's going to be me fucking you. Get used to that."

I slide out of her, still hard as hell, and move down to her feet. I check the position of her hands, then flip her over to her stomach. The tie on the headboard twists tighter.

"I want your legs together, but that ass as high as you can get it. That's perfect, baby," I tell her as she maneuvers into position. "It's going to be rough and I'm taking that ass. Can you handle that?"

"How are you still hard? When did you learn that trick?"

It's not something I learned. In fact, it never happened before she came back.

"Can you handle it, Lorelai?"

"Yes, please."

"You're leaking," I say, watching the cum start to slip out of her. I slide two fingers over it, dragging it back up and inside her. "I'm going to fuck it back into you."

"Oh god."

I drag one of her ass cheeks to the side, so it allows me access to the other hole I'm dying to be in. Gently, slowly, I move it in. I repeat the motion several times, wetting my fingers in her cunt to loosen up her ass. It's going to sting regardless, but I can lessen the pain.

"Did I punish you for teasing me in the car earlier?"

"No," she says on a gasp. Her ass wiggles for me.

She's fucking perfect. Her ass is still red from the other spankings. That doesn't mean I'll take it easy on her now as I smack the cheek I don't already have a solid grip on. After the first handful, the height of her ass starts to lower, but she quickly corrects, pulling her knees closer to her core and raising up again.

"Good, baby."

If a body can sigh, that's what hers just did. She obviously likes spankings, but I maintain that it's praise she really needs. Every muscle in her body relaxes into a happiness at two simple words.

Positioning myself behind her, I give her no warning as I slide back in, pumping into her vagina a handful of times. To get my dick wet and to push the cum further into her. Then I re-position us both. Pulling her up to her knees, I move from my knees to feet so I can squat over her.

I grab the base of my dick and set the tip at her tight entrance. She opens for me.

"That's perfect, Lorelai. Just like that," I tell her. I push little by little, letting her adjust as she needs to, until I'm in fully. "You okay?"

"Uh-huh," she says, nodding with more enthusiasm than anyone could expect.

"You're excited by this, aren't you?"

"I've been waiting years for this. Fuck my ass, Noah Anders."

"With pleasure," I say, holding back the laughter she always brings out of me.

Then I move. Slowly, at first, making sure she's prepared. She shows no signs of distress, quite the opposite. She pushes back into me when I thrust.

"You have the perfect ass. Do you know that? So tight, so warm, the perfect sheath for my cock."

"Mmhmm."

"I want to fuck it every day for the rest of my life." Lorelai quivers, her muscles fluttering against my dick. "Fuck, baby. Do that again."

"Do what?" she pants.

"That amazing little thing you did with your ass when I told you I was going to fuck it every day."

It happens again, and I lose my fucking mind. Hands going to her hips, I grip tightly as I quicken my pace. Lorelai makes pretty little sounds under me, spurring me closer to another climax.

"Noah?"

"Yeah, baby?"

"Is your foot turned out?"

What the fuck?

I pause to check, and sure enough, it is. I can't hold the laughter back now.

Only Lorelai would be concerned for the health of my body while we're fucking like rabbits. I'm struck again with how good she is at taking care of me.

"It's not funny. I don't want you to hurt your hip," she argues.

I fall on top of her, still laughing, laying her flat and pulling her legs in between mine.

"I fucking love you," I say, still laughing and stretching my arms up so I can clasp my hands around hers.

"W-what?" she asks, voice full of watery emotion.

"I love you, Lorelai," I whisper in her ear.

"You can't say that," she cries.

"Why not?"

"Noah! Your dick is in my ass, and I can't even see your face. That is not how you tell a woman you love her for the first time."

Fair point. I untie her hands, pull out and off her. I move to sit with my back against the headboard and gesture for her to climb on my lap.

"Do you see me now, Lorelai?" She nods, and I pull her closer with my hands sunk into her hair. The feeling lighting up her face is damn gorgeous, but I'm not sure I'm reading it all right. "I love you. You don't have to say it back, not until you're ready. But you should know."

"Nobody has ever said that to me before."

"Ever? Not even your mom?"

Lorelai gives the faintest shake of her head. Fuck, I can't even imagine a life like that.

"I'm sorry I never told you before. I should have."

"I'm sorry I didn't tell you things, too."

"You don't have anything else to apologize for, Lore. We're past that," I say, pressing a kiss on the tip of her nose. "You do need to get back on my cock, though."

She reaches down to grab my dick in her hand. Instead of sliding her cunt over me, she positions me at her ass.

"Yes, right there," I tell her, pulling my knees up for her to lean back on. "You keep riding my dick in your ass, and I'm going to play with your pussy."

"Jesus, your mouth."

I half smile at her, drawing her attention to my mouth so she doesn't notice my fingers moving toward her until they're in. Two inside, and my thumb rubbing softly on her clit.

Within seconds, her eyes glaze over, and her stomach flutters. I know she's close. I am too. I just need that shiver from her ass again.

"Lorelai?" Her eyes clear slightly. "You're perfect, baby. Just fucking perfect."

Fuck, there it is. I keep hold of her hips, moving her at the same pace as she explodes into a convulsive orgasm, pulling me along with her. I want her to ride it to the end, but she's too blissed out to keep the movement herself.

She's beautiful—the flush that waves across her cheeks and how she bites her lower lip when her muscles tense back up. And then a few moments later, she becomes completely languid, falling forward onto my chest. I wrap my arms around her, holding her tight, taking in her scent. Savoring everything that's happened tonight. Even sex with Lorelai is more fun than with anyone else. Never have I laughed and still stayed impossibly turned on.

Only with her.

"Let's clean you up, then get some sleep." I carry her into the shower, tend to her, then spend the most peaceful sleep I've ever known with her curled in my embrace.

31
LORELAI

I wish I could say I woke up this morning still blissfully satisfied. With the dawn of the new day comes the apprehensive gloom that Noah might have regrets. His arms are still wrapped around me, his leg thrown over mine. Steady chest movement tells me he's still asleep behind me.

Taking a few minutes, I assess the situation myself.

We didn't use protection. None. Not only did he not pull out, he shoved anything that leaked out back in. With anyone else, I'd be really weirded out by that.

But I'm not. Not even a little.

When I give it the attention it needs, I find that *I* don't have regrets. Even if he does, in the very off-chance that last night results in a baby, I'm okay with it. Because last night was the most perfect night of my life and nothing that comes from it will be anything but equally perfect.

Besides, I know I'm strong enough now to be a mother. Single or not. I can do it. And I'll be damn amazing at it. My children will never lack for love or support.

My hand moves to tummy. Seconds later, Noah's follows.

"Are you worried?" he asks, sleep still clogging his throat.

I spin my body to face his. "No."

"Good. I'm not either," he says. Because he doesn't think I got pregnant or because he doesn't care if I did? I don't know. He doesn't say. "Good morning."

"Hi."

"Do you want to talk about anything that happened last night?"

I nod my head.

"What part?"

"What happens if I'm pregnant?"

"The same thing that happens if you're not. Only you'll have my baby inside you."

"What does that mean?" I ask, ignoring the stupid flutter that ravishes my body from those words.

"It means that we take this a day at a time until we're both on the same page. We don't have to make any fast decisions. I'm here. In your life and for you, regardless."

"Are we not on the same page?"

"Are you going to move back in with me?"

"What?"

"No, we're not on the same page. But, as I said"—he presses a kiss to my forehead—"we don't need to make fast decisions."

"You're very overwhelming," I tell him.

"I've been told."

"We should get up. I'd like to be home before Livi gets up."

"One more thing," he says, his arms tightening around me. "I can't be here this Wednesday."

"Okay," I say, not understanding why he's looking at me with concern.

"It's June's birthday. Drew planned a big party."

"Okay."

"That's it?" he asks.

"Yes, Noah. I get it, she's your friend. Of course, you should be there."

"Right. But I don't like that I can't have you with me."

I wiggle out of his grip, getting off the bed and grabbing Noah's shirt to wrap around my naked body.

"June is never going to forgive me, Noah. If we're going to try to have a relationship, I'll never stand in the way of your friendship with her. You need to decide if you're okay with that. With a separation of your best friend and whatever I am. Is it worth the struggle to you? And will it be to June?"

"If that's not good enough for me?"

Fastening a few buttons of his shirt, I go stand in front of him.

"It has to be, Noah. I'm not afraid to miss pieces of your life, so long as I'm getting the pieces that belong to me. I can share you. That way, at least."

Noah pulls me down onto his lap.

"Why did you say it that way?"

"It's just something you said last night got me thinking."

"Explain."

"You brought up pegging," I say, almost bashfully.

"Does that turn you on?"

"Yes, but that isn't the issue. If we're doing this, I want us to be upfront and clear about our expectations with regards to sex. You don't only have sex with women."

"Lorelai," he says, smiling from ear to ear. "From now on, I only have sex with one person. The one woman my whole heart is in love with. If I need dick, we'll get you a strap-on."

"Oh my god, you say the sweetest things." I laugh. Noah kisses me until I'm not laughing anymore.

"Thank you," he says when he finally pulls back.

"For what?"

"For taking care of me. For understanding. For not being jealous of my friendships. For being strong enough to give me a chance."

I still have my moments where I don't feel strong. But time between them gets longer and longer every day. It helps to hear it from Noah, the only person since childhood that I wished for validation from.

"You're welcome. Thank you for *seeing* me."

Noah presses another kiss on my mouth before telling me to get ready and playfully smacking my ass.

When we get to my house, he walks me to the door hand in hand.

"Let me talk to Livi about Wednesday. If she's upset, I should be the one to deal with that fallout."

"Okay," I agree, unlocking the front door.

"Good morning, Lorelai," Olivia squeals, running to me and wrapping her arms around my waist.

"What did you just call me?" I ask, picking her up so her face is level with mine.

"Lorelai." She giggles. "Miss Grace teached me."

"I taught you, Miss Olivia. Not teached," Grace says, coming in to meet us. "I was a speech therapist for thirty-five years."

I mouth a thank you to her, and she smiles earnestly.

Noah hauls her out of my arms, turning her upside down and tickling her as he carries her to the bedroom, presumably to discuss Wednesday.

"How was she?"

"She's a joy, Lorelai. We had one small spill while making cookies, there was a flash of panic, but she controlled it quickly. She's doing very well," Grace says. She sits on the sofa, patting the seat next to her as invitation. "How was your night?"

"It was wonderful. Thank you for staying with Livi. I wouldn't have trusted anyone else."

"It was my pleasure. Both in spending time with such a sweet child, and in letting you and Noah have some time to reconnect. Noah's different since he's been coming here to Mobile every week. He's lighter, happier, healthier than he's been in years. You and your sister are good for him."

"I'm glad."

"Is he good for you, too?"

"He is, Grace. We're figuring it out, you know. He's stubborn and likes things to be his way. But if he can make some concessions where June and I are concerned, I think we'll be okay."

"What sort of concessions?"

"The sort that will require one or the other of us to miss out on certain occasions. Like her birthday."

"That isn't upsetting to you?" she asks.

"No. I made my choices and I'm paying the consequences. I wish those didn't involve Noah having to make decisions he'd rather not. But it's past the point of fixing. We can only do our best to keep each other happy now. June and Drew's friendship makes him happy; I won't stand in the way of that. But I also won't walk away from him again."

"I'm happy to hear that, dear. And how are you? It wouldn't be surprising if some of Olivia's issues triggered past traumas in you. Are you doing as well as her?"

I adore her for asking.

"Actually, I think she helps. I feel less triggered, not more. I credit having something more important than myself to focus my attentions on."

"Yes, I can see that. But you take care of yourself. And I'm here if you ever want to talk."

Just then Noah comes walking back in, resembling something like a raging bull.

Uh-oh.

"What happened?"

"She didn't know what a birthday was?" he rage-whispers.

Well... shit. She wouldn't. I hadn't even considered that.

"We weren't allowed those. Only my father's was celebrated, but it was called something different."

Noah's hands go to his head, and he stares up at the ceiling for a minute.

"She's missed four birthdays," he says. "You missed twelve. Wait, did you celebrate them at Alice's?"

"No," I say with a shake of my head. "By then, they didn't seem important. I was focused on school."

"Jesus. How many have you celebrated? Any?"

"Just the one I spent with you in college."

Grace whimpers softly next to me. I reach over to grab her hand, reassuring her with a squeeze that I'm okay.

"When is her birthday?"

"September 8th."

"We start celebrating on the fourth this year. She gets them all. And you get the entire fucking month of January. Every fucking day, you understand me?"

He's so pissed about it. Frankly, it's hot as hell.

Grace and I both nod in agreement, stunned by his anger.

"Mom, get your stuff. Say goodbye. I told Dad I'd have you back by lunch."

She stands to do as he says, patting my hand on her way up.

"Come here."

When I get within a foot, he pulls me into a tight hug.

"I have a busy week. I'm not sure when I'll get back here."

"You'll show up when you can," I reassure him.

"I will. If you need me, you call me. Okay?"

"We don't need you, Noah. We want you," I say, making his head tilt in thought. "We'll be here when you're ready."

Noah's mouth opens, probably to argue with me, but his mom walks back in telling him she's ready to go. Olivia follows behind her and comes to stand next to me, taking my hand. I look down to see her staring at Noah. Likely a little sad to see him go, not knowing when he'll be back. I can relate.

I've done all I can do. I've put my trust in him, more than I've ever given to anyone. The rest is up to him. As much as my heart swelled with satisfaction when he told me he loved me, he has to do more than that.

He has to show us he wants us.

Noah bends down to kiss her head, then places one on my lips.

"I love you," he tells me, not pulling away. I nod. I can't say it. Not yet. Not until I know he means all he says. It makes me feel too vulnerable and that's not a place I want to go back to.

We watch as they leave.

"I think tonight is a good night for pizza and ice cream. What do you think, bug?"

"Oh yes, please," she says, finally smiling.

It tells me we're going to be okay. No matter what, Livi and I, we're going to be okay.

32
NOAH

"I'm quite certain you are a cheater, Jolie."

"I'm not a cheater, Mr. Noah," she says. "You're just really bad."

She's not wrong, this sprite of a girl. We're playing chess through an app on my phone. She's won three times straight. I can't even blame the whiskey.

Which I've had more of than I should.

I'm using it to lessen the hate of the karaoke that's been happening all evening. Because, of course, it wouldn't be a party for June without that.

She looks as beautiful as ever, glowing under the attention. It's nice to see. After everything she's been through, I think she's finally happy. Fully loving her life. She's worn a radiant smile all day. For my part, I've been careful not to make it falter. But when she isn't near, I'm boorish.

That's how I ended up hanging out with Jolie. She's one of Bryce's kids. Bryce is a teammate of Drew's who has more daughters than I can keep track of. This one is about Olivia's age. Jolie is smart, like Olivia. She makes me laugh, like Olivia.

In other words, I'm a fucking mess. I miss my girls. Watching Bryce play with his daughters, all while his wife, Candace, laughs at his side, is making me hate my situation.

"Checkmate."

"Damnit. Again?"

"You should stick to Go Fish." She laughs.

"You should run, because if I catch you, I'm going to tickle you until you're red in the face," I tell her, standing and make my hands look like big claws.

She runs away, giggling the entire way across the room and into her father's arms. I wink at him, and he nods. Scanning the room, I find Reed sitting at a corner table with nothing but a bottle of whiskey as company.

"Looks like you're having as good of time as me." I sit and he pushes the bottle my way. I pour two fingers into my glass.

"What the fuck is your problem?" he asks.

"Maybe not so different than yours. I didn't claim the woman I love when I should have."

Reed is doing what he always does when his sister's best friend is in the room. He tracks Leighton's every move. Currently, she's dancing in front of the stage with Connor. Reed looks like he's ready to commit murder.

"You love the woman that almost ruined my sister's life."

"That was your best friend, if we're being truthful, Reed. You love him. Lorelai played a part, but she isn't that same woman. She's kind and she's strong, and more caring than you'd guess. So watch your mouth about her with me."

"It's not fair for you to ask June to forgive her," he says, then takes a big swallow of his drink.

"Nobody's asking that of June. Not even Lorelai. But what truly isn't fair is how incredibly misogynistic it is to forgive the man who cheated, the man who took vows and broke them, but continue to see the woman as an unforgivable whore. Is that what you're doing, Reed?"

"Of course not." He looks disgusted. "I know nothing about Lorelai. I'm just looking out for my sister. I've already failed her enough."

"I don't want to hurt June, either. You know that. As for Lorelai, all you need to know is that she never wanted to break up that marriage. She had a horrible childhood, one without guidance, and hasn't always made the wisest decisions. But she doesn't make excuses. She owns her mistakes, and she's doing her best to be a better person and helping others along the way."

"That's good, Noah. Good for her. I still don't trust her, but I can't even say those same things about Drew. That fucker was full of excuses for months."

"I remember. But he's doing right by your sister now. I don't see signs of that stopping."

"Me either," Reed says.

"Now what the fuck are you going to do about Leighton?"

"I don't know yet. I'm vacillating between kidnapping her and locking her in a cage, or just murdering your brother."

I laugh.

"There's an easier answer."

"Yeah, what's that?" he asks me.

"Move your dumb ass to New Orleans. My brother shouldn't be a problem for you much longer."

"Really?"

I nod and then I'm pelted in the side of the head by a grape.

The fuck?

I turn just in time to see June throwing another one. This one hits between my eyes.

"June," I warn.

She smiles and daintily picks up a strawberry next. I'm not fast enough to dodge it and it hits the shoulder of my new, very expensive, suit. I stare at the spot for a few seconds, then look back to June. Her eyes are narrowed on me.

"What are you doing?"

"What are you doing?" she parrots.

"Minding my own business."

"You're being broody and you're bringing me down," she says. "Both of you."

Well, fuck.

"I apologize. That's not my intention. I'll remedy the problem," I say, trying to sound contrite. I honestly don't want to sour her day.

"You'll talk to me about it?"

"Not today, no."

She throws another grape, but I catch this one and toss it back, bouncing it off her nose.

"Brute."

I laugh, then so does she.

"We'll talk tomorrow, okay?" She nods in agreement, then heads to the stage with Grabbing Leighton from the dance floor and dragging her along.

An ABBA song starts up, and I grimace. How on earth some old Swedish foursome became the go-to karaoke song list for these two, I'll never understand. Reed and I watch them as they dance around each other, singing their silly song. But the lyrics hit home as they sing about wasting emotion and sharing devotion.

Which is exactly what I'm doing. I've waisted my anger and my rage for years. I lived off the fuel of hating Lorelai, thinking she betrayed me, thinking she was anything but what she really was. Lost, alone, and trying to give me everything through her misguided actions.

It shatters me when I think of how lonely her life must have been. And now I'm fueled by guilt. Because I didn't see the things I should have. I didn't stay focused enough to take care of us both. Fuck, instead, I treated her awfully.

We could have prevented so much if we'd just been a team.

Still, here I sit, without her. Without my family. The two people I love most in the world are living without me because of my devotion to another woman.

I fix this shit tomorrow.

Tonight, I make sure June has a great birthday.

"Come on in," Drew says, opening the door to their home the next day. "Junie's in the kitchen scouring over paint chips."

"What room is she on?"

"Laundry, but you'd think it was the exterior of the house the way she can't decide on the perfect shade of periwinkle. Whatever the fuck that color even is."

Grinning, I follow him to the kitchen. The house is a ramshackle, but they don't mind. June is painstakingly planning the full remodel. They completed quick fixes to the main bedroom and bath, and one spare room. It's livable, by their standards. Just barely.

"Hi," June calls as we walk in. "Coffee?"

"No, thank you."

She gestures to the chair on her right.

"Talk, Noah."

To ease into the subject or...

"I love them." *Jump right into the deep end.*

"I know," June says, pushing the paint samples further into the center of the table and resting her hands in the now blank space.

"She doesn't expect your forgiveness and she doesn't want to stand in the way of our friendship."

"What do you want, Noah?"

"I want them, June. Someday, I want to marry Lorelai and adopt Olivia. I want them here, where I can give them all the love and security they've been denied. There's nothing I want more than to build a family with them, the likes they always deserved but never dreamed."

We're all quiet for a time, Drew's hand going to rub June's back. I wait, letting her digest, letting her gather her thoughts.

"Will you tell me about them?" she finally asks.

I think about it before speaking.

"No. Other than they're wonderful people and so good together," I say. "The rest, no. I'm not here to convince you to like Lorelai. She wouldn't want that. I don't want to use your empathy to persuade you. Only to let you know my intentions."

She drags her eyes all over my face, seeing everything I'm not trying to hide.

"I told you once before I wouldn't be the villain in your story," she says, calmly. "I may even be offended that you're treating me like I am."

"I'm not treating you like a villain, June. I'm giving you the respect you deserve as someone I care greatly for. You are my best friend. I need that friendship. But I need them more."

"What are you asking of us, Noah?" Drew finally speaks.

"Only to be my friends. Who are understanding and sure of the knowledge that I wouldn't tie anyone to me so thoroughly if I wasn't sure of who they are. I'm asking you to trust me."

"If June can't do that for you?" Drew asks, causing June to turn toward him.

"I'll hate it, but it won't change my decision. Had I not so easily let her walk away before, this all could have been prevented. I won't fail her again."

"That's not exactly true though, is it?" June says, looking back to me. "It wouldn't have prevented it all. Had you and Lorelai worked things out back in college, had you stayed together, it wouldn't have stopped what Drew did."

"Junie," he says, frowning in pain.

"It's true, Drew. You still would have cheated, just with someone else. Lorelai wasn't the catalyst for all of this, you were. I don't hate her for it more than I hated you for it." She turns back to me. "I can't see us ever being friends, Noah. Woman to woman, she broke something in me where she's concerned. But I'm not blind, I see the change in you. Since Olivia showed up, since you stopped your games. You're happier. Much happier. I'll accept anything that keeps that smile on your face and that joy in your heart. If that's Lorelai, so be it."

June teaches me something new every day. Through her strength, through her passion, through her compassion. Most importantly, she's taught me the importance of surrounding yourself with people who genuinely care about you.

She stands, places her hands on my cheeks, while she looks in my eyes.

"Go get your family, Noah. You wouldn't stand in the way of what was best for me. I won't stand in the way of what's best for you. I love you." She presses a kiss on my forehead and leaves the room.

"You are married to a remarkable woman, McKenna."

"I'm aware," he says smugly, then sobers quickly. "Has she heard from her mother?"

"No. And I'm not discussing it with you. If you gave shit, you wouldn't have abandoned them when they needed your help the most."

"That's not completely fair, Noah. I had to think of June."

"I know you did, but there must have been a way. I'm not mad about it, since it brought her back to me. But I'm not going to sugarcoat anything to spare your feelings either."

"I'm not asking you to. I'm owning up to everything I've done, all my mistakes. And I'll pay every consequence that comes from them. For what it's worth, I'm glad she has you. I think that's all she's ever wanted, someone fighting in her corner. If you recall, I told you she wasn't what you thought," he says.

Touché.

33
LORELAI

It's been six days since my date with Noah, and he hasn't been back. He calls every night, asks about my day, tells me about his. The closer it gets to the NFL season, the busier he gets with his co-hosting duties for ESPN, and with the consultation he does for the New Orleans' Saints.

It's nice, feeling a part of his life. Feeling like a priority to someone.

Miles is over tonight. He leaves for California tomorrow, to begin filming. Olivia and I made him a farewell dinner. Vegetable curry was on the menu, and luckily, Miles isn't a steak and potato type guy. He also doesn't cook, so he was looking forward to a homecooked meal.

I looked forward to cooking for an adult again. Olivia's pallet isn't horrible for a four-year-old, but she gets stuck on new foods and then that's all she wants to eat for days. She's not like that with just food, I've noticed. It's kind of everything. New stuff fascinates her and there is a lot of new stuff to work through.

Including the game Connect Four, which she currently has Miles playing with her while I finish up the dishes from our meal. Laughter erupts from her every few minutes as Miles lets her win over and over.

I dry my hands, then go watch the spectacle. Olivia's laughter is the best sound in the world. I don't ever want to go a day without it.

"I'm terrible at this, lil' miss."

"Uh-huh." She laughs at him, making me join in. Miles sends me a side-eye, but the grin on his face tells me he's enjoying making her laugh. She has that way about her. Everyone loves Livi. It's a sobering reminder of what my family would have subjected her to if she hadn't gotten out.

Those aren't thoughts to linger on, though. She is out. I got her out. And I'll keep her safe.

"I should get going. I have an early flight in the morning," Miles says, standing up from the sofa.

"Thanks for playing with me, Miles," Olivia tells him, sticking her hand out to shake. It's another new thing.

"Thank you for dinner, lil' miss." He gently shakes her hand.

"I'll walk you out," I say. "You should go put your jammies on, bug." She nods and rushes off.

"Thank you for all your help," Miles says when we reach the front porch.

"You did all the hard work, Jameson. I just helped guide you."

"Well, you were an amazing guide. I don't know that I'd feel this great if not for you."

"I think you'd surprise yourself," I tell him. "Now go break a leg or whatever it is they say these days."

Miles pulls me into a hug, holding me tightly for a few long minutes.

"You stay safe, Lore. And happy, you stay happy."

"You too, Miles," I say, and he presses a small kiss on my cheek before he walks away.

I hear him when he turns the corner to my driveway.

"That's really creepy, Tight-ass."

Noah rounds the corner on a beeline straight toward me. He doesn't stop until he's just inches in front of me.

"That was a sweet goodbye."

"It was," I agree, tilting my head. "Are you jealous or do you not trust me? Because if it's the latter, you can turn your ass around right now, Anders."

"Have I ever told you how much I love your temper?" he asks, a huge grin taking over his face. I roll my eyes at him. "It was a sweet goodbye. And yes, I was jealous because Hollywood got to put his lips on you, and I haven't done that in nearly a week."

"Well, there's nothing fucking stopping you now," I taunt.

"Good point." He moves the step closer, picking me up by the waist as he goes, until my back is up against the front door. "Kiss me, Lorelai."

"You kiss me, Anders," I counter, locking my legs around his waist.

The words are barely out when his tongue hits my skin, licking his way from my neck to my mouth. I meet him with the same intensity. With the need and desire that's been building up all these days. My arms wrap tighter around his neck, and I grind my core against him. One of his hands creeps under my shirt, making my flesh pebble. A shiver takes over and he pulls back.

"We should go inside. You need to pack your stuff," Noah says.

"Why?" I ask, leaning in for another kiss. God, I've missed him.

"Hurricane," he says in between kisses.

"What?" This time, I'm the one pulling back.

"There's a hurricane coming. You two are coming home with me."

"It was a tropical storm last I checked," I say.

"It changed. I don't trust your roof, so I came to get you."

"I just checked the status twenty minutes ago and you live two hours away. You're a shit liar, Noah."

"Sue me. But go pack some bags first."

"I can't just leave. I have a job."

"Which won't matter if you die in a hurricane."

"Wow, Noah."

He reaches behind me, opening the door and hauling me inside.

"Noah," Livi yells, excitedly.

"Hey, baby girl." Noah sets me down, then picks her up. "You and your sister are going to come stay at my house. Doesn't that sound fun?"

Olivia squeals as I sternly say his name.

"Go start packing a bag. I'll be in to help in a minute." He sets her back down and she runs off.

"What the hell are you doing?"

"Taking you home. We've established this."

If I didn't love him, I'd kill him.

"If I just up and leave, what do I tell Janelle?"

"I don't know, Lorelai. Tell her you're fleeing a potential hurricane. Or, better yet, tell her you're opening a satellite office of her business in New Orleans, because that's where you'll be living from now on. She won't have to do anything; I'll take care of all the expenses, and we'll send her twenty-five percent."

"You'd do that?" I ask, astonished.

"That's just the beginning of what I will do to get you home," Noah says, coming to kneel in front of me. "Don't fight me, Lore. The storm can change quickly. I can't rest until you, Livi, and any potential baby are safe. With me."

Noah places a kiss on my stomach at the same time his phone beeps with a notification. Pulling it out of his pocket, he swipes it open.

"See," he says, holding it up. "You've never been through a hurricane. I'm not leaving here without you."

Sure enough, the notification shows that the storm has been upgraded.

"Fine. We'll pack a few things."

"Anything you can't live without. You understand?" he asks, all stern like.

"Yes, Daddy."

"Maybe," he whispers, planting another kiss to my belly.

I swear my uterus quivers.

Twenty minutes later, we're on the road and I'm trying my best not to feel overwhelmed. Noah is a bulldozer. He always was, but I've been on my own for so long, it's not so simple to just default to his authority. Even if I like that sort of thing.

He's made me no promises, not really. Saying he loves me and he's going to be in my life is wonderful, but they're just words. Yet here I am, uprooting myself and Olivia on his whim.

Maybe I haven't learned as much as I thought these past few months. Or maybe I'm just grasping on to the idea of a happy ever after with the only man I've ever loved.

"Get out of your head, Lorelai."

"Is it that easy?"

"No, baby," he says, reaching across the center console to hold my hand. "It's not that easy. But everything is going to be fine. I promise."

I turn to see Olivia in the backseat. She's wiped out.

"In my experience, things are never just fine. They've been good these past several weeks, but now I'm leaving that all behind," I say. "It's a lot, Noah. You showed up out of nowhere and practically demanded we come with you."

He pulls my hand up to his mouth and kisses my knuckles.

"You're right, I should have called when I was on my way. In my defense, I'm not used to making a decision with someone else. Also, I was focused on getting to you. It's going to be a learning curve for each of us, since neither of us has much experience with relationships. You could just defer to me on everything and make it easier for us both."

"Asshole." I laugh.

"You've never hand anyone truly have your back before. You do now. I'm not going anywhere and I'm not letting anything bad happen to you again. Okay?"

I turn in my seat to stare at his profile. So strong and handsome, it's hard to believe this is real. That I'm here with him because he wants me so desperately. It feels like a dream. So, I close my eyes and try to settle all the toxic instincts that tell me not to trust it.

"Lorelai, wake up, sweetheart. I can't carry you both in."

"Mmm, okay," I say, waking up. I must have dozed the entire drive.

Getting out of the car, I pull bags out of the trunk while Noah moves Olivia from her seat to his arms. She's still passed out. Closing the trunk, I get the first look at Noah's new house.

"Holy shit."

"What's wrong?" Noah whispers.

"It's huge."

"I know. It's ridiculous. You'll love it." He grins.

His enthusiasm breaks through some of my awe. Not all, but some.

"Follow me," he calls.

He manages to unlock the front door while balancing Livi. We step through to a beautiful mix of old-world charm and modern décor. My eyes don't know where to look first, where to land. So, I focus on Noah's back, following him up a wide curving staircase and down a long hall. Nearly at the end, he uses his hip to open a door and flips a switch with his elbow.

"Noah," I whisper, wanting to cry but trying hard to keep it together. I drop Olivia's suitcase inside the door, dazed. Just dazed.

This room would be any little girl's dream. The light he turned on cloaks the aquamarine walls in motion. There is realistic sea life painted on the walls, making the whole room feel like a saltwater fish tank. A canopy bed with plush pillows sits center on the wall ahead and Noah gently lays Olivia down, removing her shoes, and tucking her in with a kiss to the top of her head.

He pulls me out into the hall with him, closing the door behind us, but not all the way.

"That room is magical."

"You think she'll like it? I wanted it to be perfect for her."

"You did that for her?"

"Of course, I did."

"Take me to your room, Noah. I've never wanted to suck your dick more in my life, but we shouldn't do that here in the hallway."

He laughs loudly, and I reach up to muffle his mouth with my hand. He stops laughing and nips at my fingers.

"This way."

Noah opens a door at the end of the hall, giving me entry to a large corner bedroom. I take a few minutes to wander around. It's sparsely furnished. The same king-size bed, dresser, and nightstand from his condo. Basically, nothing more. There are two closets, one full of his suits, the other completely bare. This room, like Olivia's, has a sitting room. That is also very bare.

"Did you run out of money before getting to this room?"

Noah takes my bag and drops it into the empty closet.

"Our room. Not *my* room, or *this* room. *Our* bedroom, Lorelai," he says in his stern voice. "My designer was a woman. I didn't want her, or any other woman, in our room making decisions on how it should look. The room I sleep with you in, the room I fuck you in, will look like how you want it to look. However you want it to look."

"What are you saying, Noah?"

"You want me to be very clear?" he asks, smiling with half of his face as his eyes dance.

"Very."

"Now that you're here, you're going to be very hard pressed to get me to ever agree to your leaving. I wasn't kidding about opening your own office here," he says as he draws closer to me. "Because I want you with me. But if you need to split time for a while, we can make that work, too. And, someday, when you're ready, I want to give you and Olivia my name. So, everyone knows we're family."

Oh, my heart.

"Noah, you can't say that if it's not real. I need you to mean it."

"I mean it, sweetheart. I mean it, more than I've ever meant anything. We're a team now, baby," he says, then kisses me slowly.

One of my hands winds its way around his neck, the other moves to his waistband. It's a struggle to undo his belt with one hand, but I manage. He's no help, due to his hands diving into the back of my yoga pants so he can roughly grab my ass.

"Is that a yes, Lorelai?"

"I never heard a question. I'll answer you if you ask something. Right now, I want your cock in my mouth, Noah."

"Fuck," he groans as I finally grab ahold of him. There's already precum, so I swirl around the head with my thumb. "Get naked."

"Okay," I say, licking up the line of his throat.

I undress slowly, keeping eye contact with him while he does the same. When naked, I grab a pillow off the bed and toss it at his feet. Then I kneel.

Noah watches like a predator as I squirm under his perusal. Heat radiates through me as my need for him increases. He takes his time, his hand working over himself. Up and down in languid motions. Every few strokes, his thumb circles the head, just as I had.

"I love you, Noah," I say.

"I know. But thank you for finally saying it."

"Thank you for making me feel safe enough to," I reply.

"You will always be safe with me, Lorelai."

"I know. Now quit teasing me," I say, running my hands over my breasts, then farther. Farther. Until I can dip them in, making myself moan.

"Did I tell you to touch yourself?"

"Huh-uuuuuh," I moan again. "But you weren't doing it and I need something fucking me."

"That damned mouth of yours."

"Come shut me up then. Choke me with that fat cock."

"Jesus," he curses, but finally he takes the small step. "Hands on me. I make you come, Lorelai. Not you. You don't use your hands unless you're using them on me."

"Okay," I agree, moving them from my own body to rest on his thighs.

"You ready for me to fuck that mouth, sweetheart?"

I nod and open wide for him to slide into. He doesn't ease into it; he plunges in all the way and holds himself there. Leaning forward slightly, he steals my air as easily as he's stolen my heart. He pumps in over and over, his strong grip keeping my head where he wants it.

"This mouth is mine to fuck, Lorelai. So is that cunt. You touch it if I tell you to, not before then." He pulls out and squats in front of me. Two of his fingers find easy passage into me. "You're so wet, sweetheart. Give me your hand."

I slide a shaking one to his.

"Insert two fingers with mine. Feel how wet you are. How wet sucking my dick makes you."

"Noah," I say on a moan.

"Hands back on me, baby," he says, once again standing in front of me. Offering me his hungry cock. I immediately suck him back in and he begins thrusting. His head thrown back in pleasure, arms corded in muscles... it's a magnificent feast for my eyes.

Every so often he pulls up long enough for me to swallow, to regulate my breathing. When he does it this time, I remove my mouth completely and move to lick everything I can reach. His hand takes the place of my mouth, and he rises on his toes enough for me to suck his sack into my mouth.

Moving my still slick finger to his crease, I find his hole and rub around it. He widens his stance as I tease it.

"Noah?"

"Yeah, baby?" His voice is so labored, he nearly stutters the words.

"Will you marry me?" I ask and push my finger into his asshole, while I run my tongue up the crown of his dick.

He explodes with a grunt, spilling all over my lips. The last drops land on my chin and throat.

"Fuck. Jesus, Lorelai," he pants as he comes down. "What the fuck did you just ask me?"

"Did you not hear me?"

Noah steps back so he can pull me up and guides me to sit on the edge of the bed. He stands between my legs, peering down at me, his carved chest still moving rapidly from his release, his dick still standing proudly tall.

"Did you just propose to me with your finger in my ass?"

"It seemed only fair," I playfully pout.

"I'm going to punish you for that," he says through a smirk.

"For how long?"

"Until death do us part, Lorelai."

EPILOGUE

"Good work today, Eve."

"Thanks, Lore." She waves as she leaves the studio.

True to his word, Noah opened a branch of Janelle's business in New Orleans. It's mine in every way, except for a small amount of profit we send to her once a month. She fought us on that, wanting me to be happy was her priority, not business. But that didn't sit well with either of us. She gave me the support I needed at a crucial time in my life. I'll always owe her something for that.

I grew a lot in those short months we spent in Mobile. With the help of Janelle, Miles, and most especially Olivia. Looking back, it feels like a rebirth. Or a shedding of old skin to reveal the fresh, stronger skin beneath.

The person I am today is not at all the same one that came to New Orleans all those months ago.

Noah is, of course, a big part of that, too.

But I don't want to give all the credit to the incredible support Noah gives me. Or the unconditional love Olivia does. It wouldn't be fair to me and the work I put in. There's more to do. Episodes are far and few, but I still have them. Those times I hear my father, the times I feel unworthy and in need of discipline for no valid reason—they still exist. If only occasional.

It's different now, though. Noah gives me the security and the space to work through them. He recognizes my triggers; he sees the signs even before I do. He's good at helping me recognize them and change my pace so I don't rush down the wrong way.

When I need a release, he gives it to me in our bedroom.

I wish me being in his life was as easy for him as it is for him to be in mine. I didn't arrive with luggage full of family and friends like he did. There's still judgment by some. Not his family, not anymore. His parents and brother have embraced me and Olivia as their own.

June and Drew keep their distance if I'm around, of course. Mostly, that's fine. The McKennas split time between here and Seattle. The only real issue is when there is a function that we're all expected to be at. ESPN had one not too long back. It was awkward, to say the least.

Between the McKennas' polite yet cold shoulder, the gossip mills, and the mutual acquaintances who know the sordid tale… I felt like a black cloud hanging over Noah's head. He stayed by my side all evening, though. A sentinel beside me in case anyone tried to take shots.

Nobody dared. Noah is a presence. A force. And he makes it clear he'll use it fully to defend me.

Some have warmed up to me. Sally, his producer, for one. She's great and has become a friend. My first girlfriend, ever. We do lunch regularly and it's maybe the most normal my life has ever felt.

I also have Eve. Another physical therapist that I hired through a program that helps victims of domestic violence find places in the workforce. She ran from an abusive husband in Texas and found me. Well, us. I gave her a secure job, and Noah found her a therapist. Together, we found a safe place for her to live in.

She's thriving and helping our business thrive, as well.

I'm locking the door for the night, about to head home, when my phone rings.

"Hello?" I answer the number I recognize.

"Lorelai, it's Erin with Giving Hope."

"Hi, Erin."

"Hi. Listen, we have a situation that I need to discuss with you. Is this a good time?"

Oh god.

Panic immediately sets in. If there is anything wrong with the paperwork my mother signed regarding Olivia, I'll die. Fuck that, I'll run. I will take Olivia and flee the country before I send her back there.

"What's wrong?"

"We have another girl here. From your family's ranch."

My panic subsides, only to be replaced by other feelings. Elation, apprehension, too many others to name.

"Who?"

"Delilah. She's one of your uncle's daughters."

"Okay. What do you need me to do? I can fly out tomorrow."

"Well." Erin sighs. "There's a problem with that."

"What?"

"She's only seventeen. She's not legal for another nine weeks."

Shit. That changes everything. My uncle would never give up custody willingly. Delilah won't be in the same position as Olivia was. Emancipation won't be an option either, the courts would notify him of that, and he'd instantly fight it. And I can't very well forge the paperwork like I assume my mother and aunt did for me.

"Can you keep her until I find a safe house for her in Nevada?" I ask. Nevada has lax runaway laws. As long as she's safe, stable, self-sufficient, the police won't get involved. I'll just need to find someone to help her.

"I have one already. A woman we've worked with in the past. She has a room. But Delilah has expressed wanting to be with you and Olivia as soon as possible," Erin says.

"Of course. The day she turns eighteen, I'll be there to get her."

"Good. That should help her relax, she's very anxious. She was due to wed tomorrow."

My stomach turns violently, and my hand moves to comfort it. Noah didn't get me pregnant the night of our date. But it happened just a couple months after. I'm four months along now. Early days still and nausea occurs randomly.

"Give her my cellphone number. Have her call me every evening. I'll do my best to help her through it from here. Best we get to know each other, too," I say. "Wait. How does she know about me?"

Erin is quiet for a beat.

"Your mother helped her escape. Delilah says to expect more."

"Oh. I... I don't know what to say to that." Certainly, Erin can hear the emotion in my voice.

"Delilah thinks that's why your mother went back. To help get others out."

Erin and I talk for long enough to make plans. Then I place a call to the FBI agent who is still working on the case. It's an excruciatingly slow process. I've become used to not hearing any news for months on end. But any person we get out is essential to the investigation. Though, I won't put Delilah through that if she doesn't choose. It's still important information that we may have my mother actively working from the inside.

I use the ten-minute drive home to get control of my emotions, and immediately go looking for Noah when I walk in the house. I hear him before I see him.

"Do you know what getting married means, Livi?"

"Uh-huh. Father and uncle got married a lot."

Oh boy.

We haven't married yet. There's been enough on our plates, enough change in Olivia's life, that we didn't feel the need to rush it. Besides, I'm a little in love with the idea of being fat with Noah's baby and Olivia standing beside me as my maid of honor. We're taking vows two months from now. Privately, here at our home, with just those closest to us. He invited June and Drew, but they haven't given an answer just yet. For Noah, I hope they'll attend. But either way, it won't dampen our day. This wedding is for us, not anyone else.

I don't expect they'll come. But we didn't want to exclude them, either. June is still a big part of Noah's life. They work so closely together, travel together on occasion. I'd go as far as saying they've become better friends than what they were when I first arrived in New Orleans.

I'm happy he has a friendship like that. Jealousy plays no part in my world. Noah and I are both secure in our relationship. We have no secrets, and we still have our lazy morning talks. Even when he's away, he wakes me up with a phone call. When he comes home, he's eager for oxytocin boosts.

He's still just as ridiculous. And just as perfect.

We're building a life without animosity, bitterness, or even regret. All our past choices led us here. To this moment, with this family that is full of unconditional love.

"Right, but that's not what I want. I want to get married just one time."

"You'll have just a first wife?"

"I'll have an only wife."

"Do you want Lorelai to be your only wife?"

"I do. Very much," Noah answers. "When that happens, your sister will have my last name."

"Oh," Olivia answers dejectedly. Her name officially changed to mine just before we moved in with Noah. She won't like this.

"But I was hoping I could adopt you. Do you know what that means?"

"No."

"It means I would become your parent in the same way Lorelai is your parent. You'd get to have my last name, too. If you wanted it. Would that be okay with you?"

"Oh! Oh yes, please."

"You sure you want that, Olivia?" Noah asks, his voice breaking over the words.

"What would I get to call you?"

"What would you want to call me?"

"Ummm, Daddy Noah. Could I call you that?"

"I'd love it if you did."

"It's a deal," Olivia squeals before she comes running out of the kitchen and down the hall. "Hi, Lorelai!"

"Hi, Livi," I say as she twirls by in her mismatched outfit. Today it's a lime green long tutu with a navy and red striped button up shirt. She's been playing with her style and we're indulging it. Noah doesn't know how to say no to her, and she now has a closet full of brightly colored clothes to pick from every day.

"Hey," Noah greets, sliding up behind me and wrapping his hands around to my belly. "How was work?"

"It was good," I say, turning my head to kiss his jaw. "It sounds like you're going to have a lot of us calling you daddy."

"Mmhmm." He nuzzles into me.

"I need to talk to you about something." I turn in his arms to face him.

"What's happened?"

"Giving Hope called. My mother got another one out."

"Lorelai." Noah's hands come to cup my cheeks. "That's amazing. Another one of your sisters?"

I shake my head. "A cousin. Delilah. She's only seventeen, so she'll have to go to a safehouse in Nevada until she turns eighteen in two months."

"Then she'll be able to come to us?"

Fuck, I love this man. There's absolutely nothing he wouldn't do for me and our family. Which automatically includes every stray member we can save. He doesn't question that at all. He told me after I moved back that he'd become a benefactor for Giving Hope. He also showed me the old pool house out back that he had his designer renovate into a guest house. In the event your mother, or anyone else needs it... he'd said.

It's not possible to love Noah more than I do. But he challenges me to every day with how much he shows he loves me, Olivia, and our baby on the way.

He doesn't love us by halves. He loves us wholly and eternally. Just as we do him.

ABOUT THE AUTHOR

Alison lives somewhere in the shadow of a Pacific Northwest Mountain, bordered by the Puget Sound, and not too far from the country roads she grew up on. When she's not reading, she can be found avidly reading, traveling with a youthful wanderlust, or slowly turning the inside of her home into her own personal houseplant jungle.

Subscribe to Alison's Newsletter for Early News and Bonus Scenes
More from Alison Rhymes:
Broken Play

ACKNOWLEDGMENTS

Broken Play was a therapeutic book for me to write. Not because the content of it was personal to me, but because the timing of it was. I wrote it during the worst time of my life. Brutal Play has been an entirely different experience for me. Yet still a therapeutic one.

Writing Lorelai has taught me so much. Maybe this is a strange thing to say, but I'm a better person because of her. Her story taught me a lot about how I judge people, and it's also started me on my own journey to healing some religious trauma I didn't realize I was still holding on to.

I'm motivated to keep writing stories that push at the roadblocks I've placed in my way throughout my life. And I truly see it as a blessing to have you all holding my hand along the way. Thank you, dear readers.

Chanpreet, Mylene, and Saher – Thank you so much for always being in my DM's when I need a little support and inspiration. You all never fail me.

Zainab, thank you, once again for being the best cheerleader (and editor) a person could need. I am forever grateful for the circumstances that brought you into my life. I trust you beyond measure. Thank you for cleaning up my messes.

Autumn, again, thank you for having my back and keeping me on track. I couldn't do this without your support!

Kris at Temys Designs, you know what I put you through. THANK YOU.

To my crew of beta readers:

Annie Hall, you were the MVP for the first part of this book. Your feedback was invaluable and I'm forever in your debt.

Lauren Seale Taylor, you put everything aside to jump on this when I needed help most. I appreciate you beyond words.

Nicole Mullinax-Luna, I feel stronger with you sitting next to me on this ride. I hope you're in this for the long haul because you're going to have a hard time shaking me loose now.

And a super special thank you to Natasha Madison for constantly talking me up and inspiring me to do all the things I suck at. Things like organization and plotting. I want to be you when I'm all grown up in this business. I owe you a Harry Styles concert.

Lightning Source UK Ltd.
Milton Keynes UK
UKHW041931101122
411987UK00004B/262